HOUND DOG

RICHARD BLANDFORD was born in 1975. He lives in Brighton.

RICHARD BLANDFORD

HOUND DOG

JONATHAN CAPE
LONDON

Published by Jonathan Cape 2006

2 4 6 8 10 9 7 5 3 1

First published in Great Britain in 2006 by
Jonathan Cape
Random House, 20 Vauxhall Bridge Road, London SW1V 2SA

Random House Australia (Pty) Limited
20 Alfred Street, Milsons Point, Sydney,
New South Wales 2061, Australia

Random House New Zealand Limited
18 Poland Road, Glenfield,
Auckland 10, New Zealand

Random House (Pty) Limited
Isle of Houghton, Corner of Boundary Road & Carse O'Gowrie,
Houghton 2198, South Africa

The Random House Group Limited Reg. No. 954009
www.randomhouse.co.uk

A CIP catalogue record for this book is available from the British Library

ISBN 0224077759
ISBN 9780224077750 (from Jan 2007)

Papers used by Random House are natural,
recyclable products made from wood grown in sustainable forests;
the manufacturing processes conform to the environmental
regulations of the country of origin

Typeset by Palimpsest Book Production Limited, Polmont, Stirlingshire

Printed and bound in Great Britain by
Mackays of Chatham, Chatham, Kent

Many thanks to Emily and Dave

CHAPTER 1

Wednesday afternoon, **Gay Elvis** brings the van round to my place for us to load up the equipment.

'Hi, Gaylord,' I say. 'Been hanging round any gay bars lately?'

He grins awkwardly and opens up the back doors of the van. 'You going to be getting that new *Comeback Special* DVD?' he asks.

'Not fucking likely,' I say. 'What would I want with that crap?'

Gay Elvis isn't really gay, he's just effeminate-looking. In fact he's been married for years and got three kids. But like I say he looks like a fruit, so he's Gay Elvis. And that's all he ever wants to talk about, fucking Elvis. Always bloody Elvis this, Elvis that. I'm not remotely interested, but it doesn't stop him. I mean, what is there to say about Elvis? He was born. He grew up. He drove a truck. He made some records and got famous. He joined the army and went to Germany. He came back and made some shit films. Played Vegas. Got fat. Died. That's it, that's all there is. And do I give a stuff about a single bit of it? Not fucking likely, mate. To be absolutely honest with you, I can't stand the fucker. But you know what, that doesn't stop me from trying to make a living as an Elvis impersonator, the premier one in fact, of the Cambridgeshire region.

Now, I'm the top-dog Elvis in this operation, which means I have to do all the actual work, keeping the punters entertained with snappy patter and authentic-sounding Elvis vocal tributes. Meanwhile, Gay Elvis just prances about with Fat Elvis in the background, doing silly dances and occasional backing vocals. The fact I give them a third of the income to split between them is pretty fucking obscene, but that's me all over, generous to a fault. Fatty's not helping load up the van today because he's too fat and lazy. He's so fucking fat he's almost too big to be Elvis, and that's saying something. Anyway, me and Gayboy get the van loaded, get the fuck out of the Fens and drive off to Luton.

'Can I put a tape on?' asks the Gayster once we're on the motorway.

'Would it, by any chance, be an Elvis tape?'

'Well, yes.'

I put on Radio 4. Not because I want to listen to it, I just know it will annoy the Gaylord.

Fatboy is driving himself down there in his fatmobile. He turns the steering wheel with his knees, that's how fat and lazy he is. My van's got a great big picture of Elvis on the side, which we thought was a great idea until it kept on getting vandalised by kids nearly everywhere we played. Don't get me wrong, I think Elvis looks great with a great big giant cock coming out of his trousers, but it's not very professional.

So we get to the social club, the usual concrete bunker in the middle of a council estate that we always end up playing in, set up the PA and wait for our soundman, Soundcheck Stu, who's an arsehole, to turn up. Nearly all he's got to do is mix my voice with the backing tape, but he can't even do that. No matter how much I belt it out, it's too fucking quiet. Or else the backing vocals will be far too loud. He's a sodding amateur, but the only guy we know who can even half do it. Worse, he's got a poodle perm that he's always swishing about and swatting you in the face with. He finally turns up tagging along with Fat Elvis, arriving just in time for the free nosh the social club people have got together for us.

'Awwright, boss,' says the Fatman, 'sorry I'm late. Been a bit busy today.' The head of the organising committee hands me a ploughman's on a plate. She's a little woman with a bowl haircut, thick glasses and buck teeth. She makes me think of a giant mole as she scampers away muttering, stressing out about something or other. Mind you, I'd be stressed too if I had to run a dump like this, providing entertainment for the living dead.

About half-seven, people start shuffling in. It's our usual mix of the old, the alcoholic and the long-term unemployed. I guess that's not exactly true, but unless someone reeks of loneliness or desperation, I tend just to phase them out. I'll be straight with you, from where I'm standing, planet Earth is just one big ball covered in victims and losers. I'm not saying that's how it is, but it's the way I see it. One thing I can always spot, though, is a good pair of tits. You don't get many of the young 'uns in social clubs, but the ones you do get are as common as muck and know how to show off a decent pair.

'All right, lads,' I say to Fatty and Gayboy, 'time to disappear.' Now, I have a policy of never letting the paying public see us without our costumes, so once the doors are open I shove

Gaylord and Fatman into the dressing room for us to get changed. It's all Vegas stuff of course. We don't wear proper jumpsuits because they remind me too much of being in the nick, but they're two-piece outfits that look the same, topped off with capes, scarves and big belts, and of course an Elviswig complete with big sideburns. Gay Elvis's wife Jen made them, and she did a pretty decent job, I reckon.

Half-eight and we're nearly on. I tell the Gayster to watch the door while I do a line or two of charlie before, like always. Then we go out and do the act we always do. It's a tried and tested formula and it usually works. We open with a tape of *Also Sprach Zarathustra,* or the *2001* music to you and me, just like Elvis did, then I bound in singing 'See See Rider'. Then, after I've been on for a bit, Gayboy and the Fatman come out and dance about like arseholes while I sing some songs from the films. They're not well known, and no one really likes them, but you've got two hours to kill. Tonight, they go down OK. Once I've done about twenty minutes of that, I go into the audience and sing some love songs to the ladies, leaning over their shoulders and right into their faces. Their blokes always hate it, but they never do anything about it. If someone did it to a bird of mine, I'd kick the cheeky prick in the bollocks. But that's just me.

After that, it's novelty numbers, with the boys wearing grass skirts and hula dancing to 'Blue Hawaii' and stupid stuff like that. There are always some idiots in the audience who you can persuade to join in and put on the skirts, both blokes and birds. Why they subject themselves to it I don't know. To be honest I don't understand why people enjoy what we do at all, it's all fucking shit as far as I'm concerned, but they do. I sometimes look out at all the smiling faces, and I want to ask them, why are you smiling? What the fuck is there happening here that's even remotely entertaining? I'm not even sure why I do it myself, seeing as I fucking hate Elvis. That's half the reason I have to do the charlie before I go on.

It's the interval and everyone gets up for their ploughman's. The boys head to the bar while I do a bit more charlie in the dressing room, and I'm just getting my head off the table when some woman walks in. She doesn't even bother to knock. She's pushing fifty, but she's still wearing a skirt the length of Gay Elvis's cock, with a bright green top that you can see her nipples through. She's got fake tan, bright red nail polish and lipstick, and smoker's teeth. She reminds me of a horse for some reason, but not in a bad way. She stands very close, the way slappers like her always do, and of course straight away I'm hard as granite.

'Elvis, love,' she says, 'I was wondering, will you be singing "The Wonder of You" tonight?'

'Sure, honey, we always sing that song.' Right then I'm hoping she doesn't look down. It's pretty hard to hide an erection in an Elvis jumpsuit.

'Well then,' she continues, 'it's me and my husband's twenty-third wedding anniversary this week. Would it be at all possible for you to dedicate it to us? You see, it's always been our special song. It's Roy's favourite, anyway.'

'I'll, uh, certainly do that for you, honey.' I call her 'honey' because I always try to stay in character when wearing the outfit, and make Gaylord and the Fatboy do the same. It's weird, I take pride in certain things, even though the whole act's a total fucking joke as far as I'm concerned. I've never been good at impressions, so my Elvis voice consists pretty much of speaking in something almost recognisable as an American accent and trying to fit an 'uh' into every sentence, then every so often going 'welluhthankyouverymuch'. It's pretty basic, but people accept it. I've seen some Elvis acts who do it with an English accent, which is fucking shit in my opinion. Meanwhile, I think I might still have a ring of charlie around my left nostril, not to mention the plank of wood shoved down my trousers. 'What's, uh, your name, honey?' I ask.

'Sheila,' she says, and smiles at me, flashing her yellow teeth. She leaves the room, her arse wiggling away behind her.

In the second half of the set we do the hits. 'Hound Dog', 'Heartbreak Hotel', 'Suspicious Minds', 'American Trilogy', the lot. When it comes time for us to do 'The Wonder of You', I scout the room for those lovely green tits of Sheila's. I spot them in a corner next to a tiny crab man, balding with a comb-over. Even though he's a little fella, his arms are workman's arms, thick with muscle and tattoos. 'I'd like to, uh, dedicate this song to Roy and Sheila,' I say, 'whose, uh, wedding anniversary it is, uh, today, uhthankyouverymuch.' Then I stride over to them with the radio mike, and I sing right in their faces for the entire song. The boys are doing that 'Aah-ah-uh-oooh!!' backing part behind me, and make it sound like they've dug up Elvis's corpse and are having sex with it, which to be honest, is what I sus-pect they actually spend most of their time thinking about. Meanwhile, Roy and Sheila both have an expression of almost obscene happiness on their faces, with Sheila beginning to cry, and Roy grinning like only the clinically deluded can.

I reach the climax of the song – 'That's the wonder, the wonder of yooooooooou!!!!' – then I get them to stand up and take a round of applause. 'Roy and, uh, Sheila, ladies and, uh, gentlemen, childhood sweethearts, married for, uh, nine hun-dred years, nearly as much in love now as back then, an, uh, example to us all.' It's the charlie talking of course, and now that I've taken my second hit, I doubt I'll say anything else that coherent for the rest of the performance. Still, never did Elvis any harm.

It's after the show. According to the tape, 'Elvis has left the building'. Except I haven't, I'm just in the dressing room taking my gear off while the boys talk to their adoring public. I'm down to my belt and Elvistrousers when the door opens. It's Sheila. She walks in on her horsey legs, closes the door, and stands an inch away from me. Of course I go hard again instantly and the distance between us is shortened to a quarter of an inch.

'Oh, Elvis,' she says, putting her arms around me, 'I just wanted to say, on behalf of Roy and myself, thank you for making our anniversary so special.' Now, I'm a man of some considerable experience, but even I'm surprised by the force with which she full-on snogs me. Her tongue tickles the roof of my mouth. Then she pushes me into a chair and tries to undo my enormous buckle. 'Let me do it,' I say, and while I unbuckle myself she pulls off her green top, unleashing her remarkable tits which shoot towards me like incoming missiles.

'Funny way to celebrate your anniversary,' I say, as my Elvistrousers gather at my ankles.

'Roy's hasn't been interested in sex for years,' she replies, 'I've celebrated most of our anniversaries like this.' She doesn't say much after that, and I'm wondering if this is on behalf of Roy and herself as well.

Now I'm not saying this sort of thing always happens after our gigs, but it's not the first time either. Fact is, I have a way with the ladies, a certain magnetism that just compels them to offer their bodies to me. I don't know what it is, it must just be a gift that I was born with. Only seems to work on the older lady though. Now if I could only compel some of the younger, more attractive ones, I'd be laughing.

The door opens. Obviously knocking is seen as some bizarre foreign custom that's treated with suspicion round here. In walks the mole lady. Who looks at us. And we look back at her. She stands there for a second making odd shapes with her mouth and gibbering, before darting out.

Sheila looks pale. 'Fuck,' she says. 'Fuck. Fuck. Fuck. Roy's going to go mental.' She pulls her top back on and on her way out, says to me, 'I'd get out of here if I were you, or you're going to get fucking killed.'

I pull up my Elvistrousers while I try and work out what to do. Instantly I shoot my load into them, which makes a big sticky stain on their brilliant white crotch. 'Fuck!' I say to myself. I decide to worry about it later.

I run out to the car park. I have to pass through the bar to get to it, which is taking my life in my hands, but nothing seems amiss, yet. Roy's standing at the bar laughing with his mates. Big blokes, his mates. When I get out, the boys are loading up the van, still in their Elvis gear because of there being punters about. The Fatman steps out of the social with an amp. 'Fatboy, I need your car.'

'What's wrong with the van, boss? You've come in your trousers by the way.'

'Never mind that, I've just been caught being blown by some guy's wife and I need your car now!'

Fatboy sighs. Then he starts to walk off in the opposite direction.

'Where are you fucking going?' I shout at him. 'Didn't you hear anything I just said?'

'Calm down, boss. I'm just going to put this amp in the van, and once I've done that I'm going to see if I can find my keys. I think they're in the dressing room.'

'Never mind,' I say, 'I'll get them my fucking self.' Useless fatty, he'd be too lazy even to piss on himself if he was on fire. Anyway, I leg it back into the dressing room, grab the keys and shoot back out again. As I make my way out at high speed, I see out of the corner of my eye two figures in the corner of the bar area. One is the mole woman. The other is Roy. He's looking like he's just lost World War II. And Sheila's nowhere to be seen.

I dive into the car and start up the engine. Over the top of it, I hear a shout – 'There he is!' Piling out of the social is Roy, his head purple like a boil, accompanied by his bigger friends. 'Oi! Elvis, you cunt!' he shouts, and they charge towards the car. I reverse as fast as I can, and nearly hit some of them. Meanwhile, another one of them manages to give the passenger door a good kick, snarling as he does so. But still, I get out of the car park OK, and I'm bombing it up the road, several miles away, before it occurs to me that the madding crowd might take out some of their anger on Fatboy and Gaylord, or worse still, our equipment. Oh well, I think to myself, that's another thing I can worry about later.

It's the early hours of the morning before I make it back to the Fens and arrive home. There I throw off my Elvistrousers, lie on the sofa and smoke a spliff to cushion the downs from the charlie. I try not to think about the equipment, and instead recall the sight of Sheila's lovely tits, which I fear I will never be given the opportunity ever to see again. I mourn their loss with a quick fiddle, before putting myself to bed.

CHAPTER 2

'**Well, hello again dear** boy,' says the voice from behind me. 'Be a good chap and sing "Hound Dog" for me one more time, like you used to in the good old days.'

'No, I don't want to,' I reply, as fat, stubby hands massage my shoulders.

'You seem to be under the delusion you have some choice in the matter. Now pull your trousers down and sing it, you sorry little bastard!'

A door opens at the end of a long hospital corridor in front of me. 'Quick, this way!' says my sister Bridget. I slip out of the fat hands' grip and make a run for it, getting through the door just as Bridget is closing it. She bolts it behind me, and I can hear the sound of panting from the other side.

'All right, shrimp,' says Bridget. 'You nearly didn't make it that time.'

'No, that was close. Thanks.'

I look around the room. It's Bridget's bedroom from when we were growing up. 'Look,' she says, 'you know what I have to do now, don't you?'

'Yeah,' I say, 'but I don't understand why.'

'Yes you do. You know why I have to do this.' She makes a noose out of her school tie and attaches it to the light fitting.

The phone rings.

'Awwright,' says the voice from the earpiece, travelling through a haze of sticky sleep as I lift it to my ear.

'Jesus, Fatty, do you have to phone so early?'

'I know it's only eleven o'clock, boss, but we've got a bit of a situation. Ah, after you went, the gentlemen who you managed to get on the wrong side of decided to take their frustration out on the van in your absence. And the equipment. And the Gaylord.'

'Jesus. How bad is it?'

'Well, he's got a big fat lip, but he'll live.'

'No, I meant the van and the equipment. Look, tell you what, get yourself and the Gayster down here, we'll have to sort this mess out.'

'That may be something of a problem, boss. The van's not exactly roadworthy and Gayboy is sulking. He's not talking to you right now. For some reason, he blames you for his taking a beating. I can't imagine why. Anyway, you've got my motor.'

'OK, listen. Meet me in the Golden Lion and bring him with you. Tell him I'm very, very sorry and want to make it up to him.'

'All right, I'll tell him,' said Fatboy, 'but he's really pissed off. I don't think he'll come.'

Of course, I know he'll be there. As long as I've known him, Gay Elvis has always been like a little puppy hungry for my attention, and although he's aiming for praise, he'll settle for abuse. Fatboy, on the other hand, is untrainable. He's just too lazy ever to go out of his way for anybody, no matter how much you try to bully him into doing it. The only reason he's even involved in this whole thing is that he loves Elvis. He's absolutely fucking mad on him, maybe even more than Gaylord.

I hang up on the Fatman. I want to hide in the covers for another five hours or so rather than have to go and spend time with those two cretins, but instead I force myself out of bed and crawl downstairs, an idea involving breakfast half formed in my mind. There, waiting for my attention in the living room amongst all the other crap scattered around, are the spunk-encrusted Elvistrousers I'd left on the floor the night before. Christ, what are you meant to do when something like that happens? I fill up the sink with water and leave the trousers in to soak. Some of it comes off in flakes that float about in the sink and bump into each other. It's pretty fascinating to watch, and I only stop because I realise that I'm watching my own dried spunk float about in the fucking sink. At times like this, I wish I was still married because birds know what to do with stuff like this, whether to put washing powder in, give it a good rub or whatever it is birds do with clothes in sinks. Everyday things are definitely easier with a bird around. I should know, I've been married three times – never for very long, mind you. Always some problem or other that means everything goes wrong. Either I get sent to the nick or – OK, the fact is, I have a pretty high sex drive, and when I say high, I mean it's through the fucking roof. It's been that way since I was thirteen, and it hasn't dropped off one bit. I only have to see a person of the female persuasion and chances are I've got the horn. On the street, on the telly, wherever. Now you try staying faithful under those circumstances. It's damn near impossible, I can tell you.

Anyway, the trousers are in the sink. Maybe it's the right place for them, maybe it's not. Maybe they need to be coated in some weird cleaning product I've never fucking heard of that only birds know about, I really don't know. I should wash myself too I guess. After all, my pubic hairs are stuck together. Abandoning thoughts of breakfast, I drag myself back upstairs to the bathroom. I have the misfortune to catch sight of myself in the mirror on the way in. Jesus, I'm in a state. I'm fat, I'm bald, and I'm old. Well, I'm not a porker like Fatboy, but I've got a gut. And a lot of my hair's still there, but it's long gone grey, and there's a great big patch in the centre of my scalp I have to hide by brushing what's still there over the top of it. And now there's hair sprouting out of my ears. Why is it coming out of my ears and not the top of my head? Guess that happens to you when you're old. Well, I'm fifty-two. I suppose that's old isn't it? Maybe it's not so much these days, people don't seem to get properly old until they're seventy-five or something now, but when I was young, it was bloody ancient. Anyway, I feel old. Probably because I'm in such bad shape. Christ, when I was young, I was a handsome fucker. I mean, I could pull any bird I wanted, practically. They're not exactly beating down my door any more though. Don't get me wrong, I still have lots of ladyfriends. It's just that these days I've had to lower my standards a bit. Basically, I'm just banging old birds now, nothing younger than forty-five. Really, I have no choice. Being such a highly sexed individual as I am, I just can't afford to be choosy. Yes, I'd be happy to have something with a few less miles on the clock, but unless it suddenly becomes fashionable to shag fat old cunts, I can't see it happening.

I take the opportunity to sort myself out in the shower. You'll find I have to sort myself out a lot. Five or six times a day in fact. You see, if I don't get a chance, I just can't concentrate on anything at all. It can really be a curse sometimes. No matter where I am, no matter what I'm doing, at some point I'll have to visit the lav and have a good fiddle. You never know what will set it off. Maybe I'll see a fit bird in the distance, or in a photograph on a wall. Or I'll just remember something. Then I have to go and fiddle in the lav or I will lose control of myself and whip it out wherever it is I am. And if that's at the supermarket checkout, then so be it.

I get out of the shower, put my clothes on, and get in the Fatty's car. There's a dent in the side where one of Roy's heavy friends gave it a good kick last night. Hope the Fatty's insurance covers it or the tightwad will be hassling me for cash, I think to myself as I put the radio on and reverse out of the driveway.

Fatty's fatflat is in Arbury, over in Cambridge. It's funny, when you think of Cambridge you think of toffs in stupid fucking gowns and mortar boards arsing about in boats with inbred toff birds neighing by their side. You don't think of common scum like Fatboy living here. But they do obviously, because they're always going to need people to clean the toilets or work in Tesco's, or tear their ticket when they go to listen to their fucking Mahler. Cambridge has its share of scumfolk, not that the toffs ever notice them, getting drunk in their own common scum pubs, shopping in their own common scum shops and watching their own common scum telly. And listening to Elvis of course. When you've got common scum, you've always got Elvis.

Anyway, by the time I'm parking down the road from Fatlad's local, the Golden Lion, I need to sort myself out again. It was the centre of Cambridge that did it. All those gorgeous student girls, with their rucksacks and bicycles. It's just too much. They come from Europe to learn English here. They come from bloody Scandinavia. And they walk down our streets. They walk down our streets wearing shorts. I just want to get into that pub lav and sort myself out, while thinking about dormitories and tutorials and saunas.

I'm not even conscious of what it is I'm meant to be doing here in the first place as I jog up the road to the pub. All I'm thinking about is getting some relief from the tickling itch in my trousers. So I get a surprise when I walk through the pub door to find the pair of them waiting for me inside, Fatboy with his usual jovial moronic expression, the Gaymeister with a lip like a thick black German sausage. 'Awwright' says Fats and grins, just like he does every time he sees anyone he knows, while Gaylord just nods and grunts, no doubt to signal that I'm in his bad books. Fatty's two-thirds of the way through a pint of bitter, while Gayboy's nursing some gay drink, trying to make it last.

'Hi, lads,' I say, 'aah, just got to go to the lav. Back in a sec.' Maybe I imagine it, but I'm sure I hear the pair of them giggling to each other as I hurry past. 'Get a round in, someone.' I'll give them something to fucking laugh about, I think to myself. Then I push the lav door so hard, I nearly fall over when it opens easily on its spring hinges.

CHAPTER 3

It takes about thirty seconds. I didn't even get as far as thinking about the saunas, I just had to contemplate the existence of student halls of residence and I was practically there. It's got to the point now that I don't even need to think about sex, just a location where some people might conceivably have it, and that's enough to make me come. If nothing else, it shows I have a very active imagination.

For a minute afterwards, I feel amazing. But inevitably, like always, I've hardly mopped myself up and zipped up my trousers, and I'm already hitting a low. I just feel so fucking ridiculous that my life should be dictated by it to the extent that it is. I mean, I'm a clever person, right. OK, I haven't got that many qualifications but then I've never had the opportunities.

Still, I've never got into the habit of reading books because I can't concentrate long enough on one before I have to go and fiddle with myself. You see, books are full of descriptions of people, in places, and even though they're probably not having sex in them, they potentially could do. And that's what I imagine, every time I read one. TV's not so bad though, because I can sort myself out while I watch that, and I've learned quite a lot off the telly, stuff you wouldn't expect a bloke like me to know. For instance, I know who Ernest Hemingway is. And Arthur Conan Doyle. I'm quite solitary when I'm not shacked up, so I've got to watch a lot of telly over the years.

There's no drink waiting for me when I get back. Before I sit down, I put out my newly soaped hand to Gay Elvis.

'Sorry, mate,' I say.

'Yeah, whatever,' he replies, his big black lip wobbling as he speaks. He takes my hand limply in his and shakes it.

'So lads, what's the damage?'

'We're fucked, that's what the damage is,' replies Gay Elvis.

'How fucked?'

'Totally fucked,' says the Fatboy. 'The van's a write-off. They've battered it to buggery. The back lights are fucked, the back windows are smashed, the windscreen's cracked. They only didn't slash the tyres 'cos if they had, then they wouldn't have been able to get rid of us.'

'What about the equipment?'

'Fucked,' the Fatboy continues. 'Speakers are fucked, monitors are fucked. Mixing desk . . . fucked. Amp's OK.'

'Christ, we're fucked.'

All this time the Gayster has been evil-eyeing me, which, along with his fat lip does not make a pretty sight. 'So that's it then,' he scowls, 'it's over, we're fucked. And all because of you and your fucking cock.'

'What else am I supposed to do with it?'

'Cut it off.'

'Well, never mind my cock right now, how much is this all going to cost us?'

'Could cost a thousand for a new PA, two grand for a second-hand van that's decent,' says Fats.

'Shit, we've a gig on Tuesday in Elk.'

'Christ, we're not going to Elk are we?' says the Fatman. 'They're all fucking weird in Elk.' He's right. Elk's a fucking strange place. I was there just yesterday afternoon buying some charlie. If you're not from the village, they all whisper to each other and back away, then watch you from a distance. But we've got a gig there and that's that.

'Yes, we're going to Elk,' I say. 'That means we've got less than a week to get three grand together. I'm a bit short right now. What about you, Fatboy?'

'Nah, sorry mate. Don't really have any spare cash right now, what with being out of work for so long and all.' Fatlad took a break off work after he quit his last job. That was four years ago. Fortunately his wife makes an OK amount so they get by. I suppose you could call him a house husband if it weren't for the fact he does fuck all around the house. Even though he spends all his time playing video games, watching telly and downloading porn, if you ask him what he's been up to he'll always tell you he's been busy. Elvis is about the only thing you can get him out of bed for, and even then he's a lazy fat cunt about it.

Gayboy's pretty well off, though; he's got a decent job working for the local council doing boring crap that only a gaylord would find interesting, but brings in a fair enough wage. His wife Jen works a bit too, so they're doing all right. They've got a nice house and the children are well looked after. He's definitely got three grand stashed away somewhere in some special gay bank account. 'How about it then, Softlad,' I ask. 'Surely you could come up with the dough. It's for Elvis, after all.'

He glowers at me with all his wimpy might. 'You must be fucking joking,' he says, and glowers some more.

I lean forward and fix him with my gaze. 'Come on,' I say, 'we really need this money. Please?'

'Go fuck yourself,' he says.

I'm shocked, I have to say. It's never been like this before. He always used to go out of his way to please me. Now he's suddenly treating me with open contempt. My hold has slipped. Something has made him lose respect for me. It couldn't just be the incident last night. We've been through much worse before and his faith in me has been unwavering. Christ, what could it be? I'm just figuring how to deal with this when I realise that we're being looked at from across the pub. A tall, awkward-looking man with ginger hair and glasses is smiling at me. Oh god, not another fruit to deal with, I hope. It's funny, I'd swear I've never seen him before, but there's something very familiar about him.

'I'm just going for a gypsy's kiss,' I announce.

'You've just been,' says the Gayster.

'I know, but I'm old. I'm falling apart.'

On the way to the lav, I look to see if the speccy monger is following me. Sure enough, he is. Once I'm inside, I stand at the urinal nearest the door and unleash the trouser snake. I'm pretty fucking large so I have to stand well back. Four-eyes walks in and stands two urinals down. I can see out of the corner of my eye his is a tiddler. He's standing so close to the urinal he's practically shagging it. I nod at him. He nods back.

'Are you Elvis?' he asks. His voice is nasal and squeaky.

'Could be,' I say. 'Who wants to know?'

'Me. You see, I'm Buddy Holly.'

'Yeah, course you are, mate.'

'No, I mean, I do an impersonation of him, like you do one of Elvis.'

'I'm pleased for you.'

'Yeah, well, the reason I wanted to speak to you was, well, I was wondering, like, if you'd consider me as being part of your act.'

'You mean, have you perform with my lot?'

'That's right, yeah.'

'And why would I want to do that?'

'Well, I was thinking, maybe it would be good for your business, because not everybody likes Elvis, some people just like Buddy Holly. So an Elvis and Buddy show might get more gigs.'

'Look mate, I don't really need any help getting gigs right now. We've got work coming out of our ears, and—'

'Sorry to interrupt, but I was talking to your friends the other day and—'

'They're not my friends.'

'OK, your, uh – anyway, they said you're only averaging one gig a fortnight these days, and you used to have loads more work but it's all dried up for some reason.'

'Yeah, well, I wouldn't believe everything those two charlies tell you, so – you don't happen to have three grand do you?'

'No I don't, sorry.'

'OK, never mind. Look, I can't be bothered to think about this right now, so I'll give you my card and you can phone me sometime next week and if I've come round to the idea I'll have a look at you do your stuff. Happy?'

'Oh yes, thank you, very happy.'

He finally leaves me alone and scurries back to his place at the bar. So that's the speccy stalker problem taken care of. I just wish I could deal with the bigger issue of coming up with three grand so easily. My credit rating's shot to hell, which means the only people who are going to lend me anything are loan sharks or hardened criminals. Having been in the nick as much as I have, I know quite a few of those, but one in particular has proven very useful to me in the past. Mind you, he got value for money out of me all right. I signal to Fatty and Gayboy that I'll be back shortly, and it would be wonderful if they could get a round in while I'm gone, and stroll out into the beer garden. As the midsummer sun streams down on me, I press autodial on my mobile. Immediately, a male secretary answers. 'Hold, please,' he says. Pan pipes play 'MacArthur Park' all the way through twice.

'Well, hello dear boy,' a familiar voice says finally, just as I'm getting worried I'm going to run out of credit. 'How absolutely wonderful to hear from you again.'

'Ah, hello, Eddie,' I say. 'How are you? I heard you've been doing very well recently.'

'My boy, I'm always doing well. Now what can I do for you?'

'Oh, I was just phoning up to hear about what you've been up to, you know, catch up on—'

'You need some money, don't you?'

'Yeah, well, it's partly that. You see, I was wondering, I need a bit of assistance with my current business venture, and—'

'Oh, it's business is it? Well, I don't like to discuss business on the phone. Why don't you come up and see me at my lovely residence? I don't think you've seen my new place, have you? I've just had it renovated to reflect my classical tastes.'

'Uh, sure, Eddie. Would you be free any time this week at all?'

'Yes, tomorrow, twelve o'clock. I see you are calling from a mobile telephone. I'll have someone text you the address. I've got to go now. Goodbye.'

The phone goes dead. Sure enough, an address in Esher arrives just a minute later. Esher, of all places. I rejoin the pair of them inside. Still neither of them has got a round in. For two gimps who worship Elvis, a man so generous he'd buy cars for total strangers, I've got to say, they're pretty fucking stingy.

'Fats, I need the car again tomorrow, I think I've found the money.'

'Uh, now boss,' says Fatty, 'don't take this the wrong way or anything, but I don't really want you driving it. Insurance thing, sorry.'

'You let me drive it last night.'

'I only thought you wanted to open the boot. Didn't realise you were going to fuck off in it.'

'What the fuck would I want in the boot?'

'I dunno. Anyway, I just had a look at it out front. There's a bloody great dent in the side. If my insurance doesn't cover it, you're paying for that.'

'Fine, fine. What about you, Gay Elvis, could I please borrow your car tomorrow for an urgent business trip?'

'Go fuck yourself,' says the Gaylord, looking up from the very dregs of his gay drink.

'I'll drive you,' says Fatboy. It's possibly the first time he's ever uttered those words to anyone.

'I'll come too,' says Gay Elvis, 'I've taken some time off work until my lip goes down, so I'm free.'

'What do you want to come for?'

'I'm curious as to where our funding is coming from.'

'You're better off not knowing, believe me, but if you want to tag along, then fair enough. Fatlad, pick me up at ten o'clock. We've got an appointment in Esher at twelve.'

'Are you going to pay for petrol?'

'Yes, I'll pay for the fucking petrol. Anyway, what have you lads planned for the rest of the day?'

'I'm staying round his until my lip goes down,' says the

Gayboy, 'I don't want the kids to see it.'

'Aye,' says the Fatman, 'we're going to watch the new Elvis *Comeback Special* DVD. Check out all the extras. You can come round and watch it if you like.'

'No thanks, got better things to do with my time than watch that old wanker. There's business to take care of.'

'Such as?' asks Gay Elvis.

'Oh, just stuff.'

And I leave them there in the pub to nurse their empty glasses, while I walk out into the fine sunshine. I have a theory regarding the mystery of Gay Elvis's sudden change of attitude towards me. There's only one way to prove it. I phone his wife.

She picks up. 'Hi, Jen,' I say, 'it's me.'

'Oh fuck. What do you want?'

'Are you at home?'

'Could be, why?'

'Well, I was wondering if we could talk, and stuff. Can I come over?'

A pause.

'OK, but you've got to be fucking well out of here before the kids come home from school.'

'Sure, not a problem. See you in a bit, bye.' But she's already hung up on me.

CHAPTER 4

'**So you told him** then?' I ask her a couple of hours later.

'Yeah, I told him.'

'When?'

'This morning. I just couldn't resist it. He looked so fucking pathetic, with his big swollen lip, ranting on about how it was all your fault because you couldn't keep your dick to yourself. So I told him where else you've put it.'

'Well, thanks a lot. Now he's really off with me.'

'Like I give a flying fuck, my dear.'

'Yeah, I know. Jen, you're evil, you know that don't you?'

'Ah, go burn some kids, you sick piece of shit.'

It's bliss, lying here next to Jen, in my state of well-earned flaccidity. Most of the time, I'm never at rest, either because I'm too aroused, I want some drugs, or I really want to kill someone. But now, here on Gay Elvis's bed, his just-fucked wife lying beside me, and his underwear drying on the radiator, I'm happy.

I like Jen, as much as I like anybody, because she's rotten like me. You can tell when she fucks you that she's just using you, that she has no interest at all in how you feel. But being used by her feels a hell of a lot better than any of the considerate fucks I've ever had. I reckon it's because we're both parasites. We cancel each other out, and that happens to make for some great sex. Jen's probably the most evil person I've ever met without a criminal record. With Gay Elvis she did all the ground-work for me. By the time I got to him, she'd already stripped him of any sense of self-worth he may have once had. God knows why she married him. He's a skinny ugly fucker who minces about and looks like he's got AIDS. Jen, on the other hand, is beautiful, although she'll be fifty in a few years and her figure's not what it once was. But she's still a looker with a great mane of red hair, and a furry bush to match. She never shaves it, and it feels good to rest my head on it sometimes. Jen's one of the few women I've ever bothered to go down on, and I expect her big lovely bush has a lot to do with it.

I know I'm not the only fella who's been screwing Jen since they married. God knows how many others there have been. I like to think it's at least fifty but it's more likely ten. The whole thing with Gaylord puzzles me. Maybe she shacked up with him because she just wanted a good father for her kids, because he is one, I'll give him that. They've got three kids, though one of them's mine. One girl, one boy, then the bastard, who's also a boy. In a cruel twist of fate, their son looks like their mum, so when he's older he'll be good-looking, but at the moment he's just the school ginger cunt, while their daughter looks like her Gaydad, so she resembles a midget version of Larry Grayson with pigtails. My kid's perfect though. He's got blond curly hair like I used to when I was a lad, and he's got his mum's eyes. I suppose if I could ever say I've cared for anybody, it would be the kid. But I can't say that because I can't care about anybody else except myself. You see, I've been clinically diagnosed as a psychopath.

I'm not joking, I really have. Well, to be precise the results of the test were inconclusive, but there's the possibility I could be one, and I reckon that I am. They tested me for it the second time I was in the nick, because they wanted to know how come I set a building on fire, even though I knew there were kids in it. They all got out OK, but they could have fried. Anyway, they gave me this test, and afterwards the prison shrink explained to me what they were looking for. You see, a psychopath isn't a loony like people think when they hear that word, and they're not necessarily going to be a serial killer or anything. They could just be something low-key like a small-time con artist or a shifty businessman. Or maybe just a cunt who screws people's lives up, like me. The bottom line is, a psychopath is someone who doesn't have a conscience. You're just not born with one. It's a malfunction in the brain, a physical thing. Nothing you can do about it.

When the shrink told me about it in more detail, a lot of the time it was like he was just describing me. You could say it was a moment of enlightenment for me, almost religious, with the shrink being like this guru who was explaining the reason for my life being the way it was. For instance, one of the things he said was that a psychopath has no feelings for anybody else, they just fake it. Well I've been faking my feelings for other people my whole life. Can't think of a single nice thing I've ever said to anybody I've actually meant. Another thing, psychopaths don't feel guilt. Again, that's never been something I've ever had a problem with, so that's another point in favour of me being one.

Also, he said psychopaths are very deceitful, which I am. And not only that, they have problems with self-control, and that's me all over, what with my constant wanking and the charlie. So, the shoe fits, and that means I'm a psychopath doesn't it?

Well, they wouldn't diagnose me as being one. The thing is, I'm a very angry person. I don't know why, and the shrink couldn't work it out either, but there was something eating away at me, and still is. At first they thought it might be because my dad fiddled with my sister so much that she killed herself. But I really don't have a problem with my dad, one way or the other. He's been dead for years anyway. But they said if I really was a psychopath, I probably wouldn't let whatever that one thing is that I'm angry about bother me so much, because they're emotionally too shallow. I'm not buying it though. I reckon I am one. I'm just a special new type that's very angry. I mean I've got to be, haven't I. Otherwise I wouldn't be trying to cook little kiddies in burning buildings.

'OK,' says Jen, breaking my reverie, 'fuck off now, the kids will be home soon.' She throws my clothes at me and pulls up her tights. I obediently start getting dressed.

'So, I guess I'll see you soon then,' I say.

'Dunno, maybe.' She pulls down on her blouse and finds a pair of shoes. 'Look, show yourself out will you, I've got things to do.' Jen's on the phone when I leave, being a damn sight more polite to whoever it is than she's ever been to me.

Due to a lack of my own transport, it looks like I'll be riding home on the number 47 bus. It's quite a walk to the station, but I don't mind. It's a beautiful day, with the sun making the stones of old buildings glow so bright it almost hurts to look at them, and after giving Jen such a good hammering, I'm able to walk through the centre of Cambridge without getting quite such a hard-on for a change. It's funny, the things I find myself thinking about when I don't need to fiddle. It's not stuff I really want to bother myself with, but it just comes to me, whether I want it to or not. Like that psychopath thing, I haven't thought about that in ages, but there it was, in my head all of a sudden. And now, not half an hour later, I'm walking through Cambridge, and instead of fantasising about locations in which the various American tourists that I pass might possibly have sex, like I normally would be, I'm thinking about even more stuff that happened years back. I'm thinking about the first time I met Eddie. Christ, that changed everything. It made me into Elvis for a start.

I was only nineteen the first time I was in the nick. I'd fallen in with some bad boys and had been doing some serious thieving when I done got caught and sent down. Now I thought I was hard, but in the nick I was well out of my league. And with my curly blond hair and angelic features, well – to put it bluntly, I was raped. More than once. Fortunately, being the top-drawer psychopath I undoubtedly am, I wouldn't say it affected my self-esteem that much, but it fucking hurt.

Then I started sharing a cell with Eddie. We got to know each other quickly, and he seemed keen to be my friend. He was in for dubious business practices, the nature of which I would not know for some time. Eddie was about twenty years older than me, and my first impressions of him were that he was posh, polite, kind and very intelligent. He tried to get me reading, and lent me books by French writers I couldn't understand. He said they'd help me find myself. I remember one was about people catching the plague, and another was about a bloke who always felt nauseous. Anyway, when I finally felt that I could trust him enough, I told Eddie about the attacks. He gave me a priceless piece of advice. 'Listen, my dear boy,' he said, 'everybody loves an entertainer. If you can put on a bit of a show for the lads, then they'll most likely leave you alone.'

'What sort of thing were you thinking of?' I asked him.

'Well,' he said, 'a lot of the guys in here love Elvis. If you can do a few Elvis numbers the way Elvis does them, I believe that they'll love you for it. Just don't get cute and sing "Jailhouse Rock" and you will certainly be a shining star.'

He was right. The last time a load of them had been out of the nick, Elvis was still King. Most of them wouldn't even recognise a Beatle if they stepped on one. So I decided to do as he said, and practised and practised until I got it down pat. Then one day in the rec yard, I blacked up my hair and greased it into a quiff, did the thing with the lip, and sung 'All Shook Up', 'Heartbreak Hotel' and 'Love Me Tender'. Jesus, they fucking loved it. From then on, every day in the rec yard, they'd crowd around me, and they'd all shout 'Do Elvis! Do Elvis!' Sure enough, they left me alone after that, and I was the most popular guy in the block, after the drug dealer. Unfortunately for me, it turned out that Eddie was really a fairy who had a thing about Elvis, and I got buggered pretty much every night from that point on while he made me sing 'Hound Dog'. No one would ever do anything about it, even though it kept the entire block up, because Eddie was effectively running the gaff. I still have dreams about it sometimes.

So that's how I learned how to do Elvis. That was in the early seventies, and by the time I got out, Elvis had turned into a big gutbucket. Not too long after that he was dead, and then there was a big demand for Elvis acts. So in between my two stretches in the nick, I started up doing Elvis professionally, although it wasn't my business then, I mostly did it through an agency. Of course, no one wanted to see a young sexy Elvis act, they just wanted fat on-drugs Vegas Elvis, so that's what I became. I don't care really, but I can't say that it's ever been as good as it was in the prison rec yard all those years ago. I don't know, it meant something then.

I wait for the bus. The sun bakes me through the glass of the large shelter, until it finally arrives. I let it take me through the fields, and down country roads, the smell of cow shit in the air. It's early evening by the time I get to my front door, and the local kids in their hoods and baseball caps are hanging around outside, waiting for me on their bicycles. I tell them not to hang around outside and always phone ahead, but they never listen. Doesn't really matter, there are no police cars cruising around out here. That's why I moved here, I guess, it's quiet, and so there's less to get me aggravated. Anyway, I let them in and we do some business. I sell them an eighth of the skunk I buy from this hippy I know from a few villages down. He grows it in his house. It's like a jungle in there. Anyway, he grows it, I sell it and we split the proceeds. It's not something I enjoy, especially as I have to put up with scummy kids hanging round my door at all hours. But there's no way I'd be able to live off what I make with Elvis, all that just goes up my nose, and to be honest with you, proper work and me have never really gone together. But I'm supplying to half the kids on the estate here, so I make a bit of bread, and a lot of the time the kids are buying it for their parents as much as themselves. I don't do anything harder, because I'm too old to do too much more time in the nick, even though I could make a load of cash from it round here.

So I have to stay up for nearly all of the night, making myself available for business like I do most nights. To while away the time, I do some charlie and sort myself out a couple of times while I think about Jen. Thoughts of Eddie keep me awake, and when I finally drop off as the sun rises, he's already waiting for me in my dreams.

CHAPTER 5

I think you could probably say that I'm in a really bad mood. Sitting here in the back seat of the fatmobile, listening to Fats and Gayboy discuss what must have been a truly scintillating experience, that is, watching all seven fucking hours of the new Elvis *'68 Comeback Special* DVD, I feel even closer to murder than I normally do. At least I can comfort myself that for one of those seven hours I was giving the Gaylord's wife a good seeing to. By God, I wish I was there now instead of stuck in this car with these two idiots, listening to them analysing every one of Elvis's costume changes while Fatty steers with his knees. I try to comfort myself with the possibility that I've knocked Jen up again, but to be realistic at her age it's unlikely.

The pair of them are even more Elvis-mad than usual at the

moment. It's because it's meant to be the fiftieth anniversary of rock 'n' roll which, we are now being told, was invented by Elvis in Sun Studios in Memphis on 5 July, 1954. That's funny, because they always used to say it was invented by wife-beatin' Ike Turner when he recorded a song called 'Rocket 88', in the same studio, three years earlier. The problem with that of course, it that it means that rock 'n' roll was the idea of a violent, coke-snorting, sex-addicted psycho. But I guess making Elvis the inventor of rock 'n' roll is more convenient, seeing as he's white and never beat up Tina Turner.

Meanwhile, I'm uneasy about the whole situation here. I mean, the Fatman actually offered me a lift. He never normally does favours for anyone because he's such a lazy fat oaf, but here he is driving me at a moment's notice and I didn't even have to ask. Something's definitely up with all this but I don't know what it is. Right now, they've started singing 'If I Can Dream', the song Elvis does at the end of the *Comeback Special*, at the top of their voices. I find myself unlocking the door and fingering the handle, and have to use all my will power not to open it and throw myself onto the motorway. At the song's climax Gay Elvis takes the female backing singers' part, and screeches in a high operatic voice, 'Please let my dream come true riiiiiight noooow!!!'

God help me. I can't hold it in any longer. 'Gay Elvis,' I say, 'you truly are a gaylord. You are lord of all the gays. Other gays bow down before you in awe and say, "Surely no man could be more gay, he is our lord and master." In fact you have a government post as Minister of Gay Affairs at the Homo Office. You tried out for the Village People but didn't get in because you were too gay. You own a box set of the complete works of Gloria Gay-nor, you want to move to Para-gay, you—'

'For Christ's sake, knock off the gay stuff!'

'I beg your pardon?'

'I'm sick of this constant abuse. My name's not Gay Elvis, it's Derek, so would you please be so kind as to call me that, and knock off all the fucking gay stuff!'

'Yeah, and I don't want to be called Fat Elvis any more either,' says Fat Elvis. 'It was funny about five years ago, but we're both kind of sick of it now.'

'Hmmph. If that's the way you feel.'

'Yeah, it is, sorry.'

We sit in sullen silence for a few minutes, until they start talking about fucking Elvis again. Then, I don't know why but I get the horn. I know I won't have a chance to do anything about it before I meet Eddie, by which point I'll be rubbing up against his antique chair legs in frustration. This could be something of a problem. I want to just whip it out in the back of the fatmobile and be done with it, but I can't see any tissue.

After what seems an eternity of Elvis analysis and ball-ache, we finally arrive on the outskirts of Esher. It's funny that Eddie should end up here, but then he's always had class, and it's certainly a classy neighbourhood. I just wonder if anybody here realises that Eddie's linked to one of London's major crime families. He's a millionaire of course, made a fortune running discos and strip clubs in the seventies and eighties, then cleaned up again with lap-dancing clubs in the nineties, but other than his irrational and perverted love of Elvis, he's very cultural. At least I think he is. I don't have the education to be able to tell the good stuff from the bad, so when he tells me something is the height of good taste, I've always tended to believe him.

The fatmobile drives up to a pair of enormous gates, through which we can see what looks like the fucking Parthenon about a mile off. There are various signs, warning of armed response, dogs and general nastiness. And by the gate, there's an intercom. As I'm in the back seat I have no choice but to let Fatty speak into it. And I swear I will kill him, because he has to fuck about and pretend to be Elvis.

'Hello?' says the intercom.

'Thisiselvispresley,' he mumbles.

'What?'

'Elvispresleyhoney,' he says to the very male intercom voice. Fatty-Fatty-Fat-Fuck and Gaylord burst out laughing.

'Drive away from the gate now sir, or you will be very sorry.'

'Welluhthankyouverymuchhoney.'

I clamber between the two front seats and over Fat Elvis, an experience that I never want to repeat, and shout into the intercom who I am and that I have an appointment.

'Letting you in,' says the intercom, with an audible sigh.

'You stupid fat cunt,' I scream at the Fatboy as he drives up the path. 'You don't mess with these people!'

'I was just having a laugh with them.'

'You'll be laughing out of a fucking bullet hole in the back of your head if you do anything as fucking stupid again.'

'Just having a laugh, that's all.'

Honestly, it's like talking to a wall of lard.

We drive to the front of the house where a gaggle of men in suits and sunglasses show us where to park. I'm hoping none of them were just working the intercom. If they were they give no sign. They're not your usual security. Of course, they're big and threatening, but also very clean and, well . . . moisturised. I never thought Eddie was that high up the totem pole, but he now seems to have more protection than any of his bosses ever did. Once we've parked, the men in suits open the car doors for us, carry out a body search, and form a cordon around us as they lead us up the steps to the house. It's as if they're afraid Fatboy's going to explode or something. We go through the front door and into a hall that's about the size of an aircraft hangar.

We're made to wait in some sort of study, decorated with old paintings and statues. At least they look old. In any case, they're all of naked men. And naked boys. As I walk in, I feel panic rising up in my chest. The realisation that I'm about to come into physical contact with Eddie overwhelms me, and it's all I can do not to run out the door and up the driveway. Why did I do it? I ask myself. Why did I get back in touch? The same reason you kept in touch with him all those years, says a calmer, more reasonable voice in my head, you needed him. It's true. Although when I left prison the first time I never wanted anything to do with the dirty bastard ever again, the thing was, I was really just a sad little dozy twit with a criminal record and a reputation for getting caught. I didn't have any real contacts, and other than the ability to mimic the recorded works of Elvis Presley, no noticeable skills. My prospects weren't that good, in fact I might well have had to actually seek honest employment if it hadn't been for Eddie.

He was still in the nick, but he was grateful for the loan I had made of my arsehole as a depository for his spunk, and he made sure that there were people looking after me on the outside. He got me a job working as part of a fencing operation, and then when he got out and into the entertainment industry, he remembered the aural delight he received when I used to sing him 'Hound Dog', and even though he didn't get to roger me senseless any more, he still booked me in his clubs and got me established. Not only that, when I got out of the nick the second time, he gave me the money I needed to start up my own Elvis act. So I suppose you could say that Eddie made me the man I am today.

I'm calmer now, but I'll be happier once I've sorted myself out. I ask the goons guarding the door to point me in the direction of the lav. Rather than give directions, they escort me personally down the hall. The lav's enormous, and I feel quite puny sitting there on the throne, fiddling with myself. Eddie's had the ceiling decorated with paintings of cherubs frolicking about in a very gay manner, so I have to close my eyes and imagine a space where grown heterosexual people might possibly have sex. I catch it in some luxury toilet tissue, wash my hands, and let the goons take me back to the study.

I was gone too long. Eddie is in there already, and Fatboy and Gaylord are serenading him with 'Love Me Tender'. Christ, that wasn't meant to happen. My heart scuttles up my windpipe and nearly chokes me. I don't know what I'm more afraid of, what Eddie might still want to do to me, or the possibility that Gay and Fat Elvis will screw everything up. Letting them both tag along suddenly seems a very bad idea indeed. Still, there's nothing for it but to let them sing now that they've started. I stand in the doorway, simultaneously wishing that they'd stop and also for them to carry on forever, thus delaying the moment when I have to reveal my presence to Eddie. I haven't seen him for nearly a decade, but I can see that the years have been kind to him, which they often are if you have the money to beat them back with. Maybe he's fatter, more jowly, but he's still the same old Eddie, that same combination of cuddly old poof and cold-hearted killer. Depends which angle you look at him. He's wearing flip-flops and a dressing gown, and his hair is wet and slicked back, still with no noticeable bald spot. The performance ends and he gives the boys a round of applause and cheers, 'Bravo!' I push myself forward into the room.

'Hello, Eddie.'

'My dear boy, it's simply wonderful to see you. They're very, very good. Where did you find them?'

'In a kebab shop.' This is actually true.

'How are you my boy? Still wowing the crowds?' He hugs me in a way that brings back bad memories, but I suppose might possibly be genuinely affectionate.

'Still am, Eddie. Of course you know I could never have done it without you.'

'Oh, you. You're embarrassing me. Shall we conduct our business out by the pool? I've been having a dip.' The four of us make our way outside, flanked of course by the super-clean security guards.

CHAPTER 6

'**Are you sure you** won't join me?'

Eddie has taken his dressing gown off to reveal a pair of tight blue Speedos, which make his dreaded penis look like the snout of something from outer space, or the bottom of the sea. I decline, and he climbs down the pool ladder and splashes about for a bit, before treading water. Not long before, he'd ordered two of the security goons to play a game of kick-about with Gay Elvis and Fatboy on the lawn. His men are playing skins. Without their shirts they are tanned, muscular, hairless and oily.

'So what can I do for you, my boy?' he asks.

'I need three grand right now.'

'Is that all? I thought you'd want a hundred thousand, or have someone wiped out in some drug turf war or what-have-you. I heard about you selling the waccy baccy. Can't say I approve, but that's by the by.'

'No, I just need three grand. I'll pay you back the money as soon as I have it.'

'But you'll never have it, my boy, I know what you're like. It's no secret that all your cash goes straight up your nose. I've been keeping tabs on you, dear chap. I know what you're up to. Now, if I loan you this money I will end up having to have your legs broken to get it back, so I'm not going to do it.'

'Eddie, I'll pay it back, I promise. I need it for Elvis, not for—'

'I am, however, going to give you the money.'

'Eddie, I—'

'Or at least I'm going to let you earn it. Three grand now, in return for an appearance by you and your lovely assistants at the sixtieth birthday party of Mister Johnny Brooks at the Trunk Club, in just under a month's time.'

Johnny Brooks is an old-style gangster, one of the few not to be overrun by the younger, more vicious breed, largely because he's a class A psycho. Legend has it he once forced a man to eat his own eyeballs before killing him. The Trunk Club is one of Eddie's lap-dancing venues in London, and a major hang-out for Eddie's crime family. The thought of performing there fills my head with visions of me singing 'Viva Las Vegas' while naked girls writhe about on poles all around. There's a thought to keep me warm at nights.

'Of course, Eddie,' I say. 'I'd love to do that for you. You can certainly count me in on it.' The whole thing's a charade, of course. I knew that Eddie would never lend me the money. Eddie is too proud to lend anybody anything, he only ever gives it. And seeing as Eddie's been effectively bankrolling me on and off for the past thirty years, and rarely says no to anybody, if only to show off how much money he's got to spare, I had reasonable faith that he'd bail me out now. The trick is to act like I'm not expecting him to. I've learned the drill over the years.

'Well that's utterly splendid,' says Eddie. 'I was afraid we'd have to have DJs playing that awful housey housey music that Johnny's suddenly started liking, but Elvis is much better. Can you imagine, a man of sixty listening to that nonsense? It's not very dignified, is it? Mind you, I think it's far more to do with the pretty young thing he's got himself hung up on. He's not exactly using his ears to listen to it, if you see what I mean.'

'Johnny hasn't broken up with Nanette, has he?' I ask.

'No, no, of course not. He's just picked up a silly new bit of fluff, that's all. The only thing is, this time, he thinks he's in love with her, the old fool. It's all quite embarrassing.'

The deal made, Eddie has one of his beefcake goons bring him his chequebook. While he dries his hands on a towel for him to write the cheque, he says the words I'd been dreading for a long time. Words so disturbing, they sometimes turn up in my dreams. 'You know,' he says, 'I'd really like to hear you sing "Hound Dog" one more time. Why don't you and your friends sing it for me now?'

I feel sick. 'Of course,' I say, 'I'd love to. Just give me a minute to prepare.'

'Certainly, do your vocal exercises, or whatever it is that you do.'

A goon rounds up Gay and Fat Elvis for me and brings them to the poolside.

'Look,' I say, 'I've got to sing "Hound Dog" for Eddie, and he wants you two to be involved. So sing some backing vocals, and make 'em good.'

'There aren't backing vocals for "Hound Dog", boss,' says Fatboy.

'I know there aren't! But I can't just have you dancing about like twats like you usually do, it'll look fucking terrible! Make something up, for fuck's sake, and do it quick.'

They settle on some 'doo-be-do-wah' nonsense, and I motion to Eddie. 'We're ready!'

'Oh, goody,' says Eddie, and pulls his slug-like body onto a lounger floating in the pool. A goon hands him a martini. And so while Eddie lies on his lounger in his tight and tiny Speedos, we stand on the poolside and I begin to sing:

> You ain't nothin' but a hound dog
> Cryin' all the time . . .

I'm shitting bricks, afraid that the backing vocals are ridiculous and belong on a barbershop record, and terrified that I won't be able to remember the second verse when it comes. And then something unexpected happens. Maybe it's because I'm not in my usual Vegas costume, or maybe because it's Eddie, but something inspires me to slip into young hip-swivelling Elvis mode, something I haven't done since the prison rec yard all those years ago. I don't realise I'm doing it at first, but once I start I can't stop if I tried. Even though I hate Elvis, young Elvis, old Elvis, fucking *'68 Comeback Special* Elvis, every so often, very rarely these days, he gets inside of me in some way, as if he's possessed me from beyond the grave, perhaps looking for another body to ruin. Usually, it's when I'm singing some Vegas crap like 'American Trilogy', and I find myself buying into it for about five minutes before I remember how much I hate the fucker, but this time, it's young Elvis that's got inside. I become lost in my own performance. It's in rare moments like this that I under-stand why I exist, what it is I am meant to do. By impersonating a dead rock 'n' roll star I hate, my sick, psychopathic existence has some meaning. As long as I swivel my fifty-two-year-old hips at gay gangsters, or dress up in a white jumpsuit and serenade old-age pensioners, there is order in the universe. Cosmic balance is maintained only as long as I am Elvis, and if I cease to be Elvis then the forces of chaos will be unleashed. I am compelled to be, and I must be Elvis, for it is my destiny.

We're slowing it down, messing with the tempo just like Elvis used to do on television and I'm jerkily moving the way he did, when I see something that breaks the spell. Eddie is lying there with a serious erection. His lycra trunks stretch around it so that you can almost see the veins. Idly, he strokes it as he bobs his head along to the music. I feel faint, and dots appear in front of my eyes. I'm still trying to walk like Elvis as I lose consciousness and fall into the swimming pool.

The water revives me moments later, but by now I'm totally submerged and sinking. My thrashing about doesn't help, and just as I experience sudden awareness of my impending death, I feel a pair of hands grab me by the armpits and pull me up and over the poolside. Then I feel another pair of fatter hands squeeze my stomach, causing me to choke up most of the swimming pool. Fatboy lays me on my side, and I can see Gay Elvis standing there, soaking wet. The boys just saved my life. I know I should be grateful, but being a psychopath I can't do gratitude, so I have to fake it for them.

'Thanks lads,' I say. Really, that's the best I can do.

Eddie sends us inside to dry off, escorted by a pair of his goons who provide us with towels and dressing gowns and a bathroom to dry ourselves in. There's a sunken bath in it that you could easily fit Eddie into along with all of his security. He's had it decorated with his usual young-men-touching-each-other motif, which doesn't put me at ease when having to take off my clothes in front of Gaylord and Fatty.

'Shit, my mobile's fucked,' says Gayboy. I guess mine must be too. The cheque from Eddie was folded up in my shirt pocket, but it's mush now.

'Don't get too excited Gay Derek, but I'm getting my cock out,' I say, as I pull off my pants.

'Boss, we've got something to tell you,' says the Fatboy.

'Oh, what's that?'

'Well, you're not going to like it, but, we've had a long talk, the pair of us, and . . . we've decided that we don't want to do Elvis with you any more. We're going to do our own thing from now on.'

'You're shitting me.'

'No, we're not,' says Gay Elvis.

'What's wrong, you gone off Elvis or something?'

'No. Not at all. It's a number of things really,' says Fatman, 'we want to sing more, and we want to do something more informative, with the songs in historical order and appropriate outfits for different sections of the show—'

'And we're sick to death of you treating us like fucking dog shit,' says the Gaylord.

'Yeah, that too.'

'I see.'

'I mean, we don't understand why you bother doing it any more,' continues the Gayster. 'Bookings are down, because nobody wants to see someone who doesn't give a shit. You don't even like Elvis.' Of course, there's no way I could make them understand why I have to do it, not that I'd really want them to.

'We just thought we'd see it through to make sure you got hold of the money. We felt we owed you that.'

Christ, I think, they owe me so much more. When I found them in that kebab shop singing 'Girl Happy', they'd never even performed in public before. I gave them the opportunity to be

Elvis on stage, week in week out, even make a bit of cash out of it, and this is their idea of repaying me, one lift to Esher and a stab in the back. And they also saved my life I suppose, but I don't see how that cancels out an act of betrayal like this.

One of Eddie's gay goons knocks on the door. He pokes his head round and grins. 'Eddie thought you could do with a change of clothes. He said you could keep them. They're a bit eighties, I'm afraid.' The goon grimaces at the pile of neon-coloured clothes and leaves. There's nothing that would fit the Fatman, but he's not that wet. Gaylord and I have no choice but to pick out some god-awful stuff that makes us look like we've stumbled out of the fucking *Breakfast Club*. It's all way too big for Gayboy, but it strangely suits him. The smiling goon pokes his head round the door again and tells us Eddie is waiting for us in the hallway.

'I'm afraid I'll need another cheque,' I say to Eddie when we shuffle out in our new duds. He's dressed now, in a light suit.

'Keep it safe,' he says as he writes it, and then tucks it into the pocket of the black and purple diamond-patterned shirt he's given me to wear. He kisses me on both cheeks and hugs me. 'Have a safe journey home, my boy,' he says, and turns and walks into one of his many rooms. The goons open the door and show us to the fatmobile. We sit in silence as we drive away. Of course, it only lasts a few minutes until they start talking about Elvis again. I wish I'd drowned. I'd got the money, but what good is it to me now? I feel wretched. Then, in the centre of all the noise, I find an oasis, a place of calm. In my mind's eye I find Jen's furry red bush. I imagine I'm resting my head there now, and I have peace.

Naturally, thoughts of Jen's bush gets the old horn throbbing again, and then I can't wait to get home to sort myself out. And I think, why wait? What's the worst that could happen? So while the Fatman drives us down the motorway, I take a leap into the unknown and unzip Eddie's offensive bleached jeans and whip it out. It takes a while for either of them to catch a glimpse of what I'm up to in the rear-view mirror, and by that point I'm nearly finished.

'What the fuck do you think you're doing?' says Gay Elvis.

'What does it look like? I'm having a wank.'

'Not in my car you're not!' says the Fatty. 'Put it away now, you dirty fucker.'

'No. Besides, I'm almost done.'

The Fatlad frantically pulls up onto the hard shoulder, gets out, opens my door, and throws me out of the car. I point my cock in his direction as I ejaculate, but I miss, and it splatters on the concrete. Gay Elvis looks at me with contempt from the passenger seat.

'He calls you Gaylord behind your back you know!' I shout. He doesn't respond.

'You're one sad, dirty fucker,' says Fats, as he gets back in his car.

'Fucking wanker,' cries the Gaylord.

And they drive off, leaving me stranded on the hard shoulder with my cock out. I have to say I feel distressed and confused.

CHAPTER 7

What came over me? I think to myself, standing on the hard shoulder of the motorway. I let myself get dragged out of a car by a fatty, be insulted by him and his homo friend, and I didn't do a thing about it. How come I didn't kick seven shades of shit out of them? Because, you know, I'm a psychopath. I have been known to damage people. I've broken legs before, and I disfigured someone's face when I was in the nick. I admit, I've never killed anyone, but that was more down to luck on their part than any fault on mine. So it stands that I'm a very bad man, OK? So how come I just took their abuse, and the only thing I did back was try to hit them with my spunk? Is my cock the only thing I'll dare hurt anybody with these days? Maybe I'm getting soft, and I'm not talking about my erection for once.

With this thought, I slump down on my knees, and to my surprise, for the first time since I don't know when, most likely ever, I find myself crying. And through the sobbing, words that I'm not in control of emerge. 'Jen, Jen, help me,' I whimper, as I think about the warmth of her furry red bush. I must get back to it, I decide. If I get back to Jen's bush then I will be myself again, and everything will be all right.

To do that, I reason, I need to stop this effeminate sobbing and hitch a lift. So through the power of my will, I pick myself up, dry my eyes, stand on the hard shoulder and stick my thumb out. However, hitchhiking on the motorway is not as easy as I thought. Cars zoom by, and while a number of them toot their horns, no one stops. I lose track of time, but I guess I must be there for half an hour. Sometimes passengers look at me while the car drives by, and they turn around to look some more, and quite a few horns are sounded, but no one feels like interrupting their journey. Then, finally, a car drives past, slows down, and pulls onto the hard shoulder some way up the motorway. A figure gets out and waves at me, and I run towards it. As I run, I feel strangely free, with quite a breeze blowing on my nether regions, and I realise that my cock's hanging out, swinging from side to side. It must have been out all this time and I've been flashing every passing motorist and their passengers. No wonder they've been honking at me. I put it away quickly, and as I get closer, the waving figure looks more familiar and distinctly ginger. Then at last I see. It's only fucking Buddy Holly. I'm nearly there and he's still waving.

'Hi, Elvis!' he shouts.

'All right,' I reply.

'You need a lift?'

'Could say that.'

'Well, hop in the back then, if you're going back to Cambridge.'

I finally make it to the car and get in. I'm sweating like a pig and smelling like one. In the front passenger seat is a woman, in about her mid-thirties, with dyed-blonde hair with dark roots, a bit podgy and a bit simple-looking, but with huge breasts and a lovely smile.

'This is my girlfriend Emma. Emma, this is Elvis.'

'Hello, Elvis. Pleased to meet you.'

'Same here.'

'Who'd have thought, me getting to meet Buddy Holly and Elvis.' She laughs a lovely sexy laugh. I can feel the first pulses of an erection as we drive away.

'I hope you don't mind me asking,' says Buddy, 'but didn't you have your willy out just now?'

'I must admit I did,' I say. 'You see, I have a very rare skin condition that means I have to air it periodically or it breaks out in sores.'

'Sounds nasty. Don't you ever get in trouble, getting your willy out like that?'

'No, I have a doctor's note.'

'Ah, I see. We've just been to an auction of rock 'n' roll memorabilia up in London. I was outbid on most things, but I got Fats Domino's autograph. Listen,' he says, 'I've just had a thought. Now that I have you as a captive audience, as it were, why don't I audition for you now? Save me taking up your time next week.'

I'm in no mood to hear the wittering twit sing, but I don't feel like being chucked out of another car. 'Sure,' I say, 'go ahead.'

And without further ado, he sings 'Peggy Sue', in an unpleasant, nasal manner, with a range of vocal affectations that I find intensely annoying. In other words, it's a perfect Buddy Holly impersonation. I have to say, I'm impressed.

'OK, you're in. We'll get you an outfit and some gear

tomorrow. We'll rehearse your act over the weekend and your first gig's on Tuesday.'

'Thank you, Elvis, you won't regret it. But don't worry about the outfit, I've got one already.'

'Oh, Mister Elvis, I'm afraid Buddy won't be able to play with you this Tuesday,' his bird pipes up. 'Any other day is fine, but on Tuesday we're going to my parents' for drinks.'

God save me from stupid women, even ones with enormous and inviting breasts. 'Well,' I say, 'I'm afraid I will need him on Tuesday. And to be honest with you, if I can't get the hundred per cent commitment I require, then I will have to consider other artists, possibly even another Buddy Holly tribute act.'

I can hear Buddy swallowing. In the rear-view mirror, I catch a glimpse of his eyes as they dart towards her. I know that look all right. It's the look of a man thinking dark and violent thoughts. 'Em,' he says finally, 'tell your parents I won't be able to make it for drinks on Tuesday.'

'Buddy, you said you'd be there. You can't just mess people about like that, it's not nice.'

'Em, this is more important.'

'Oh, is it?'

'Yes it is.'

You could say it's an awkward moment. Buddy's face turns as bright red as his hair, while Em vibrates, although whether it's from annoyance or fear I can't tell from where I'm sitting. They both stare out at the road for a good few minutes. Then the silence is broken by the sound of Buddy singing 'Heartbeat'.

Her stony face crumbles and she breaks out her big idiot grin. She puts her hand on his shoulder as he sings, and he turns towards her and gazes with his now soft eyes. For the second time this day, I have the feeling I am about to die. 'Keep your eyes on the road, love,' she says gently.

For the rest of the journey, I'm treated to Buddy's life story, how he's worked as a postman since the age of eighteen, but has dedicated his life to rock 'n' roll, or at least listening to it and obsessively collecting memorabilia. He's particularly devoted to Buddy Holly of course, and once spent five grand on a letter written by the four-eyed twat.

'How come you managed to afford that?' I ask.

'Well, to be totally honest with you, I suppose I didn't have that much else to spend it on. I was living on my own, and I didn't have a girlfriend at the time . . .'

'Yeah, Buddy didn't have a girlfriend until he met me, did you, Buddy?' Em interrupts suddenly.

'No,' he snaps.

'Oh, that surprises me,' I say. He's quiet for the rest of the journey.

Buddy drops me off in the centre of Cambridge. I arrange for him to pop round the next day to begin his training, and say goodbye to both him and Em, who gives me a lovely, silly smile as I stare at her huge tits. I catch the bank just in time to deposit the cheque, and while waiting in the queue I think about all I've been through in the past few days, and come to the devastating conclusion that I need to get very drunk very quickly. I don't get drunk that often, at least, not as much as I used to, and charlie will always be my main vice, not including wanking. But sometimes, I just really need to get absolutely bladdered. Flush the shit from out of my head. First though, I'm starving, so I stuff my face in McDonald's before I go looking for a suitable pub. I wander down Hills Road and chance upon an old haunt which I knew as the Blind Beggar, but which since my last visit has been renamed the Frog 'n' Ribbit and painted all over in vomit-green gloss paint. It's half-five when I walk in, and I'm nearly the only person there.

Behind the bar is a young man with dreadlocks and piercings all over his face.

'All right,' he says. 'What can I get you?'

'A pint of Guinness please.'

'Right you are.'

'It's quiet in here.'

'Yeah, it is now, but this evening it'll be packed.'

'Really?'

'Yeah, students mostly.'

My interest is piqued. I resolve right then that tonight will be the night when I finally get into the pants of something that's younger than forty. Although eighteen or nineteen years old would be ideal, I'll settle for anything in its twenties or thirties. Between forty and forty-five would be a compromise, and anything older than that would not be acceptable. I must admit normally I find it pretty impossible to chat up the younger birds, because I can never think what to say. Old birds I can charm the pants off, literally, because being a psychopath I have great powers of manipulation, but with the young 'uns, I get nervous, my brain stops working, and I blow it. Tonight, however, I'm going to be so pissed there's no way I can possibly lose my bottle. Yes, tonight is definitely going to be the night, oh yes indeed.

The barman's name is Oliver. He'd be quite handsome, I reckon, if he hadn't shoved fifty pieces of metal through his face We talk for a bit. His company's pleasant enough, I guess. As more people come in, Oliver finds less and less time to talk to me, and after a while, he just nods at me as he passes, even when he doesn't have anybody to serve. At quarter past seven I'm pleasantly drunk. That's when they really start arriving. And my god, they're all so beautiful. Or at least, they're young and female, which in my book amounts to about the same thing. There are boys there too of course, some of them with the girls, but I don't pay too much attention to them. They all look pretty weedy and I could easily break their windpipes if the situation called for it. I think I'm going to play it cool for a while. After all, I want to have the choice of the widest possible selection, so I'll wait until the place is full before making my move. I sort myself out in the lav in the meantime so I don't come over too desperate, and go back to drinking at the bar, looking the part of an enigmatic and intriguing loner. I keep this up for another hour, and by half-eight the place is packed. However, it's still not time to make my move. They need to be drunker, I think, and besides, there's so much choice. Too much choice, in fact. There's so much cleavage on display, so many legs, arms and midriffs, just so much flesh, I don't know where to begin. I find myself getting over-heated and decide I'll be able to make an informed decision if I go and sort myself out in the lav again. When I get back, some local old drunk with a red face and a tache comes up to me, no doubt mistaking me for a kindred spirit. 'Didn't you used to be a boxer?' he slurs. 'I was on *Nationwide*.' I tell him to fuck off. He does, but takes a good five minutes about it before going off to talk to a bunch of students, who take the piss and laugh at him. He's just grateful for the company.

A couple or so more pints and suddenly it's half-nine. Oliver takes pity and talks to me again, enquiring what it is I do for a living. I tell him I'm a drug dealer and Elvis impersonator. He thinks both jobs are pretty cool. Now he likes me. I give him my number should he need anything. He says he'll keep it in mind. Then it's ten o'clock, and I realise I'll have to make my choice pretty soon, but I'm still no closer to deciding. Until I see her. Her hair is long and black and makes its way right down her back. She's small but not skinny, and she's wearing a dress that makes her look quite bohemian, although I can tell she's wearing a Wonderbra underneath. There's something mystical about her, spiritual and in touch with nature. Her face glows with kindness, and her eyes sparkle with magic. Now, surely she wouldn't turn me away?

I'll go to the lav to sort myself out, I decide, then I'll make my move. I do, but when I come back, I can't see her. I search all over the pub looking for her, afraid I've lost her. Then I find her again, standing with her group of friends upstairs on a crowded balcony. Any minute now. First I watch her for a while, trying to read her, looking for clues. And then it's quarter to eleven. I can see some of her friends getting ready to go. It's now or never, I say to myself, or Elvis says to me from beyond the grave maybe, and I launch myself forward. Walking is difficult, I find, and I stumble towards her, bumping into people, spilling my pint. 'Oi! Watch it, mate,' they say. And then I'm right next to her, but she doesn't see me. So I stand there for a few minutes, and some of her friends glance at me uneasily. I can't think of what to say. I've frozen, just like always. But I have to do something, I tell myself, now or never.

'I like your dress.' That's what I come up with.

She doesn't hear me. I say it again.

'What?' she says.

'I like your dress.'

'OK, thank you.' She smiles half-heartedly, then turns back towards her friends. They mumble between themselves and make moves to go.

'No, don't go!' I shout in her ear, 'I'll buy you a drink, what do you want?'

'No, thank you,' she says. I realise with horror that I'm still wearing Eddie's old eighties gear. Where is my head at today? I think to myself.

'Is it the shirt? It's not mine, I borrowed it.' I stumble forwards after them, knocking drinks out of people's hands as I go. I'm losing them, so I lunge towards her, and grab hold of her long hair. She cries out, and I find my arm being grabbed so hard that it makes me lose my grip. Some surprisingly strong students restrain me until one of the bouncers gets me in a headlock, takes me downstairs, and throws me out the door. 'We don't want to see you in here again, now fuck off,' he says.

I look up and down the street hoping to see her, but she's nowhere to be found. I wander into a small, quiet pub as last orders are served, pick up some alcoholic old hag who must be in her late fifties, and I try to get her to give me a blow job in an alleyway in exchange for a bottle of whisky I've just bought her, but she only gets halfway through before she has to stop to be sick. By now I feel very tired and I just want to go home.

CHAPTER 8

I wake up in my own bed. Don't ask me how I got there, because I don't remember. There's an unpleasant smell though, and it occurs to me that I'm caked in my own sick. I'm lying in a hardening pool of it, and have to peel bits off my face. That was a close one, I think to myself, I could have choked to death on it. I sit up, and as I do so, my head spins and my vision disintegrates into a psychedelic display of dots. I want to go back to sleep, but my bed's covered in sick. Maybe I'll just lie in it anyway. No, I'd better sort this mess out, I guess. I'll start with me. I drag myself into the shower. Just as the water hits me, I realise I'm going to be sick again. I stumble out of the shower towards the toilet, but just end up spraying the bathroom floor and the toilet seat with sick. Now there's more of a fucking mess to clear up. I head back to the shower. I'm going to be systematic about this, I decide. I'll clean myself up first, then the bathroom, and then the bedroom. Anyway, I manage to get myself clean and put a few clothes on. I'm just about to start mopping up the bathroom floor when I have to be sick again. I get most of it in the toilet but I still spray the T-shirt I've only just put on. I'm thinking I might go to back to bed. Then I remember that the bed's full of sick. And then the doorbell rings.

I stagger downstairs and open the door. It's fucking Buddy Holly, the real one. Only joking, it's the Buddy Holly that I know, dressed as the other Buddy Holly, the dead one. He's a dead ringer for him in his outfit, except for him being a ginger. I'm not sure what he's doing there, and I almost slam the door in his face and go back to bed, but then I remember that I told him to come round, and that my bed is full of sick.

'Where the fuck did you get that outfit?' I ask him.

'Its authentic fifties gear this. Well, the jacket is anyway.' The jacket is pale blue, worn with a white shirt and a black bow tie. 'I thought I'd wear my blue one, because blue was Buddy's favourite colour. Did you know that?'

'No, I didn't, funnily enough. Better come in then.'

He's brought his own guitar, a red and white electric Stratocaster. 'Can you play that thing?' I ask.

'I can actually,' he says. 'Well, I can't do solos, but I can play chords.'

I sit him down in the living room and make him some tea.

'Hope you don't mind me saying,' he says, as I offer him a biscuit, 'but there's a bit of a funny smell in here.'

'Yes, that'll be sick. I've thrown up all over two rooms upstairs.'

'Right.'

'Yeah, went on a bit of a bender last night. Probably drunk nearly thirty pints. Not sure really, can't remember anything much after nine o'clock. I think I might have pulled.'

'One of those nights, eh?'

'You could say that.'

'Could I just use your toilet before we start?'

'Wouldn't recommend it.'

'Ah OK.'

He's brought a Buddy Holly karaoke CD to sing along to. I put it in my portable player and get him to stand in the middle of the living room. 'OK,' I say, sitting on my sofa, 'hit it.' The backing starts up, and he launches into that 'Rave On' song. He's only pretending to play guitar, but he's miming the real chords. He's got the moves, he's got the voice, he's got the clothes. I hate to say it, but he's fucking brilliant. He's as good as I used to be in the prison rec yard all those years ago, well almost. Buddy must be pushing forty but right now he looks nearly as young as the real Buddy was when he snuffed it.

He finishes and gives me an approval-seeking look the likes of which I haven't seen since the days of training Gay Elvis. 'What do you think, was it all right?' he asks.

'Yeah, it was all right,' I say. 'You need to work on a few things, though. Firstly, you're closing your eyes too much. If you stand up singing with your eyes closed in some of the places we play, they'll think you're taking the piss and bottle you off. So always look at the audience, but only make eye contact with birds and kids. If you make eye contact with a bloke you may as well ask him to shove a snooker cue up your arse and be done with it. Also, couldn't you do that stupid dance he used to do?'

'Uh, not sure what you mean. Buddy didn't do a stupid dance.'

'No, he did, I'm sure. I saw it on TV once. He used to kick his legs up behind him and hop from foot to foot. Made him look like a spaz.' I stand up and show him the dance I mean.

'Ah, Elvis, I think that was Freddie and the Dreamers,' says Buddy.

'Are you sure? Not Buddy Holly?'

'Yeah, I'm pretty positive on that one, Elvis.'

'You could still do the dance, though,' I say.

'I'm not sure about that. It wouldn't really be accurate.'

'OK, but here's something to think about, how about a joint tribute to Buddy Holly and Freddie and the Dreamers? You look like both of them, so you just have to change your jacket. Then you could do the dance.'

'I don't know if it would really work . . .'

'Look, it's something to think about, that's all. We'll leave it for now and come back to it later, OK?'

'Uh, yeah, OK . . .'

Now, as you know, I'm not a total fucking moron. Of course I realise it was Freddie and the Dreamers who did the dance and not Buddy Holly, but right now I'm faced with some kid who has every chance of upstaging me, and the only way I can stop that from happening is undermining his confidence to the point that not only does he think he's nothing special, but that he's not even normal. To do this, I'm already formulating a three-step plan in my head, which at the moment goes something like this: step one, trick him into portraying his hero, Buddy Holly, in a disrespectful and unflattering manner; step two, find his weak spot and tease him about it, ideally working up to giving him a derogatory nickname; step three, and this is more of a long-term goal, shag his girlfriend. All of this plotting leaves me feeling a bit more my old bastard self again, and that feels good. As well as feeling good, however, I also feel sick, and before I know it, I'm spewing my guts out on my living-room carpet.

'Are you OK?' says Buddy, edging quickly backwards.

'Fine, fine, just a bit of sick that's all. Nothing to worry about.'

'Uh, I'll get a cloth, shall I?' Buddy scampers off to the kitchen, leaping across the vomit pool on the way.

'Oh shit, oh fucking shit, oh fucking bumholes,' I hear him rasping to himself.

'What's the problem, Buddy?'

I hear running water and more muttering. 'Fuck, fuck, fuck. Fucking, fucking hell.'

'Are you OK in there?'

'Uh, yeah, hang on a minute.'

Eventually he comes in damping himself down with a cloth. 'Um, Elvis, I think you may have caught me with some of that, look.'

He takes the cloth away. There's a brown patch of vomit stain on the right sleeve and across the pocket of his blue rock 'n' roll jacket.

'Um, right,' I say, 'not sure what to suggest really. You could leave it in the sink to soak.'

'Nah mate, best get this down the dry-cleaner's straight away. Could be ruined otherwise.'

Dry-cleaner's, now there's an idea. I still haven't been able to get rid of that spunk stain on my Elvistrousers, no matter how long I leave them in the sink. Hadn't occurred to me I could take them to a dry-cleaner. In fact, I'd forgotten such places existed. Now, if I had a bird, she would know when to take things to the dry-cleaner's, or at least remember what they are. Buddy's of a younger generation where men can remember that dry-cleaners exist all by themselves. It's progress of a sort, I guess.

'Buddy,' I say, 'can you do me a favour? Could you drop my Elvistrousers off at the dry-cleaner's as well? We'll split the cost between us, yeah?'

'Ah, actually Elvis,' he says, looking down at the ground, 'you couldn't pay for all of it, could you? It was your sick after all.'

'Yeah, I guess you're right,' I say. I don't want to push him too far, too soon. There'll be all the time in the world for that once I've broken him. Having said that, I'm beginning to think he'll be a tough nut to crack. Even though he's dying to be part of the act, he actually seems keen to hold on to some self-respect and dignity. Also, it has to be said, I vomited on him far too early in our working relationship. It'll take a lot to recover my position of superiority after that.

The rehearsal has clearly reached a natural conclusion, so I pack Buddy off to the dry-cleaner's with my Elvistrousers in a plastic bag. We arrange to try again on Monday, by which point my stomach will have calmed down and I'll hopefully have cleaned up some of this mess. I wouldn't put money on it though, because I have three rooms full of sick, and no real idea about what cleaning products to use to get rid of it. So unless I find that out, I may well have to live with it. It's probably seeped right into the mattress of the bed by now, so that'll smell forever more for a start. I could just turn it over I guess. No, that won't do. I must concentrate hard on solving this problem, or I may as well just move out and live under a bush with the village tramp. Now, I think there's such a thing as carpet cleaner, because I'm pretty sure I've seen it advertised on telly. I could buy some of that. And isn't there some spray you use for getting rid of stains in carpets? Fucking hell, I'm making some sort of breakthrough here, thinking maybe I can do this after all. I'll just go down the local shop, load up on all this stuff, and read the instructions.

But as soon as I even think about leaving, I feel so tired and drained that I don't want to leave the house, even though the smell is almost unbearable. God, I'm feeling rough. I haven't even wanked today, in fact I've barely had the horn. I think about having a quick fiddle before I leave the house, and get as far as letting my cock out, but it refuses to respond to my touch, and just sits in my lap, semi-erect and shrinking. Looking at it deflate somehow makes me recall the details of last night. With sudden horror I remember talking to the girl with the long hair and the angelic smile. I remember grabbing at her hair. And getting thrown out of the pub. I remember the aborted blow job in the alley from the old drunken hag. I even remember the ride home on the last bus, shouting, 'I am Elvis! I am the fucking king of fucking rock 'n' roll!' and singing Elvis songs to embarrassed teenagers and shift workers. And now I'm in a house full of sick.

The doorbell rings. 'Fuck off!' I shout, instinctively.

It rings again. Through the window I can see a swarm of baseball caps and rat-faced youths. They've probably been told to fuck off so many times they've forgotten what it means. I say it again, but when it has no effect, I give in and open the door.

'What do you lot want?' I say. 'I told you lot a million fucking times to phone ahead.'

'You got any puff?' asks the head baseball hat.

Oh well, I need the money for the dry-cleaning. 'Yeah. Get inside.'

I leave them in the hallway and make my way to the stash drawer and scales upstairs.

'Fucking hell, it stinks in here, mate,' says one of them as I climb.

'Do you want it or not?'

'Yeah.'

'Then shut your fucking mouth then.'

I complete the transaction and tell them to sling their hooks. Then, I find some clothes that don't have sick on them and, feeling like a man with a mission, finally walk to the village shop.

CHAPTER 9

After several hours of following the instructions on the back of cleaning products, I lie triumphantly on my bed, which admittedly still smells quite a lot of sick, high on charlie, and celebrate a job well done with a hard-earned wank. I got my horn back sometime in the mid-afternoon, and now it's throbbing like a good 'un. I come, and I relax as the spunk forms a puddle in my belly button. Coupled with the post-orgasm bliss, I feel a real sense of achievement at cleaning up my sick without the help of any woman. I've been thinking recently about how maybe it would be easier if I got hitched up again and had someone to look after me and the house, but now I realise, if I learn a few new skills, like I've just done with sick removal, it might not be necessary. Granted, I wouldn't say the sick clearance was entirely successful, there's still an outline on the carpet of where it was, like a chalk drawing at a murder scene, and I have no fucking clue how to stop this mattress from smelling, but it's a first effort, and chances are next time I'll crack it.

Still, a wife or live-in partner would be handy. Not that getting one would be so easy these days, seeing as I'm so much older now, as well as a bit of a porker, which isn't surprising seeing as I pretty much live on takeaways and ready-meals. Nothing new there, but I used to be able to eat anything and my body could deal with it. Now I'm just getting fatter all the time. If I had someone looking after me, I'd get to eat proper food and I might lose some weight, but I'm getting to be such a lard-arse that no bird is going to want to. Also, even though I try to keep the house clean, some of the time anyway, it's never as good as when a woman does it. It always whiffs a bit, even if I spray the place. Birds know how to do this stuff properly, birds and gaylords. But I've been on my own so long, I've got so I feel nervous about having someone else around the place. I actually enjoy being left alone, and if I had a woman around I'd never get any peace. It's not like I'm lonely. I've never really got lonely, but now I'm on my own so much, sometimes I get bored.

So there are pluses and minuses to getting a bird. Also, I wouldn't exactly say I've a good track record of holding down a serious relationship. Like I said, I've been married three times, and all of them ended in tears. The first time was way back when I was living where I was born in Colchester. I was just a kid, so it's not surprising it all went tits up. I mean, I really was, I had to get my parents' permission. You see, by the time I was fifteen, it was pretty apparent I was a sex addict. I was wanking constantly, even more than usual for a teenage boy. I was skiving off school just so I could wank. I was already shagging by the time I was fourteen, but back then it wasn't like it is now. It was really hard work getting into a girl's pants, they were all waiting for someone they loved, or even saving themselves for fucking marriage. You don't need that crap when your dick's opening your flies all by itself. Obviously, there were some dirty slappers about, just like there always are, but really, if you wanted it from a bird you really fancied, you usually had to convince them that you loved them, and might even marry them one day. I remember I used to say things like, 'I thought I'd died and gone to heaven, but now I can see that I'm still alive, and heaven has been brought to me.' They'd laugh when I said that, but they still slipped their knickers off. So I said these things to a fox of a girl called Karen, and of course right away she's up the duff. She went and told her parents when she found out, and next thing I know, her dad's beating seven shades of shit out of me in his garden shed, telling me I had to marry her or he'd make sure I spent the rest of my life in a wheelchair.

So I got married at sixteen years old. I was still in school, but I had a wife and a kid on the way. I was made to move in with Karen's parents, even though her dad hated me and was always threatening to thrash me if I put a foot wrong. I had to play the role of the dutiful husband and then, when the baby was born, the dutiful father. So, in order to appear responsible, I got a job as an apprentice in the butcher's, but that hardly paid anything at all, and I wasn't exactly good at it, in fact, I nearly caused an outbreak of food poisoning. And after the baby was born, of course the sex dried up, although it was already hard enough getting any with the in-laws skulking about all the time. Under the circumstances, I don't think there was any way that I could have stayed faithful. Three months into the marriage I had two other women on the go regularly, with the occasional odd bits of stuff as well. Both of the women were quite a lot older, in their late thirties. One was married, and the other was a divorcee with a kid nearly my age. After five months of a wife I couldn't shag, a little brat who wouldn't stop screaming, and a father-in-law who was always looking for an excuse to give me a beating, I did a runner and went to live with the divorced lady.

She was pretty well off, so I didn't have to work. I chucked my job and spent my days being looked after by her. She also had a maid that cleaned up after the both of us. I didn't leave the house much because if Karen's dad tracked me down I'd be mincemeat. So we pretty much just shagged all the time and lived off her ex-husband's money. I remember she had a poodle that would always try to bite me, until I booted it across the room one day and it learned its lesson. It was an all right way to live, but pretty soon I was getting bored and claustrophobic. Then her daughter came home from boarding school. She was gorgeous, a real classy young thing, and before long I was banging her too. Course, her mum didn't know, and when she came home one day and caught us, I was out on my ear. Years after I found out I'd got the girl pregnant, but her mum told her to get rid of it. So anyway, I moved on to Luton and fell in with a bad crowd. A couple of years later I'm in the nick and you know what happened there. Once I got out, I found myself struggling to make ends meet until Eddie intervened and I spent that time in London working as a fence, moving electrical goods and kids' toys and the like that had fallen off the back of a lorry.

Me being connected with Eddie meant that I ended up with some good contacts. That doesn't mean that I was taken that seriously, I was treated like a bit of a joke to be honest with you, but I got to hang out in the right clubs and was allowed to say hello to the right people. Anyway, that's when I met Nanette. Now Nanette was what I'd call a top-looking bird. She always dressed like a model, I mean you never saw her wearing jeans or stuff like that, and she had one hell of a bod. Long legs, big tits and she wasn't afraid to show them off. It was impossible for a man to look at her and not think about what she'd be like in bed, and it's not just me that's said so. Her family were all part of the scene, and she was meant to be the girlfriend of Brian O'Sullivan, who was a real psycho, but he was in the nick and wasn't coming out for a very long time. Now like I said, I was a small-time fence who got the piss taken out of him, so it was a bit of a surprise when it became obvious that Nanette was interested. I swear I never made a move on her, because I didn't want to get my neck broken by O'Sullivan's goons, but Nanette told me to relax, that O'Sullivan would never dare do anything to upset her dad. Now her dad was Harry Roscoe. If you want to know who he is, go down your local library, because they're writing fucking history books about him now. He's an under-world legend. Young posh lads now who've never done a bad thing in their entire lives fucking worship him. Mind you, these days he's going straight and does adverts for breakfast cereals on telly. Anyway, Nanette started to make the moves on me. First I just catch her looking at me a few times in the club, and then when she sees she's got my attention, she looks away. Then another time, I'm standing at the bar when she walks up and tells me I should stop drinking. I ask her why. 'Because you're driving me home,' she says. And of course, next thing I know, I'm banging the hottest property in gangland. Not unreasonably, this won me new-found respect.

Why Nanette chose me I've never been sure. I guess I was pretty damn good-looking. I still had my blond, curly hair, and I was in good shape. A lot of the other guys on the scene had been in so many punch-ups their faces looked like train wrecks. Still, she must have known the way people thought about me. Anyway, thanks to Nanette, I was doing pretty fucking well for myself. I got promoted and ran laundered money through a car lot. Of course a lot of people were jealous, but if O'Sullivan wasn't going to mess with me, they sure as hell weren't going to. I was living a charmed life, it seemed, and even Nanette's dad ended up liking me and put a few little earners my way. After a while, however, old Harry took me to one side, and suggested that if I wanted to carry on enjoying intimate relations with his daughter, it would be only right for me to do so within the bounds of holy matrimony. It was up to me of course, but if I enjoyed breathing, proposing to her was probably my most sensible option. So for the second time in my life, I married a girl in order to avoid the possibility of her dad doing me some serious damage.

We had it all right for a while, me and Nanette. Lots of cash, a nice house in the suburbs, cars, foreign holidays. Even staying faithful was easy for me, I think partly because Nanette chose me instead of the other way round, and partly because there's no telling what her dad would have done to me if I was caught putting my pencil in the wrong case. Now, I can't say that I loved her, because I honestly don't know what that means, but at least I respected her, and I don't have too much of that to go round. So things were good, I'd say. Until Johnny Brooks got out of the nick, then it all went tits up. At first it was just a few dropped hints in conversation by friends, words to the wise that Johnny and Nanette had a history, and that I should keep an eye out, that was all. Then acquaintances would tell me they just happened to see them together down the club on a night I was working, and they looked quite friendly. Nanette wouldn't always be around when I expected her to be, but that wasn't anything new, and besides, I'd never kept tabs on her before, and I didn't think I'd get away with starting to now. Finally Harry Roscoe cornered me and said outright that Johnny was having an affair with Nanette and what was I going to do about it. Even Harry was scared of Johnny. He wasn't going to eat his own eyeballs just for the sake of his slutty daughter's marriage, so if anyone was going to teach him a lesson it was going to have to be me.

Well, could I do it? Could I take on the hardest mental case in the London underworld in order to preserve my dignity? Of course I fucking couldn't. One day I came home and heard them at it in the bedroom. I thought about walking in on them for about half a second, but in the end I just stayed downstairs and had a stiff drink, and waited for them to finish. I guess I found out how the lady felt when she caught me screwing her daughter that day. Anyway, they both came downstairs afterwards, and I said hello to Johnny and offered him a drink. He said no and that he ought to be going, things to do, nice to meet me. I was going to tell Nanette I wanted a divorce but she beat me to it. She and Johnny got married as soon as it was finalised and they're still together to this day, although of course Johnny has always had about a hundred girls on the side as well.

Meanwhile, as soon as word got around that Nanette had left me for Johnny, I was dropped like a stone. Respect for me went out the window now I was just the dozy twit husband of Johnny Brooks's new girl. Opportunities stopped coming my way, and eventually I was forced out of the car lot, even though I was doing a good job. With the work drying up, and Nanette running off with half my cash, it was hard to make ends meet. I was in a pretty sorry state when Eddie suggested I do Elvis again at his club. So that's where I ended up, dressed as Vegas Elvis in a wig and a jumpsuit and singing to a bunch of gangsters and their birds, including of course, Johnny Brooks and his new wife Nanette.

Well, there you have it, a little insight for you, a little glimpse of how I got to where I am today. And where am I? Right now, I'm booked to sing at the birthday party of the man who fucked my wife in my house, and stole her away from me. Not only that, I'm doing it in the club of the man who raped me pretty much every night in the nick for nearly three years. And I bet you're thinking, what the hell's wrong with him, where is this man's pride? Well to be honest with you, I don't recall ever having any to begin with. Maybe I traded it in years ago in order to stay alive. Since then, I've been fucked over again and again, but I've stayed alive, and that's what's important.

There was a wife number three of course, but I don't think you'd want me to go into that right now. Anyway, these trips down memory lane leave me in fucking dark moods I can tell you. So forgive me if I spend this evening watching telly, doing some charlie, and masturbating until the top comes off. Anything to stop me thinking about wife number three.

CHAPTER 10

I wake up from the dream again. It's always the same thing. Eddie's after me, sometimes he even gets me, but always, I'm rescued by my sister Bridget. Sometimes me and Bridget talk, but I don't remember much of what we say when I wake up. All I managed to cling on to this time was her telling me that I looked like my dad now I'd gotten old. That's it really, except, just like I always do, I asked her, why. She still looked eighteen, of course. Every time I have that dream it puts me in a weird frame of mind for the rest of the day. It's like my brain's a shingle beach, and everything gets shifted about in the tide, so things that are buried underneath just turn up on the surface. I suppose I think about it that way at the moment because it's made me remember a seaside holiday we went on when I was little. Donkey rides and sandcastles, Bridget wearing a grown-up swimming costume for the first time. My dad smiling for once, Mum as sullen as always. I've been having the dream a lot lately, although I've been dreaming various versions of it for years. Its one of the few things that makes me want to get out of bed in the morning, rather than just lying there and playing with myself like most days. Right now I'd do anything to forget it, so I head straight for my stash and do a line of charlie.

It takes my mind off it all right, and lets me work out what to do with the day. It's Sunday, I can't get on with anything useful, so that means I should spend it in relaxation. The time is long overdue to see my ladyfriends, I feel. And seeing as I've neglected them all for so long, and my head's such a mess from all that's happened to me and the dream coming back, I'm not going to stop at just one. Oh no. In fact, I am going to fit as many of them into this one day as is humanly possible. I am going for gold. You probably think that's being greedy, and maybe it is, but they get as much out of it as I do, if not more. Anyway, you'll see what I mean.

It's important that I make the necessary phone calls, get myself dressed, and be on my merry way before the charlie wears off and I go on a downer. I make a start immediately with Shirley, getting the phone to autodial her number while I look for my good pair of pants. Shirley's the head of the entertainments committee at the social club in the next village to mine. Her husband walked out on her years ago, and I've been servicing her since '98 or thereabouts after she booked me at the club and demonstrated her own unusual approach to artist hospitality. She's not exactly a looker, and her body's sagging like nobody's business, but she's got a cheeky smile and she's pretty good in bed. I've got one leg in my underwear when she picks up the phone.

HOUND DOG • 73

'Hi, Shirley,' I say, 'this is Elvis, and I'm phoning to say I'm going to get you All Shook Up this morning.'

'Well, Elvis,' she replies, 'how do you know that I'm not busy? I might just be on my way to church.'

'I don't believe you.'

'No,' she laughs, 'it's not very likely is it?'

'I don't think they'd let a naughty girl like you into church.'

'Elvis, you're a very bad man.'

'I'll see you in half an hour, you naughty, naughty girl.'

Next I call Maureen. Mo's an old time rock 'n' roll fan who goes out jiving with ageing Teddy boys. When I met her at a fifties festival in some pub, she was going out with a genuine rocker who'd beaten up mods on Brighton Beach. Then he died of a heart attack, and she started turning up at all my gigs. I could tell what she was after, and I ended up giving it to her partly just to get her to stop following me. It ended up just encouraging it, but fortunately her health took a turn for the worse and I was saved. Mo must be gone sixty by now, but she still dresses like she did when she was fifteen. It's pretty sad to look at, and I only go round there when none of the other girls are available because she gives me the creeps. Still, I'm trying to set a personal record here, so she's on the list.

'Hello there, ma'am, this is Elvis Presley.'

'Good golly gosh, is it really Elvis speaking to me on the telephone? My girlfriends are gonna be so jealous . . .' She speaks in an American accent. It's painful to listen to.

'Uh, I was wondering, if it's not too much trouble that is, if I could maybe come round and visit this afternoon . . .'

'Oh yes, Elvis, I would love that! Are you going to Love Me Tender?'

'Uh, I'm going to give you a Big Hunk O' Love baby.'

'Ooooh, I can't wait.'

'I'll be round at two. Make sure to Treat Me Nice.'

'Yes, Elvis, yes!'

It's funny how many old birds will sleep with me just because of the Elvis thing. Mind you, it's not just women who come on to me. After a gig, sometimes I catch blokes who are meant to be straight as a post nervously trying to rub up against me in the car park. Of course, I'm having none of it, and tell them to fuck right off or they'll be sorry, but Elvis must do something to them. It's like that actor, Nicolas Cage. He loved Elvis so much, he married his daughter, just so he could get to have sex with him and for it not to be gay. It would be nice if some of the younger birds reacted to Elvis like that, but they never do. I had high hopes when that 'Little Less Conversation' song got to number one, but it didn't change anything.

I try to call Sue, some bird I know in Cambridge who breeds dogs, but no one answers, so I decide to take a risk and phone Sandra instead. I hang up at the sound of her husband's voice. Anyway, its time to get a move on, so I get out the door and start walking down the country roads, whistling as I go, past the fields and on to the next village.

'Hi, Elvis,' says a stoned voice from behind a hedge.

I look round, and poking his head out from behind his privet is Lawrence, the hippy whose skunk I sell. His eyes are saucer-shaped and red. 'Hey there, Lawrence,' I say. 'How's tricks?'

'Oh man, I broke the rules. I got high on my own supply.'

'Lawrence, you're always high on your own supply.'

'Yeeeah.' He breaks into a strange whistling laugh, like an old kettle boiling. 'What are you up to, man? Got any gigs lined up?'

'I'm playing Elk on Tuesday.'

'Elk? Oh man, that place is full of trolls.'

Trolls. I couldn't have put it better myself.

'See you later, Lawrence.'

'Yeah, see you. Tell me when you need more stuff, yeah?'

I wave goodbye and make my way to Shirley's house down the road. I ring her doorbell. She opens the door a part of the way and beckons me in with a finger. The hallway is dark, and as I close the door behind me, I find her standing by the stairs in a black silk dressing gown. 'Hello, Elvis,' she says, and it falls to the floor. She's wearing some tarty negligee underneath.

'Elvis, take me upstairs and fuck me like a bad girl,' she says.

'Hmmm, put it in your mouth and I'll think about it,' I reply, and she takes it out and does just that in the hallway. Then we go upstairs and I fuck her hard from behind. You know, of all the ways you can do it, I like going from behind best, because it feels like you're really fucking somebody. None of this making love crap, you're just doing it to them, fucking them really hard and giving them a good seeing to. It's honest, and there's usually very little honesty when it comes to fucking. You have to lie to get it, then you have to lie about how amazing it made you feel for you to get it again. Shirley screams her head off all the way through, so even though I can never make her come, I'm pretty sure she's had a good time. I hold out as long as I can, then when I've finished I lay myself down on the bed next to her.

'That OK?' she asks.

'Oh, it was wonderful, honey,' I say. It wasn't really, but it was OK.

I know I'm about to go on a downer from the charlie, so I roll a spliff to smooth it over and share it with Shirley. I think its fair to say my honeymoon period with charlie is well and truly over. Now, I wouldn't say I'm addicted, although I suppose I do take a hell of a lot of it. And it always gives me a buzz, even though the downs are getting more severe. But it's certainly not as much fun as it used to be, that's for sure. But then, neither is sex. Mind you, the charlie's still good for something. I always take it when I have to do Elvis, because it helps me get into the role, and seeing as he was out of his mind on prescription pills anyway, it actually makes it more authentic. On the downside, I have nosebleeds all the time, and one of these days I'm going to sneeze and my whole fucking nose is going to come off. Then I'll have to do Michael Jackson impersonations. At the end of the day though, I guess I take it because for half an hour or so it gives me a bit of rest from all the noise in my head, which comes on three times stronger once the downs hit me. But for the moment of quiet it's worth it.

I tell Shirley to lie still, and I lay a line of it down between her breasts.

'What are you doing?' she asks.

'You'll see,' I reply, and in one big snort, I hoover it all up. She giggles like a naughty schoolgirl. I offer her some but she shakes her head.

'Shirley, do you reckon you could do me a favour and run me into Cambridge?'

'Off to see another one of your girls?'

'No, don't be silly. Got to see a man about a motor.'

'The Elvismobile pack up on you?'

'Yeah. Need a new one.'

'Course I can, love. Just get your head down there and get me to come before we go.'

She drives a hard bargain. Suffice to say we both get what we want and three-quarters of an hour later, Shirley drops me in the vicinity of Mo's house. On the way, I try Sue again, but still get no answer. So I phone Sandra. She answers this time and she's not happy.

'I told you never to phone here at the weekend. What is it?'

'I just want to see you babe. Uh, listen, honey, I was wondering . . . if I was Elvis, would you screw me?'

'For Christ's sake . . . OK, Bill will be out at seven. Come round at half-seven but don't stay long.'

'Don't you worry, I'll be in and out in no time.'

'Yes, I daresay. Bye.'

Sandra's a schoolteacher. I found her on a park bench one day last year looking lonely and I persuaded her to take me home for the afternoon to see if a good orgasm wouldn't cheer her up. It did, and I've been providing her with the odd one ever since, usually whenever it's the school holidays or half-term. Her husband is a dull fuckwit, but she can never quite bring herself to leave even though she detests the very sight of him. I think they have kids, but they've grown up. She's prim and proper and stern, and needs a good seeing to now and again to stop her from being too uptight even to breathe. She's never seen me as Elvis, but I do it anyway to wind her up, which is funny.

Meanwhile, I get to Mo's, and she answers the door to me in a pink prom dress straight out of *Grease*. In the background I can hear some slow Elvis playing. I walk right in, put my arm round her waist and ask her to dance.

'I'd love to,' she sighs.

I gently lead her into the living room, where it's still 1959, or at least the 1959 that had the Fonz in it. It's not even her own youth that she's reliving, but some crappy TV version of it. An old vinyl record plays 'Love Me Tender'. I softly sing along, catching the last verse before it ends. I pull her close to me and kiss her.

'Maureen, I want to make love to you,' I say.

'Really?' she gasps.

'Yes, Mo, very much.'

And I take her upstairs to her pink fifties bedroom and fuck her slowly, as 'Treat Me Nice', the next track on her original copy of *Elvis's Golden Records* plays underneath us. I fake it pretty good, but all the time I'm wanting to fuck her hard. So to calm myself down, I just think about Jen's furry bush, and daydream about stroking it and resting my head there. Mo comes long before I do with a whimper. I just want to finish it off and pound her, but I know from past experience it would make her scared, so I politely move it in, move it out, move it in, and out . . . until I come. Then I have to get out of there. I've only been there barely ten minutes, but it already feels like some freakish pink prison, with the sickly taste of someone else's misery heavy in the air.

'I've got to go,' I say, in my normal voice.

'So soon? Couldn't you stay just a bit longer?' She's still speaking in her awful American accent.

'No, sorry. I'd like to, but there are things I have to do.'

'You'll come again soon, won't you?'

'Of course I will. Very soon.'

'Next week maybe?'

'Probably not that soon. Business is very busy at the moment.'

'Of course, of course. I'm being selfish.'

She shows me to the door, puts her hands to my face and kisses me gently on the lips. 'I love you, Elvis,' she whispers to me.

I don't say anything and close the door behind me.

I wasn't expecting that to be quite so traumatic or so quick. Now I have hours to kill before my next appointment at half-seven. There's really no other option but to find a pub for a quiet pint or three, which is exactly what I do. There, I lose track of time daydreaming between the pints, as well as mis-judging how long it will take to get there by a long shot, so when I finally get to Sandra's it's gone quarter past eight.

I can tell she's pissed off from the moment she opens the door.

'Look, if I say half-seven, I mean half-seven. We've barely got three-quarters of an hour before Bill's back home. And you smell like a brewery, Jesus.'

Even on her day off, she's dressed like a schoolteacher. Smart shirt and skirt, sensible shoes. She leads me into her immaculate minimalist living room, takes off her shoes and pulls down her tights and knickers.

'Well come on then, what are you waiting for?' she asks.

'Aren't we going upstairs?'

'Don't be silly, you'd make the sheets smell. Now will you please stop messing about and get on with it?'

She takes off her shirt, skirt and bra, and lies on a wool rug with her legs apart. I get undressed and on top of her as quick as I can. I haven't touched her at all but inside she's soaking wet. She presses down on my buttocks to make me go deeper inside. We both come quickly and nearly at the same time. I'm exhausted by the end of it, but immediately start to make a move, seeing as we're running late.

'No, don't go just yet,' she says gently, and caresses my chest. We lie there for a few minutes, stroking each other in silence. Then she gets up and sprays the room with air freshener to get rid of the smell of beer and sex.

CHAPTER 11

It's Monday afternoon and I now possess a new Elvismobile, a white Volkswagen diesel that's just crying out for a large stencilled Elvis on the side, crudely drawn-on cock optional. In the back of the van is a new PA, loud enough to bring down the roof of your average social club, or at least cause serious structural damage. Picture the scene – Buddy Holly's round my house again, where I'm giving him further guidance on stage-craft. This time he's not made the mistake of dressing up for the occasion.

'You're singing too close to the mike,' I tell him. 'You need to push the top half of your body way back, so you can get deep breaths and you don't pop your Ps and Bs. No, no further back . . . further, a little bit further . . .'

'If I go back any further I'll bloody fall over,' he says.

'That's a risk we all have to take in live performance. Luciano Pavarotti once fell backwards during a concert and killed two members of the chorus.'

'That's not true is it?'

'Absolutely true, mate. Now deep breath, bend back . . . that's it . . . don't breathe out, not yet! Now sing!'

Buddy lets out a strangled asthmatic squawk.

'I can't sing at that angle,' he says, 'I can't get the air out.'

'You've got to train your stomach muscles. Practise at home every day for quarter of an hour and in a week you'll be able to do it.'

'OK, but I'll sing standing up straight for the time being, if that's all right with you.'

'Well, just this one time, but it's a bad habit that you've got to get out of.'

Teaching Buddy to be not so fucking good is proving tricky. He's not clever, but nevertheless seems to evade every trap I set for him, even though he doesn't actually know that they are traps. He's like Road Runner, but I don't particularly feel like being Wile E. Coyote. I've now got just over a day to stop him from showing me up, so I need to get something to work pretty damn quick.

'Have you had any more thoughts about the dance?' I say.

'What do you mean?'

'You know, the dance I showed you, the Buddy Holly dance.'

'But it wasn't Buddy Holly, it was Freddie and the Dreamers.'

'Oh yes, that's right. Now, doing a tribute to Buddy Holly's all very well, but don't you think it's a bit old hat, you know, a bit passé? What you need is a twist. So, how about . . . a tribute to Freddie and the Dreamers doing a tribute to Buddy Holly.'

'I'm not sure I follow.'

'OK, I'll break it down for you. Freddie and the Dreamers are doing a tribute to Buddy Holly, right?'

'Um, are they?'

'Yes, they are. Now you are doing a tribute to them, which means you are pretending to be them while they are pretending to be Buddy Holly. Follow?'

'I . . . think so. But did Freddie and the Dreamers ever do a tribute to Buddy Holly?'

'Not sure, but that doesn't matter. It's what they call postmodern.'

'What's that, then?'

'It's when you nick someone else's idea and everybody thinks you're clever for nicking it. If we were postmodern and clever we could play student unions and graduation balls. It could really open doors for us.'

'They might not get it in the social clubs though. I don't get it anyway.'

'True, true. I suppose it's best not to go over people's heads. But still, there's an idea there we could come back to.'

'I guess . . .'

This obviously isn't working. Which means it's time to change tack and skip right to stage two of my plan, this of course being psychological torture centring around the use of a derogatory nickname.

'Buddy,' I say, 'you've almost got the hang of this, you're nearly there, you really are. But there's one thing missing from your performance.'

'What's that?'

'I can't see the fear.'

'Eh?'

'A bloke on telly once said, for a great performance, you need drama, and for great drama, you need conflict. So, if we apply that thinking to your performance, it means that you need to be in a state of emotional conflict when you sing. What I mean is, you have to be experiencing inner turmoil. Now, unfortunately you can't always conjure up inner turmoil to order, so the easiest way to fake it is to think of something you're really afraid of, and imagine it's right next to you. Now, do you think you can do that for me?'

'Dunno, maybe. And that would work would it?'

'Abso-fucking-lutely would. Do you want to give it a go?'

'Ummm . . . OK.'

'Right. So what are you really afraid of? What gives you the willies?'

'Umm . . . needles, maybe. But then, if I have to have an injection, I suppose I just grin and bear it OK.'

'Anything else?'

'Uh, I don't know if I can think of anything really scary off the top of my head.'

'Of course you can,' I say. 'Something from your childhood perhaps, something buried deep inside you, just waiting to upset you all over again.'

'Hmmmm . . . well, there might be something . . .'

'Do you think you could get in touch with it, remember what it was like?'

'Don't think I want to.'

'Please, Buddy, for the act. It will be OK, I promise.' I look at him with the most trustworthy expression I can muster. He looks back at me, no doubt evaluating exactly how trustworthy that expression is.

'OK, then, I'll give it a go,' he says finally.

'Right,' I say, 'what I want you to do is close your eyes, and think back to that time. I want you to remember what happened, and how it felt. Then, I don't want you just to remember it, I want you to imagine that you are there. I want you to live it all again, right now. Can you do that for me?'

'Um, OK.' He just sits there for a minute, then suddenly, all the blood drains out of his face and he starts to mutter to himself very quietly. It's inaudible at first, but gradually its gets louder and it becomes possible to make out some words.

'Leave me alone . . . not my fault . . . it just happened . . . Don't you laugh at me! I couldn't help it! It was an accident!' By now he's shouting and his eyes are wide open. I shake him hard.

'Buddy! Buddy! Come back now. It's OK!'

'Whaa – where am I?' he gargles.

'Everything's OK. You're back in my living room.'

'Oh . . . Sorry, mate, I just lost it for a bit there, it was like you said, like I'd travelled back in time, and I was actually there when I was nine years old again.'

'So what happened, what did you see?'

'I was on a school trip to Yorkshire. I didn't want to go, but my mam thought it would be good for me to try and spend some time with kids my age. I wasn't very popular you see. Anyway, we were staying in some hostel, and things weren't going well. Some big kids were pushing me about all day and giving me a hard time. I was getting more and more miserable, and then one night, I was in the dormitory with all the other boys, and they were making fun of me because I'm ginger, calling me names in the dark, and I got so upset that . . . I wet the bed. And they smelt it, and called me dirty and smelly and they laughed at me. Then . . . they stole my pyjamas and locked me out of the dormitory, so I had to walk round the hostel in the nuddy looking for teacher. Only, because we were little, they'd put us to bed at half-nine and loads of people were up and about, some of them were ladies, and they all looked at me as I walked about with my hand over my willy, and some of them laughed, but some of them asked me what was wrong and I had to tell them and then they laughed as well . . .'

He breaks into tears. My god, I think to myself, this is fucking gold dust. I put my arm round him and tell him everything's OK, it's over now, he has a good life and a smashing girlfriend, and the boys who bullied him are either in prison or, worse, in middle-management, and therefore must hate themselves with a passion.

'You're right,' he says through the tears, 'I won really, didn't I?'

'Of course you did,' I say, 'of course you did.'

'They can't do anything to me now, can they, not now I'm Buddy Holly?'

'No they can't. And do you know how you can really get one over on them?' He shakes his head. 'You use the experience of what they put you through to make your performance even better.'

'Really, how?'

'When you go on stage, just before you sing, think about that experience and feel the pain, the humiliation, the sense of utter worthlessness that the memory evokes. Dwell on it all for a minute, and really feel it, and then, just before the misery completely swallows you up, think about who you are now, how strong you are and how good your life is. Your performance should be an emotional journey for you from then to now. And it will make it brilliant, trust me.'

'I-I'm not sure I can do that.'

'Yes you can do that, because you are strong!'

'Yeah, I am. I'm strong.'

'That's right. Now for this to work, we've got to keep the moment fresh in your mind. You've always got to be aware of how it felt to be abused, bullied and demeaned.'

'I don't think I want to be reminded!'

'Please Buddy, it's necessary for this to work.' He looks at me uncertainly. 'I'll tell you what, we'll try it for this gig, and if you don't think you can hack it, we won't do it again.'

'OK, I'll try it out. Just one time.'

'Right, now the most effective way of keeping it fresh in your mind is for me to simulate for you the experience of being bullied. Effectively, what this means is I have to pretend to bully you.'

'You do?'

'Yes, and as you know, the bully's main weapon is of course the nickname. One that's really personal and upsetting. So for you, I think that should be . . . Bedwetter Bud.'

'God, you're right,' he says, 'that really is very upsetting.'

'Well that's good, it needs to be to work. Anyway, I will be calling you Bedwetter Bud at various points over the next couple of days, and making little comments about the whole bed-wetting incident. It will be quite traumatic but it will be worth it. And tomorrow, you will shine, because you are a star.'

'I hope so.'

'Of course you will, you smelly bed-wetter.'

And so we work on the act a bit more, and I mention bed-wetting a couple of times, but not too often, because you have to build that sort of thing up. Just little remarks like, 'Fancy a cup of tea, Bedwetter Bud? Careful you don't piss yourself once you've drunk it,' that sort of thing. By half-five, we decide to call it a day and relax. We discuss rock 'n' roll a bit, and how music's rubbish now they do it all with computers. Then, he looks at me seriously and says, 'Thank you, Elvis, for everything you're doing for me. This is really my dream come true.'

'That's OK, Bud,' I say. 'Just think of me as Jim'll Fix It in an Elvis suit.'

'I'm really grateful, you know that, don't you.'

Of course I know it, and I think he's a moron for it, but I just put my hand on his shoulder, smile, and tell him not to mention it.

'You know,' he says, 'if you're not doing anything tonight, you could come round to ours and I'll play you some of my records. I've got some real rare ones, even some rock 'n' roll 78s.'

Now don't get me wrong, I don't like the speccy bed-wetting twit, but his proposition strikes me as strangely attractive. I suppose that's because I don't have any friends, just people I owe money to, and maybe I just feel like having company for a change. Also, I might get to look at Emma's huge tits all evening.

'Sure,' I say, 'I'd love to.'

'Great,' he replies, 'Em will be picking me up in a few minutes, so you can follow us if you like.'

Sure enough there's a knock on the door and I see an enormous pair of breasts through the frosted glass as I go to open it.

'Hi, Elvis!' she says, flashing her lovely idiot grin. She's wearing a stripy top that makes her tits look even larger than they are. She and Buddy have a big noisy snog on my doorstep.

'Elvis will be coming back to ours this evening if that's all right, love.'

'Yeah, course it is. You boys have fun?'

'Yeah, smashing,' he says.

For the first time I can properly see her arse. It's a lovely big round thing and I want to bite it.

CHAPTER 12

Half-six Tuesday evening and I'm parking the new Elvismobile in the social club car park of the godforsaken Fen village of Elk. I've never done Elvis here before, but I have a feeling it's going to be a tough gig, what with me not knowing any songs from the film *The Wicker Man*. Lawrence had it right. They're all trolls here, and they think you're trying to steal their gold.

I can see Buddy Holly and Em waiting for me as I drive up, but there's something not right. Buddy seems to be having a go at her from what I can see. He's in his outfit already, his blue jacket back from the cleaners. Once they realise I'm pulling up, they snap their usual idiot grins back on, and keep them fixed on as I walk up to them. I expect after last night they think I'm their new best mate. And even though my estimation of the pair of them didn't go up, I mean, I still think they're cretins, I must admit I had an OK time. It was just nice to do stuff like sit and talk and listen to old records, instead of the usual routine of bullying people or begging for money. Mind you, they didn't have anything decent to drink in the flat, just gay drinks like Baileys, and at eight o'clock they both wanted to watch fucking *Heartbeat* on telly, but it was fun to look at Buddy's collection of rock 'n' roll memorabilia, even if it is fucking sad that he's got it in the first place.

'Hi, Elvis,' says Buddy, 'are you ready to shake, rattle and roll?' Buddy hands me a plastic bag. Inside it are my trousers.

'No, I'm ready to arse about in a stupid jumpsuit singing crap songs while sweating like a pig. But I guess that's what you meant.'

'Oh Elvis, you're so silly,' says Em. 'Will you excuse me just a minute, I've got to go for a wee.' She goes inside the social club, her big arse wobbling behind her, giving me the horn. Now despite being a bit of porker, and obviously retarded, I've come to the conclusion that Emma is a very sexy lady. I put this down to her big fat arse and enormous breasts, which are just lovely. Now, I've never been one for fat birds, but to be honest, if a woman's got large knockers and a big arse, it can't help but give me the horn. I just look at tits like that and I'm imagining how much fun it would be to play with them, or to give an arse that big a good wobble. On a good arse you can even get a ripple effect going if you wobble it right. I'm not saying I don't like skinny birds, of course I do, but when it comes to tits and arses you need something that will keep your hands full. Looking at Emma's big fat arse in her tight jeans, with half of it spilling out the top as is the fashion these days, Christ, I want to bite it so much. Then after that take her from behind and have it make a great big slapping sound as I ram it in.

But that's not for now. Right now I have to concentrate on Buddy. 'So how's it going, Bedwettin' Bud?' I ask. 'Wet any good beds recently with your stinky piss?'

'Uh, no I haven't, Elvis.'

'Are you sure? Are you sure you haven't sprung a leak and soaked the bed in piss, then walked around in your wet pyjamas, dripping all over the floor making a big puddle?'

'Um, yeah, I'm quite sure on that one.'

'Because if I found a big puddle of piss, with you standing in the middle, I'd have to call you Smelly Buddy Piss-Pants, and you wouldn't want me to do that would you?'

'No, Elvis, I certainly wouldn't.'

It's working a treat. He's avoiding eye contact, staring at the ground, shuffling and fidgeting about nervously. With a bit of luck he'll be wetting himself on stage at this rate, which gives me an idea.

'Buddy, you know I'm just messing around, but in all seriousness, have you had a little tinkle recently?'

'Uh, not for a while actually. I was thinking of going when Em got back.'

'Don't!'

'I really need to . . .'

'No, listen, it's another top performance technique. What you do is hold it in all the time you're on stage, and the strain adds a whole layer of intensity to your act. It really works. Bet you'll never guess who came up with it.'

'I don't know, who?'

'Enoch bloody Powell! Now he was a great performer. Total fucking nutter, but a great performer. And, you know, when he gave his "Rivers of Blood" speech, he was holding in a whole river of piss.'

'I did not know that.'

'Well, now you do. So I don't want to see you anywhere near the urinals until after you've been on. Because I want to see the best Buddy Holly show imaginable tonight, and that means I want to see Buddy Holly singing with a full bladder.'

'OK, Elvis, you know best.'

'Well yes I do. Now if you'll excuse me, I must go for a piss.'

The sight of Em's wobbling arse-cleavage earlier means that my piss is swiftly followed by a wank, but that doesn't stop me getting a hard-on when I see her at the bar about five minutes later. 'Hey, Elvis, what are you drinking?' she asks as I sidle up next to her.

'I'll have a pint of Guinness, cheers.'

The troll at the bar grumpily pours our drinks, all the while keeping a yellow eye on us. No doubt he's just waiting for us to make a beeline for his chest of precious things he keeps behind the crisps.

'Buddy's been telling me about the tips you've been giving him,' says Em. 'I don't know much about this sort of thing, but they seem pretty unusual.'

'Not really, it's what's called method acting. Like what people like Marlon Brando and Robert De Niro do when they're making a film.'

'They don't go to the toilet?'

'Very rarely. It's a little known fact that Robert De Niro was desperate for a leak all the way through the car chase in *Ronin*. That's why he was driving so fast.'

'Really, that is interesting. Listen, Elvis, do you fancy sitting down for a bit? Buddy's just running through a few things in the dressing room.'

'Sure,' I say, 'love to.' We sit opposite each other at a round table. Whenever she leans forward I can see right down her sparkly V-neck top. For a second I feel like we're on a date. She grins her idiot grin at me and raises her glass of orange birds' drink. 'Cheers,' she says, and clinks my pint glass.

There's definitely some kind of connection between Em and myself. Last night at their flat, she was asking me all sorts of questions about what I did and my life. I had to make up lies to cover most of it of course, but she seemed genuinely interested. Also, she was always fussing over me, offering me snacks and drinks, and sometimes, when I'd said something particularly outrageous, like how Elvis was really just a second-rate Dean Martin impersonator, she'd just think I was joking, and grab my shoulder and shake me, going, 'Oh, Elvis, you're terrible!' Then, when it was time for me to go, she pulled me toward her and kissed me on the cheek, and I swear, I felt a hard nipple brush against me. The only stumbling block is that she's nearly twenty years younger than me, and of course there's that whole problem I have with younger ladies. Like with the bird in the pub, I mean, 'I like your dress.' What was that all about? The trick is, of course, to make women feel special – get them to talk about themselves and appear really interested, even if their lives are in fact dull as fucking dishwater. I suppose it's easier to apply that trick to older birds because they're not that pretty any more and their self-confidence has gone. Still, Em can't have that much confidence herself, not when she's that size. So maybe I can work my magic on her after all.

'So, Em,' I say, 'what is it that you do?'

'Oh, I work in a nursery.'

'Really? That's fantastic. Plants or children?'

'Children. Little ones.'

'Well, I should imagine that's very fulfilling.'

'Yes, it is, very.'

'I bet you're very good with kids.'

'Well I can't have them myself, so . . .'

'What? That's terrible.'

'Buddy and me would love to have kids, but I have a thyroid condition which makes it practically impossible for me to conceive. We've tried, god knows we've tried over the past year, but we've been told that the chances are very low. We've thought about adoption, but that's a whole nightmare in itself.' She sheds a tear as she gives this unexpected confession. She must trust me more than I thought. 'I'm sorry,' she says, 'mustn't get tearful.'

'No, please don't apologise. I admire you for your strength in coping in such difficult circumstances. You're a very brave and remarkable woman.'

'No, no, I'm really not. I don't even feel like a proper woman, I can't give Buddy kids, I'm . . .'

'Now don't you talk like that. I can't believe that Buddy holds it against you in any way.'

'Oh, but he does,' she sniffles. 'He's sweet most of the time, but every so often, if he's had too much Baileys, he lashes out and shouts at me and says it's my fault he'll never have kids. He's always sorry afterwards, but it hurts so much, and he's right, it is my fault . . .' By this point her face is a streaming red mess of tears. 'Shit,' she says softly. 'I hate crying in public.'

'Why don't you come out with me to the van for a minute, give you a chance to collect yourself.'

'O-OK,' she whimpers. I lead her gently outside and open the passenger door for her. We sit in silence for a minute while I stroke the back of her head, until finally, she stops crying. 'I'm sorry, I really am, it's just that most of the time Buddy is as sweet as anything, but there's another side to him that nobody except me gets to see. He'll be fine, and then something will just snap and he'll be shouting and being aggressive. Sometimes he breaks things. And I get frightened, it really scares me. And I don't know where it all comes from.'

'You must really love him.'

'I do, I do, of course I do, but it just gets a bit lonely sometimes, you know, being the only person who knows about that side of him.'

'Well, you're not alone any more. Now you have a friend to share it with.'

'Yes, yes, I do,' she smiles and looks at me with warm, wet eyes. I take her hand and cradle it between mine. We sit there like that for I don't know how many minutes, and you know what, I'm as hard as a fucking rock. Meanwhile, she looks out of the window absent-mindedly then catches her face in the rear-view mirror. 'God, I look a state,' she says. She turns and smiles at me again, then goes back to gazing out of the window. I free one hand, unzip my trousers with it and pull out my cock, which stands up like a flagpole in my lap. Then I slowly take her hand and place it around it. A puzzled look passes over her face before she turns to see what she's suddenly holding. Her mouth forms a silent O, which I think for a second means she's about to suck it. But instead she snatches her hand away while a hurt expression crosses her face. 'Oh Elvis, you are silly,' she says faintly.

She says that she'd better go and fix her face. I don't attempt to stop her as she quickly slips out of the van. Instead, I watch her big arse wobble across the car park while I masturbate frantically. I come long before I expect it, and there's nothing I can do to stop it spraying all over the steering wheel. Christ, where did I go wrong this time? I suppose it would have to be when I got my cock out, but it just seemed the thing to do at that moment. Absent-mindedly I rest my hand on the wheel as I consider what just happened, until I'm interrupted by the beeping of a car horn behind me. Driving into the car park is

Soundcheck Stu. Hurriedly, I zip myself up and wave a spunk-coated hand at him.

'Hello there, Soundcheck Stu,' I shout out from my window, 'it's not time already is it?'

'Certainly is, Mister Elvis,' he says, getting out.

'Well you can help me lug the gear inside then. I'm running late.'

'You don't pay me for that sort of thing, you know.'

'I know, I pay you to do the sound, but seeing as you always make a pig's ear of that, you can help me set up free of charge.'

'Elvis, I don't know if anyone's ever told you this, but you're a complete and utter cunt.'

'Many times, many times.'

'Oh, by the way, I got a phone call from Gaylord today, saying him and the Fatman had left you to do their own thing, and would I be interested in mixing their sound for them.'

'Well, what did you say?'

'I said yes, of course.'

'You're a fucking traitor, Soundcheck Stu.'

'Yeah, whatever. What's that on your hand? Do you know you're getting it all over your new equipment? If any gets on the mixing desk, then I'm going home.'

'Mind your own fucking business,' I say as we go inside.

CHAPTER 13

I set up the gear with Soundcheck Stu, then run through a few numbers to get the balance right. Of course it's never right with Soundcheck Stu, and you just have to make do with whatever crap mix he comes up with. I need to get Buddy out of the dressing room for his soundcheck, but I hesitate because I can't see Em anywhere, and if she's in there telling him that I just tricked her into touching my manhood, then things could get a little messy. I put my ear to the door, but I can't hear anything inside except him singing bloody 'Heartbeat'. I take my life in my hands and open it. Inside, Buddy stands on his own, posing in front of the mirror with his guitar.

'All right Bud,' I say, 'not wanking in front of the mirror are we?'

'Nah, I'm just going over a few things. I'm still not sure about this not going to the loo thing though. I'm finding it really hard to concentrate. By the time I get on stage I'll be wetting myself.'

'Exactly. It makes you work harder. And that's what we want.'

'I guess. You haven't seen Em, have you? She popped out to get me a half and she never came back, and that was over an hour ago.'

'No, mate, I haven't, sorry.'

'Maybe I should go and look for her.'

'Yeah, well, we need you to soundcheck right now, so I'm sure she'll turn up, yeah?'

'Oh right, OK. She can't have gone far I suppose.'

'It's OK, love, I'm here.' Em's standing in the doorway, with her idiot grin intact, although it seems strained. But then, maybe I'm imagining that. 'I just had to pop into the loo for a bit, women's stuff.'

'Ah, I see,' says Buddy. She walks over to him and they paw at each other like a pair of puppies.

'Now you go out and be great for me, OK?' she says.

'It's only the soundcheck, hon.'

'Doesn't matter, you'll still be brilliant, because you're always brilliant. You're the best.'

They dribble over each other some more, until she backs away towards the door. 'Anyway, I'll leave you to it,' she says. 'Good luck, both of you.' She looks at each of us in turn with kind eyes that only seem to falter slightly when I meet her gaze. She turns to leave, but Buddy stops her, gently grabbing her shoulders.

'Are you OK?' he asks softly. 'You seem a bit out of sorts.'

'Yeah, I'm fine, fine.' She nods her head maybe a little too vigorously. 'You know, like I said, women's problems. Got to go to the toilet again.' She pulls his head towards her and kisses him. 'I love you, Buddy,' she whispers to him, although I can hear it perfectly well from across the room. Then she's gone.

'Come on, Bedwettin' Bud. Time for you to soundcheck. And don't piss your pants while you're singing, or you'll electrocute yourself and we'll have to peel you off the stage. Not that that would be too bad, seeing as we wouldn't have to listen to your bloody awful smelly bed-wetter music.'

'Um, yeah, sure.' He's not even listening to me.

Even with a bladder full of piss, Buddy's bloody brilliant. He sings just one song and captures the attention of the entire room. Admittedly the room currently has only four people in it, but it's more than I managed to do, bellowing out 'Kentucky Rain'. And of course Soundcheck Stu manages to give him a perfect mix. I realise the apparent incompetence Stu has demonstrated over all these years is obviously just an act, no doubt intended as a personal attack on myself. Why didn't I see that earlier? I immediately fill up with anger, and have to fight back the urge to slam his head into the mixing desk. But as I stand there, watching Buddy sing his speccy ginger-twat heart out, all my anger is transformed into an awful, inescapable sense that I've been beaten and there's absolutely nothing I can do about it. No matter how much I attempt to turn Buddy into a nervous wreck, no matter how much piss I make him hold in, he's still going to wipe the floor with me. Perhaps I have nothing else to do but await my own public humiliation. But still, I just can't give in that easily, it's not in my nature. I resolve to carry on with my plan, even though it's hopeless.

Buddy finishes his number, and receives a warm round of applause from the bar staff and the cleaning lady. Seems that the trollpeople like him. Soundcheck Stu also claps especially loudly. Buddy bows to his audience, puts his guitar on its stand, and walks over to me. 'Was that all right?' he asks.

'Buddy,' I tell him, 'that was reasonably good, but it lacked intensity. You've got to keep your mind on that dormitory and being soaked in piss, with the boys tormenting you and stealing your clothes, and the ladies laughing at your naked piss-drenched body, or you won't communicate. Now, what are you drinking? Half? Mate, have a pint.'

They've opened the doors and the place is beginning to fill up with the usual mix of the living dead, the alcoholic unemployed, cleaner wives and their big-titted teenage daughters. But there's something particularly scummy about this lot. It's not that they're dirty or anything, but they just seem like they don't quite belong to civilisation. In fact they look almost feral, as if they live out on the marshes instead of in houses. Anyway, it's time to retire to the dressing room to put on the jumpsuit and wig and snort up a couple of lines of charlie for luck. I leave Buddy nattering to Soundcheck Stu, and remember the bag that he handed me with my Elvistrousers in. I take it with me along with the rucksack in which I keep the rest of the gear, all badly folded and rumpled up. As I open the door, I catch a glimpse of something to the right of me. I turn, and see Em coming out of the women's toilets. We both stand, hovering at our respective doors, accidentally caught in each other's gaze, saying nothing. Then she breaks away, walking quickly towards the bar. I watch her as she goes.

Back in the dressing room I take the trousers out of their bag. They are completely spotless and indeed spunkless. The groin area, however, is now decidedly frayed. There is a hole starting right in the area of where my sizable manhood should be. It's not quite broken yet, so it will probably hold through the gig. Or maybe I'll just have a great big hole in my crotch, with my grubby boxer shorts that don't even have any buttons left on them any more exposed to the world. The hole depresses me so much that

I decide I need to do an extra line of charlie to counteract its effect. So I snort it all up and sit riding the wave of euphoria until there's a knock on the door and some trollwoman pokes her head round. 'You have to go out now,' she says, suspicious of what magic trickery I might have up my jumpsuit sleeve.

The way I've decided it's going to go is that I will do half of my set, Buddy will do his thing in the middle, and then I finish things off. That'll give me a chance to claw back a bit of the glory, I figure, although something tells me all it will really do is prolong the pain. But like the troll-lady said, it's time to start, so facing up to the inevitable, I stand in the corridor, waiting for Soundcheck Stu to start playing the opening tape of *Also Sprach Zarathustra*. It lasts forever, it lasts no time at all. And it segues into the riff of 'See See Rider'. I make my entrance. There's a ripple of hairy-handed applause, not that enthusiastic, as I make my way to the microphone. It's quite a full room, but not that many of the trollpeople seem to have realised someone dressed as fucking Elvis has just walked in, seeming more concerned with playing strange board games with wooden pieces they probably whittled themselves. Nevertheless, I start singing,

> I said see, see see Rider,
> Oh see what you have done

in a good Vegas rumble, but I can tell I'm not connecting with these people. It doesn't help that Soundcheck Stu's up to his old tricks again and making me sound like I'm singing from the far end of a long tunnel. I finish the song, and of course there's a bit of applause, but it's all but drowned out by the babble of their strange troll tongue.

Still, it's early days, and I'm sure I can warm this audience up a bit. Yeah, right. So anyway, I do a couple of love songs, go out into the audience, sing to the troll-ladies. It's a mixed reaction, and although some of them might as well be corpses, a few of them get into it so much you could swear they actually knew I was there. I mean it's ridiculous, one of them just carries on gibbering to her trollfriend even though I'm singing right into her perm. Still, maybe I can win them over with a bit of audience participation. I've had to revamp this bit of the show now that Fatty and Gayboy are no longer on board, one big change basically being that it's now me that has to put on the fucking grass skirt for 'Blue Hawaii'. 'Well, uh, I'll need some volunteers for this next here number ladiesandgentlemen, welluhthankyouverymuch,' I say. And do any of the trolls volunteer? Do they fuck. None of them want to put on a stupid fucking grass skirt and quite right too, I guess. Meanwhile, though, I'm standing there wearing one singing 'Blue Hawaii' on my fucking own, doing stupid Hawaiian dancing and looking a complete fucking tit. And then of course there's no applause. None at all. I'm dying on my grass-skirted arse up here. These trolls are the worst audience I've ever had. I can see Soundcheck Stu smirking to himself behind the mixing desk. God, he must have been waiting years for this.

And the thought hits me that, really, it's nothing to do with the audience. It's me. Maybe I've never really been the star of this act at all. What if Gaylord and the Fatman were the real stars, and I've just provided the soundtrack for their over-earnest freak show? What if it was their passion that people were responding to, and now without it, there is nothing to look at but an ageing cokehead who clearly hates Elvis, but for some unexplainable reason still has to go out pretending to be him in public? The thought drains me of any comprehensible impetus to carry on, but still some strange, buried instinct forces me to struggle on through the rest of the first half, entertaining nobody and being rewarded with little applause. As I head off to the dressing room, it seems hardly anyone even notices that I've gone. I pass Em and Buddy standing at the bar on the way, no doubt trying to hide their pity. Buddy follows me in.

'Quite a tough crowd tonight, Elvis,' he says.

'Yeah, bunch of cunts, the lot of them.'

'God, it's making me really nervous. If they treat you like that, how are they going to react to me? I'm going to bomb, I know it.'

'Have you been to the toilet?'

'No, Elvis, I swear I haven't. I'm going to wet myself any minute, but I haven't been.'

'If I call you a bed-wetting smelly freak, does it make you feel quite upset?'

'Yes, Elvis, it does actually.'

'Then you're going to be fine, my son.'

'Ah, OK.'

'Look, I need a few minutes to myself. Can you just leave me alone for a bit, then call me when it's time for the second half?'

'No problem, Elvis. Are you sure you're all right?'

'Yeah, I'm fine. Just need to psych myself up a bit. Get in the zone. Clear my head of all thoughts. Do a bit of Zen.'

'Never had you down for a practitioner of Eastern philosophy, Elvis.'

'Why not? Goes with the fucking karate.'

And so Buddy finally fucks off, and I'm free to do another line. But even the comfort of the charlie can't muzzle the thoughts that nag at me. Could I have been wrong all this time? Have I always just been totally fucking shit, and only got by because the Fatty and the Gaylord were out there geeing things up a bit? How come nobody told me? Probably because I'd have punched the living crap out of them, I guess. No, I tell myself, it can't be true, or at least it can't be that simple. I was good before I even met those two jokers, but way back then I felt that strange feeling more often, the way I felt when I sang for Eddie by the swimming pool, feeling as if I was doing what I was meant to do, what I exist for. But I hardly ever feel that now. Maybe having Gayboy and Fatman out there compensated for it, took attention away from the fact I was just coasting. But they're not there any more, and I've got to feel that way again, right away. But how? You can't force that sort of thing. But maybe you can fake it. Maybe you can fake it with charlie. Lots of charlie.

'Time, Elvis!' says Buddy from the other side of the door half an hour later. I feel like a colossus, a gigantic Elvis striding across the dressing room, down the corridor and through the bar of tiny midget-trolls towards the stage. I walk on, and the applause sounds like a helicopter, no, like a waterfall. I can't see many of them clapping, but that's what it sounds like. I perceive a great distance between me on the stage and the people out there in the audience, a chasm, or an ocean, maybe even an eternity, that I must make a bridge across. Somehow, I must reach out to the trollpeople, and convince them that we are really of the same race. I must lay down a bridge of sound, and the sound is that of my voice. Across the void, in the far distance, the little trollfolk are looking up at me, Elvis, a leader of men, perhaps a god, no – better than a god, a king, the King, Elvis Presley. For I am Elvis. Yes, I am indeed fucking Elvis! Who's the King? I fucking am, Elvis fucking Presley, that's fucking who! I feel I should speak. Yet what words could I possibly bless them with? There are no words. All words are inadequate. So instead I must stand here, saying nothing, bestowing the gift of my very being on these trolls of Elk, who, despite their deformities, are still my people.

You'd think they'd be grateful.

CHAPTER 14

'**O**i! **Elvis, get on** with it!'

'Wakey! Wakey!'

'Dime bar?'

The crowd taunt me in their troll language as I stand there, unable to articulate the wonder of my godly being in words. I can see Buddy looking at me with concern through his goggles. And then I remember. I'm meant to be introducing Buddy. That's why I'm there. I can do that. I can do that with words.

'Ladies and gentlemen, as you know Elvis Presley was the King of Rock 'n' Roll, but there were a few contenders to the throne. Yet no matter how much they tried to take his crown, Elvis always came out on top. Whoever dared to challenge him, Elvis struck them down with his almighty wrath. There was

Jerry Lee Lewis, he coveted the throne of Rock 'n' Roll-land, but Elvis filled him with desire for his thirteen-year-old cousin which made him marry her, and lo! his career ended. Then Little Richard said to the people, "Elvis is not the King of Rock 'n' Roll, for it is I – Little Richard, a gaylord with big hair." And Elvis was much displeased with him and convinced Little Richard that gospel music was interesting, when in fact it's really fucking dull. And it came to pass Little Richard no longer wanted to be the King of Rock 'n' Roll, but instead wanted to be the King of Gospel, and nobody gives a fuck who the King of Gospel is. Eddie Cochran, he was so foolish as to take on the King, and Elvis took him out in a hit-and-run car smash, also giving Gene Vincent a good mashing for good measure at the same time. But Elvis still had to face the greatest threat to his Kingship. He was a big fatty who went "Hellooooooo Baybay" down the telephone to underage girls. His name was the Big Bopper. Elvis did him in by making his plane crash and fixed it so it looked like an accident, thus vanquishing his foe. Also killed in the plane were minor musical figures Ritchie Valens and Buddy Holly, which leads me to the small matter of introducing you now to the one, the only, the dead, Buddy Holly!'

Buddy bounds on stage with overenthusiasm as the boos and laughter that have drowned out most of my speech are mixed with some slight applause. As he assumes his position, I grab his arm and mutter in his ear: 'Don't think you're anything special, you bed-wetting piece of shit. Why don't you just piss yourself now and be done with it, it's all you're good for, all people will ever remember about you. Just a big puddle of piss on the floor with you standing in the middle of it. Go on, sing! People will just laugh at you, you and your stinky piss-smelling trousers and your blue jacket with the yellow piss stains on it. Go back to your dormitory and your piss-filled bed, you bed-wetting freak!'

And I walk over to the side of the stage. Buddy looks at me for a second, pale and agitated, then shouts in my direction, 'Leave me alone! I'm not afraid of you! You can't hurt me now I'm all grown up! I'm Buddy Holly!' and launches into the most blistering version of 'Rave On' you could possibly imagine. Of course the mix is excellent – you can hear his vocals crystal clear, but there's something else going on as well. The audience lap him up as he sings like a man possessed, quite possibly by the spirit of Buddy Holly himself, or at the very least by one of the Proclaimers. By the end of the song they're even singing along to the chorus. He stands and soaks up the applause. You can tell from his teary eyes and uncontrollable grin that this alone is a dream come true for him. It would be a nightmare for me if it wasn't for the charlie, especially as he keeps on looking my way in disbelief and sticking his thumb up. 'Pisspants!' I shout at him, but I don't think he hears. Soundcheck Stu starts the backing track for his next song and he's away again. He soars, and takes the audience with him through about eight songs, nearly all hits. They just fucking love him. I know he's good, but this is ridiculous. It's as if he's tapped into some primordial tribal spirit by accident, and is drawing the trolls of this rotten village together in some sort of communal experience. He carries them with him until, twenty minutes later, he finishes with a version of 'Peggy Sue' which sounds like it's going to explode. And then, as he reaches the last few bars, something does explode, this thing being Buddy's bladder. As the song ends, he is blatantly standing in a large, spreading pool of his own piss.

First of course the trolls are cheering. Then they see the puddle. The cheers become mixed with laughter. 'He's pissed himself! Look, he's pissed himself!' they say, nudging each other and pointing to the expanding puddle. For a moment it looks like all of Buddy's hard work has been obliterated in one emptying of the bladder, as the laughter increases and his face turns an ashen grey while he mutters to himself, no doubt explaining himself to the boys in the youth hostel dormitory. Em bravely walks right into the puddle of piss and takes his hand to lead him off. But then something very strange happens. The laughter dies down and turns back to cheers, as they remember how good he was. Big burly men jump on stage, then lift Buddy up on their shoulders, pissed trousers and all.

'I'm Buddy fucking Holly!' he shouts at the top of his lungs as they carry him round the bar on a lap of honour. He punches the air as he goes, and shakes their hoofed hands. Meanwhile a woman is dispatched to mop up the puddle discreetly before it reaches the PA and blows us all to kingdom come. All the while, I'm just standing there, pondering this unlikely and strangely pagan event. What is his secret, I ask myself. And more importantly, how the fuck do I follow that?

Fortunately the clean-up operation buys me enough time to nip back to the dressing room to do some more charlie and therefore strengthen my sense of godlike greatness. I snort a couple of lines, and I'm just about to go out again when Buddy walks in with Em wrapped round his waist. He's not wearing any trousers. They are both grinning ecstatically. 'Thank you Elvis,' he says, barely holding back the tears, 'I couldn't have done it without you. Your tips took me to a level I could never have dreamed of reaching. It was like I was smashing those bullies' faces in with music! Just got to time that bladder thing a bit better, though.'

'Yeah, thanks Elvis,' says Em. She's crying her eyes out and her mascara's running down her face, but in the black smudges where her eyes used to be, I sense that I'm forgiven. 'Good luck,' she mouths at me as I begin my walk of fate back to the stage.

A wave of disappointment travels across the room and hits me in the stomach as I take the stage again. I'll show 'em, I think to myself amid the booing, I'll fucking show them who's King. I give the signal and launch into 'Blue Suede Shoes'. But of course Soundcheck Stu is working his magic and you can hardly fucking hear me. I point up at him frantically for him to raise the level, but he just smiles serenely back at me like the cunt he is. I'm not taking any of his shit now though. During the instrumental break I dive over the mixing desk and grab him by the throat. 'You mix me properly or I swear to god I'll break your fingers off and shove them up your fucking arse.'

He rolls his eyes and tuts at me, but he pushes the vocal channel up on the desk just in time for the next verse. For the first time since I came out of the nick second time round, I can actually hear myself when I sing. I finish the song, and look out to see a room of grudging, mildly entertained neanderthal faces, some of whom are even bothering to clap in a way that doesn't sound sarcastic. I've cracked it! I've reached them. Just got to keep up the momentum and they are mine. I'm hitting them with the hits now. 'All Shook Up', 'A Big Hunk O' Love', 'Viva Las Vegas'. The reaction from the trolls grows bit by bit with each number. And I am in the zone. I am most fucking definitely in the zone. I don't care that I'm dressed as fat Vegas Elvis, and I'm not even wearing padding, I'm dancing like I'm young sex Elvis in the prison rec yard. I probably look fucking stupid, but you know what, they're mildly liking it. I have quite definitely and irrefutably won them over. I am the King and the trolls are my subjects. Which means I can do what I want with them.

The time has come to go out in the audience and converse

with my flock. I spy my ideal family sitting in a booth – little man, big fat wife and bored teenage daughter with bottle-blonde hair and big tits, texting on her mobile at a hundred strokes per second to her friends she'd much rather be out with. Christ, she's got a lovely pair, I think to myself. It would only be right if I could get my hands on them. I am the King after all. As my subject it is her duty to offer them up to me, should I decree it. Or maybe I should think of her as her father's property and put my demand to him in the first instance. Yes, my understanding of feudal custom is a bit rusty, but I think that's how it works. I walk up to them, radio mike in hand. 'Well, uh, good evening sir,' I say to the little man. 'Are you having a good time?'

'Yes thank you,' he says, barely audible as his lips don't move when he speaks. Obviously evolution hasn't taken them that far yet.

'And, uh, what is your name, sir?'

'Colin.'

'Sorry sir, I, uh, didn't quite catch that. Speak into the microphone if you will.'

'Colin.'

'Did you say Colin?'

'Yes, that's right.'

'And, uh, who are these lovely ladies with you tonight?'

'Sarah, my wife, and that's Debbie, my daughter.'

'Your, uh, lovely daughter, Debbie. And how old is Debbie?'

'She's seventeen.'

'Seventeen years old, well that's just swell. Uh, does she fuck?'

'You what?'

'Now Colin,' I say, 'seeing as I'm uh, your king and all, I have the right to make your daughter what they call my concubine. What this means is that it will be her duty to, uh, service me sexually. Now, I should imagine you must feel, uh, pretty honoured by that, Debbie.' I point the microphone in her direction.

'Are you taking the fucking piss out of me?' she says.

But I'm not listening. I've become mesmerised by her smashing pair and forget where I am and what I'm meant to be doing, until someone punches me in the side of my face and I nearly fall down. I catch myself on their table, but knock over everybody's drinks. 'Uh, whoopsa-daisy,' I say.

I realise I've just been punched by big fat Sarah. She's steaming mad and bright red with it, like something out of the *Beano*. Next thing I know my arms are pinned behind my back and I'm being lynched by the trollpeople! This is no way to treat their king! One of them holds me up as various males and females of the species pound me in the face and chest. I get a good kick in the bollocks for good measure. The organising committee half-heartedly flit around asking people to stop, but you can tell their hearts aren't really in it.

'My people,' I gasp, 'why do you treat your, uh, king this way?'

'Shut it, you perv,' one of them says, then punches me in the mouth. It's a good job I'm out of my mind on drugs, or this would really hurt.

'Leave him alone!' a woman's voice cries from across the room. Through the blood congealing on my eyes I see Em and Buddy, who's wearing a pair of borrowed trousers, make their way through the mob.

'OK, that's enough!' shouts Buddy over and over again. It takes a while, but eventually the trolls remember that they like him and do what he says. The pair of them carry me by my arms to a settle, but no sooner have they put me down, then they have to move me again to a corner of the stage after the

club secretary insists that they musn't get blood on the uphol-
stery.

'Elvis, are you OK? Can you hear us?'

'Forgive them, they know not-ughhh . . .'

'Elvis, we're going to get you to hospital, OK?'

'No, no doctors. They would not understand . . . my internal
organs . . . from another dimension . . .'

'Elvis, we're going to get you out of here. Buddy's going to
bring the car round the side entrance, and I'll wait here with
you.'

'No need, my angels will take me . . . back to Heaven . . . in
the spaceship . . .'

Why have my people turned against me like this? Now I know
how God felt about that Golden Calf business. They must be
made aware of my power. I must give them a sign, but what?
Em is washing the blood off my face with a cloth. While she
does this, her huge breasts are pressed right up to me and I can
feel them squash against my chest. Naturally this gives me the
horn something rotten, and I immediately see what form the
sign must take. Using all my will power, I direct my sizable manhood out of the buttonless fly of my boxer shorts and force open
the hole that is forming in the crotch of my trousers. Soon
enough, my bulging bell-end, lustrously and vibrantly purple-
pink, is poking out like a beacon from my gleaming white
Elvistrousers.

'Oh my god, that's disgusting.'

'He's a fucking disgrace.'

'I didn't know they came that big.'

In the darkness, I see troll-like forms make their way towards
me, and I get the feeling I'm about to be lynched again.

'Oh, Elvis,' says Em, patiently. 'Can't you ever keep it to
yourself?'

Just then, I feel myself being dragged backwards out of a door, and carried for a short while before finally being laid down somewhere. There's the brief sensation of forward movement, and then I black out entirely.

CHAPTER 15

I'm pushing a shopping trolley around a supermarket and I'm naked except for a pinny. The trolley is full of toilet roll, and it's coming out of its packets and unrolling onto the floor. I'm in the fruit section, but when I give the fruit a squeeze, it shoots a sticky fluid in my eyes and an alarm goes off. Gay Elvis and Fatboy charge round the corner with their own shopping trolley and the alarm turns into them singing a Vegas-period Elvis song, 'Burning Love'. They career into me, knocking my trolley away with theirs and shout the song into my ear.

'Don't tell me you've been caught with your cock out in the supermarket, you dirty man!' screams Gay Elvis.

'Actually it isn't out, I have a pinny,' I reply.

'It's not covering it up though!' Fat Elvis points down at it, and I see that it's erect and the pinny isn't remotely covering it.

'Keep it away from the fruit!' screeches the Gaylord.

'Oh my god, you dirty fucker, you've come on the apples,' says Fatboy.

He was right, I had.

'Anyway, we're off,' Gay Elvis brays into my ear, 'we're going to sing for Elvis. You're a joke. See you.' They zoom off, and I see their trolley is full of Elvis records. They're all the same one, the *Blue Hawaii* soundtrack.

'Well hello, dear boy,' a voice says behind me. It's Eddie. I run down an aisle as fast as I can, still pushing my trolley. I turn and see that he's chasing after me with his trousers round his ankles. It doesn't slow him down at all though. 'This way,' cries Bridget, who's sitting behind a checkout in her mod gear. I push my trolley up to it, where she takes the unravelling toilet rolls and starts rolling them all up again. 'You really shouldn't have done this before you paid for them,' she says.

'I know, I know, I'm sorry,' I reply. I feel something hit the back of my legs. It's Eddie with his trolley.

'Do you think I could fit all of this up there?' he asks me, with a wink.

I look to Bridget for help, but she just says, 'I'm sorry, shrimp, I can't let you go through until I've rolled all these up.' Eddie keeps on hitting me with his trolley, as if he's working up to something. Christ, I think, this is going to be bad. But then suddenly I feel like I'm being sucked out of the supermarket by a giant vacuum cleaner and thrown into a wall of fuzz, like the screen of a detuned television. The fuzz somehow gets inside my head, and I start to wander around in it. I'm in there for what seems like hours, until I begin to think that I hear voices, but I can't make out clearly what they say. Then I can see lights and shapes. There's one final suck of the vacuum cleaner and I find myself in the back seat of Buddy's car, being held upright by Em.

'What's going on?' I blurt, making Em jump.

'It's OK, Elvis,' she says soothingly, 'we're just taking you to hospital. You've had a bit of a knock.'

'No, no, I can't. Let me out, please.'

'Elvis, you'll be OK. You just need to be looked over and stitched up a bit.'

'No, I don't want to go. I really don't.' I can't stand hospitals. Not since I was just a lad and Bridget tried to kill herself the first time by swallowing aspirin. They poured charcoal down her throat with a funnel to counteract it. I caught a glimpse of her coughing it all up before they closed the curtain round her. It's stayed with me forever. 'Look, I've got cocaine in my system, OK? I can't see a doctor right now.'

'You take cocaine?' says Buddy. 'Actually, that would explain a lot, come to think of it.'

'Oh Elvis, you big silly,' sighs Em. 'You've really got to be looked at. You're not exactly in a good way, you know.'

I catch myself in the rear-view mirror. She has a point. I look like something that should be hung on a butcher's hook. My memory of the evening is a bit vague right now, but I have a feeling I might have been a bit naughty, and I don't want to be anywhere the boys in blue can easily find me, certainly not with this amount of charlie in my system. 'Look guys, I appreciate your concern, but unless you turn this car around, I'm jumping out the door right this second.'

'Elvis, I've got central locking.'

'Can you unlock it, please?'

'No, sorry.'

'I will see a doctor, I promise, but in a day or two, when the stuff's out of my system. But right now I just want to lie low for a bit, so would you mind taking me home?'

They're quiet for a moment, and then Em says, 'OK, this is what we'll do. We'll take you back to ours, and I'll tidy you up a bit. You stay with us for twenty-four hours, then we take you to A & E.'

'You don't need to do that, just drop me off at my house and—'

'Elvis, either you let us look after you or we're driving you to the hospital right now.'

'OK.' I know when to admit defeat. Also, I find the idea of being nursed by Em and her enormous boobs quite appealing. You never know, maybe this is my chance to finally win her over.

Half an hour later and I'm stripped to the waist in Buddy and Em's flat. Turns out I've got a nasty gash on my forehead, so Em cleans it and covers it up. It needs stitches, but thankfully she didn't offer to try her hand at that. My torso's badly bruised, but it doesn't seem like any of my ribs are broken. Just in case, Em bandages it so tightly that even if my ribs aren't broken, they probably are now. For a while, Buddy sits by the record player, playing Stray Cats records in a vain effort to impress me. 'Do you like them?' he says.

'They're OK, but they're no King Pleasure and the Biscuit Boys,' I reply. Soon enough he goes to bed, as he has to be up in a few hours to do his postal route, leaving me alone with Em. We sit in silence for a bit, as she runs her hand through my thinning hair in a way that she no doubt intends to be calming, but naturally gets me quite aroused. Then finally she speaks.

'Elvis, I think you may need some help.'

'Who doesn't?'

'No, really, Elvis. I think you need to see someone about your drug use. It's a bit out of hand.'

'You think?'

'Yes, I do.'

'Yeah . . . maybe you're right.'

She strokes my hair some more, and my manhood threatens to poke out through the hole again, but I feel so sore I can't muster up the energy to do anything about it, let alone the audacity, and I find myself falling asleep.

My sleep is very deep and very long. I dream about Eddie and Bridget again of course, but when I wake I don't feel the way I usually do after it, like someone's bitten a big chunk out of my brain, but instead I'd say I feel restful, quite contented in fact. It's not that the dream itself was any different, Eddie was being Eddie, and me and Bridget had the same type of pointless conversation we always have, but the atmosphere had changed. Before, I'd always be left with the feeling that Bridg was pitying me, even though she was the one who'd hanged herself after years of Dad's fiddling, but this time it was like we were more on the same level. Anyway, back here in the flat, Em's laid me out on the sofa and covered me with a blanket. It must be late morning. On a coffee table next to me is a note. I stretch out for it and read it where I lie. In girly handwriting, with very round letters and circles where the dots should be, it says:

Dear Elvis,

  Gone to work. Buddy will be back early afternoon. Make yourself at home. Help yourself to any food in the kitchen and any drink except the champagne. Please do not try to leave as we agreed that you should go to A & E this evening and I would be very hurt if you let me down.

  See you soon,

  Love

  Em x

I can't see me staying there the whole day, and as for going to A & E she must be having a laugh, but right now I'm starving. I go to the kitchen to look for something microwaveable. On the way I find some clothes that Em has left for me, which is good seeing as I can't walk around dressed as Elvis all day. There's a pair of trousers with an elasticated waist and a big smock-like top that are obviously hers, what with Buddy being about half the size of me. Also the smock is bright pink. I can just about get my big gut into the trousers, and although they're women's clothes, I don't really care right now. Meanwhile, I find a beef curry and heat it up. It takes about fifteen minutes altogether, so I kill time by having a bit of an amble about the house. First I go into the spare bedroom which is Buddy's shrine to Buddy Holly, as well as where he keeps most of his rock 'n' roll memorabilia. Em doesn't let him have it in the living room, which is all flat-pack storage units and candle holders. Em calls it Buddy's Buddy room. It's packed full of stuff, some of it very valuable. Old 78s, sheet music, autographs, replica guitars and clothes, all sorts of stuff. Pride of place is given to a signed photo of Buddy Holly, and in a frame, the handwritten letter by the man himself that Buddy paid five grand for. It's about his income tax.

Then I go into the bedroom. It's a lovely thing in peach which Em is clearly in charge of, with so much pot-pourri you nearly overdose, and a queen-size double bed with no end of cushions, pillows, a menagerie of soft toys on top and in it. God knows how they get in the thing. I think about Em on it, naked, with her big fat arse in the air. I'm just contemplating lying there having a wank when the microwave pings. I go back to the kitchen, dish out the curry, take it to the living room and turn on the telly. Wouldn't you know it, Buddy's got Sky. I can't even get Channel 5 at my place. I must be sat there for hours, flicking channels, looking for something worth watching. Unfortunately Buddy doesn't subscribe to any porn channels, being a good boy, so I end up watching the home shopping. The presenter has a cheeky gleam in her eye, and what with my little day-dream in the bedroom, makes it absolutely necessary to have a quick fiddle there on Buddy's sofa. I'm just about to shoot my load into a handy tissue forty-five seconds into it when I hear the front door open. I manage to stuff it away just in time before Buddy walks in.

'All right, big guy, how you feeling?' chirps the singing postman.

'Oh, not bad, yourself?'

'Yeah, good, good. What are you watching?'

'Oh, nothing, really. Just flicking channels.'

'Yeah, it's like that Bruce Springsteen song, "57 Channels and Nothin' On". I've got over two hundred channels, and there's still nothing on!' He chuckles at his own joke, and I do my very best to smile. 'Do you like Bruce Springsteen at all?'

'Not a big fan,' I say.

'Yeah, he's OK, but he's not like a proper rock 'n' roll singer. So other than Elvis, what music are you into, if you don't mind me asking?'

God, what a question, I think to myself. I haven't bought any new music since *Smell of Female* by the Cramps, and I never listened to that much. I remember listening to pub rock quite a bit in the seventies, Ducks Deluxe, Dr Feelgood and all that, but really music isn't a part of my life at all these days, other than the odd bit I hear on the radio, like Dido. 'Shakin' Stevens,' I say.

'Yeah, he's underrated.'

We talk a bit more about music, mostly old rock 'n' roll stuff that I suppose I know quite a bit about, until Buddy hits me

with a startling confession. 'You know what,' he says, 'sometimes, now and then like, I just think, I'm so fucking bored with
Buddy Holly. After all these years listening to his music, learning
his songs, going to conventions, talking about him for hours with
other fans and stuff, I just sometimes think I might have had
enough of him. I feel like I've got everything I'm ever going to
get out of him, and I never need to hear a note of his music
again, if you know what I mean.'

'Yeah, I can see where you're coming from there.'

'But then, I'll put one of his records on, and I'll think, fucking
hell, I really, really love him! I expect it's a bit like that with
you and Elvis.'

'Um, something like that.'

'I suppose,' he continues, 'in a way, Buddy's the centre of my
life. If I had a choice between Em and Buddy, I'm not sure who
I'd choose. You don't mind me telling you that, do you?'

'No, of course not.'

'He's just always been there for me, see. Ever since I was a
lad – oh, hang on.'

Buddy's mobile phone is playing the opening bars of 'Every
Day'. Is there a single aspect of his life that Buddy Holly hasn't
wormed his way into?

'Hello?' he says. 'Oh right, hello. Just bear with me a minute.'
He takes the phone into the Buddy-shrine room with him, so I
can't hear what he's saying, I suppose. Of course, I can hear
perfectly, but mostly all he says is 'oh, right,' and 'sure' before
telling the other party he'd get back to them after he'd talked to
the missus.

When he comes back in, he has a rather grave look on his face.

'Elvis, that was the social club from last night.'

'Oh?'

'Um, what they were phoning me about was, they'd like me

to play there again in the near future, by myself like, on my own . . . that is, without you.'

'Cheeky fuckers. I hope you told them where to go.'

'Actually, I said I probably would, I just wanted to talk to Em about it before I confirmed for definite. That's OK with you isn't it? Me doing it by myself? Um, to be honest with you, I wasn't really thinking of playing with you again, not until you sorted out your drug problem anyway.'

'Nah, not bothered. Don't worry about it.'

'So you're OK with it, then?'

'Yeah, course I am, mate. You can even borrow my gear if you like. Come on, let's go to the pub and celebrate.'

'Yeah, OK, sounds good.'

I realise that I have no money, because my wallet is in the pocket of my trousers back in the dressing room of the social club. 'Look, Bud, you couldn't lend me twenty quid could you?' I ask him.

'Uh, yeah, sure,' he says, as he goes to change out of his postman's uniform.

CHAPTER 16

'The Beatles? Fuck the fucking Beatles. Took them fucking years to catch up with what Buddy was doing fucking ages before, then they just took loads of drugs and made bloody curry house music. "Strawberry Fields Forever", what's that fucking all about? It's not exactly fucking rock 'n' roll is it? If Buddy had lived he'd have kicked the fucking Beatles' arses. He was way ahead of them, fucking way ahead. Tell you what, Elvis, the Beatles, bunch of cunts. Cheers.' Buddy clinks my glass and spills beer down his sleeve in the process. He's in a right state. I'm feeling pretty merry myself, but I'm far more composed seeing as I've had years of practice, while Buddy's just been sipping on tiny glasses of Baileys all his adult life. Mind you, right now, I wouldn't have it any other way.

We're sitting outside a rather quaint pub on the bank of the River Cam. It's not my usual sort of place, it's even got an eating area you can take children, for Christ's sake! But still, I'm having a right merry old time, watching the river go by and Buddy getting wasted. It was a bit of an effort to persuade Buddy to drink pints instead of halves, but several rounds in and he's a magnificent fucking embarrassment. He's shouting everything at the top of his lungs, and swearing like a trooper, which is quite funny to listen to, seeing as normally the harshest word he can bring himself to say is 'bum'. I have a feeling he's going to get us chucked out pretty soon because we're getting funny looks from the posh twats and the tourists who drink here, but I hope we can get at least one more round in. It's not just Buddy's shouting that's drawing attention. My head's still bandaged up, and some blood has soaked through. I'm also wearing Em's pink smock and elasticated trousers and my Elvis boots, but then there's no law against dressing like a tit. I finish my pint while Buddy's still halfway through his, and most of that he's spilt on himself. 'It's your round I think, Bud.'

'Hang on! I've still got a bit to go.'

'Well, drink up, then. I'm getting parched over here.'

'OK, OK,' he says, and downs his pint, with a load of it going down his shirt. He burps. Then he gags, puts his hand to his mouth, stands up quickly and runs off inside in the direction of the lavs, beer pouring out his mouth and between his fingers as he goes. I follow him, the barman shaking his head disapprovingly at me as I pass, and find him throwing up into the sink. It's not a pretty sight. In fact I think he may be in need of more than one sink.

'Are you OK, Bud?' I say when he finally stops.

'Yeah, I'm fine. Just needed to be a bit sick, that's all. Oh, wait a minute.' He retches and it starts up again, like someone's turned on a mains tap. Some time later, it stops. The smell is rank, like the mattress I threw out the other day.

'Hey Bud,' I say, 'let's go and get some fresh air, eh? Do you good.'

'Yeah, I like the sound of that.'

'It's your round, though, don't forget.'

'I don't want to see you in here again,' says the barman, as I navigate Buddy out of the pub front door. I point him in the direction of the riverbank.

'Tell you what, Bud,' I say, 'why don't we walk along there for a bit? It'll be nice, and if you want to be sick again, you can just go in the river. What do you think?'

'Yeah, be nice,' he mumbles, before walking into someone's parked car and setting off the alarm.

'Come on, Bud, let's go.'

We walk along the riverbank, passing the odd houseboat moored at the side. Before long, we come to a lock, and beyond that, through the trees, we can just about make out something I didn't even know was there, a swimming pool.

'Christ, what's this doing here?' I say.

'It's a lido,' says Buddy.

'It's a what?'

'A lido. An outdoor swimming pool. I used to come here when I was a lad.'

'Outdoor swimming pool? That's a fucking stupid idea. What happens when it rains?'

'You get wet.'

'Don't try to be clever, Bud, you're not cut out for it.'

By the pool there's a grassy area, where lovely young lasses lounge about, sunbathing in their bikinis. 'Look at those beauties, eh, Bud. Bet you'd like to get yourself some of that.'

'Yeah, like they'd want anything to do with me. Until Em

came along, women wouldn't even give me the time of day. Not that I care, I wouldn't want to touch dirty sluts like those. Lying about, showing their tits off. They'll obviously spread their legs for anybody.'

'Yeah, except you, Bud.'

We pass the lido, and carry on walking. Buddy has to stop to be sick on a bush and it's not long before he's asking if we can sit down on a bench near a bridge. We do, and he curls himself up into a tight little ball, moaning to himself. It's pretty annoying, so I try to phase him out by thinking about the natural scenery around us, something I've never really been in the habit of doing, but I feel the urge to here for some reason. I suppose I'd have to say it's quite restful here, listening to the water. The smell of sick blowing off Buddy spoils it a little bit, but I can live with it. Buddy just rocks backwards and forwards in his ball, looking ill. After a while, he seems to have fallen asleep, and I sit by him silently, watching the ducks float downriver. The trees droop over us here, I think they're willows, although I might be wrong. Occasionally someone passes over the bridge, and at one point some posh twit brings his neighing children past us on the river-bank with their newt nets. He hurries them along when he sees the state of us, or when he smells it. The sun gets lower in the sky, and peeks between the branches of the trees. After a while, I've had enough of nature, and I'm getting hungry and bored. I want to go home, or at least for a curry. I wake Buddy up.

'Buddy,' I say, 'time to get a move on.'

'Ugggnugh – yeah, five more minutes.'

'Come on, Bud, Em'll be wondering where you've got to.'

'Oh, right. Oh. Oh, Christ, Elvis, if Em sees me in this state, she'll kill me.'

'She'll be more upset if you don't turn up at all. Anyway, you've got to tell her your good news.'

'What good news?'

'That you've got a gig all by yourself. You've got to go home and tell her.'

'Oh yeah, that news.' He seems to drift off for a second, his eyes gazing out at nothing in particular. Then he says, 'Elvis, I'm a total fucking cunt.'

'Why do you say that, Bud?'

'I mean I'm a total fucking arsehole. Em is a wonderful woman, a truly wonderful, wonderful woman, and I treat her really fucking badly, and I don't fucking deserve her, and that's why I'm a total fucking arsehole cunt.'

'I'm sure that's not true, I'm sure you treat her very well.'

'Yeah, right. Listen Elvis, I may seem OK on the surface, but deep down I'm angry at the whole fucking world, angry at the way I got treated all these years by fucking everybody, and do you know what, I take it out on her. It's not fair. She shouldn't be with me, she should be with someone better who treats her right.'

'You really think so?'

'Yes, I do. I've nearly hit her loads of times, but it's nothing to do with her, it's me! I'm a total piece of shit.'

He starts sobbing, and I put my hands on his shoulders. I hold him for a second while he cries. Meanwhile, I look to see if anyone can see us. There doesn't appear to be anybody about.

'Buddy,' I tell him finally, 'I think you're right.'

'What?'

'You are a piece of shit. A huge, total, stinking, disgusting, sticky, lump of steaming shit. You're absolutely right, you don't deserve Em at all. You're a fucking disgrace, and I'm going to fix it that you never have a chance to go near her with your tiny little dick again.'

The look of incomprehension on his face is truly beautiful.

I pause to savour it before I smack my fist right into his mouth. Then I push him down onto the ground and give him a good kicking. Fortunately for him his glasses fall off on the way down, but it wouldn't bother me if they hadn't. Anyway, I kick him and stamp on him until his face is a mess of blood and dirt, and he's grabbing his balls in agony and screaming. I bend down and grab his hair, and slam his head several times into the ground for good measure. 'You fucking bed-wetter,' I say, as I do all of this, 'how dare you think you can fuck with me, take my gigs, try to upstage me. You got lucky, you fucker, that's all. My Elvis could wipe the floor with you, and no one would care about your precious fucking Buddy Holly. And do you know what I'm going to do? I'm going to go right round your flat and fuck your girl-friend. And she's going to fucking love it. I'm going to go and do that right now, while you're lying here. How'd you like that, you little bed-wetting freak?' After a while, he stops screaming and his limbs aren't spazzing all over the place, which means he's dead or unconscious. I want to stamp on his head some more, but figure his screams may well have attracted some atten-tion, so I leave him where he is, look around again quickly to make sure nobody saw me, and dart into the trees, scramble up the bank before hitting upon a path that leads to the road.

Once I reach it, I decide to go in the opposite direction from which I came. By now I'm starving, so even though I'm making the effort to put as much ground between me and him as possible, I'm also looking out for a decent takeaway. I stumble across a Chinese, and while I wait for my Peking Duck, I hear the sound of ambulance sirens in the distance. They stop, and by the time I find a wall to sit on while I eat, I hear them again for a minute before they fade away. After the Chinese I'm feeling pretty stuffed and just want to go for a pint somewhere, but sitting there on the wall it occurs to me that I only have a small window of time to get round Buddy's house and make a move on Em before the police notify her. After that she might be at the hospital for days or weeks on end. Depends how long it takes Buddy to get better, I guess. Or snuff it, if he hasn't already. It takes me about forty minutes to walk back to their place, and doing it on such a full stomach gives me cramps. Anyway, it turns out it was a waste of time. From the top of the street I can see a police car parked in their road, blue lights flashing. I turn back quickly the way I came and make myself scarce. So where to now? I suppose it might make sense to head for the bus station and get the fuck out of Cambridge, but I fancy a pint and I can't be bothered with the bus right now. So instead, stomach cramps and all, I walk to the town centre and find a quiet pub with a dartboard and a telly.

So I'm sitting there minding my own business for I don't know how long, half following whatever crap's on the telly, soaps mostly. Then the landlord switches it over for the news, and wouldn't you know, Buddy's on it, sort of. Apparently police are investigating the attack on a thirty-eight-year-old man in Cambridge, who is in a critical but stable condition in hospital. They don't give out any details of a suspect, but are appealing for witnesses. I don't think anybody saw us, which means I'm safe for the time being, or at least until Buddy regains consciousness, if that should ever happen.

The landlord tuts in my direction. 'Quite near here, that,' he says. 'Never used to be like this. Now you never know what's going to happen. Could be murdered in your bed tomorrow. Christ, mate, do you want a plaster or something?' he says.

'What do you mean?'

'You've cut yourself, look.'

He points to my hand and I see that my knuckle is bleeding. 'How'd you do that?' he asks.

'Not sure.'

'You've been in the wars a bit haven't you?' he says, pointing to my bandaged forehead.

'Yeah, I guess I have,' I say. I down my pint in one and leave.

I decide that I'm risking too much, staying so near the scene of the crime. I should go home, I think, and I make my way to the bus station. All of a sudden I just want to go to bed. I almost nod off waiting for the bus, but I come to my senses when I see that blood has begun to ooze from my knuckle. It just keeps on bleeding, so I stick it in the pocket of my elasticated trousers. I feel faint as a dark red circle begins to spread across them. As the evening turns to night and the bus rolls down the country roads, I have the sensation that I might be about to die. I sense when it's my stop, although I can't see it, as everything's disintegrating into geometric patterns in front of my eyes. Yet I manage I step off the bus somehow, and start to walk. Somewhere along that country lane, I fall. I must have landed in a hedgerow or something, but in my head I just keep on falling, for hours upon hours, like I'm heading for the centre of the Earth. I pass Eddie and Bridget on the way down, of course, but neither of them has a chance to get hold of me, because I'm falling much too fast.

I don't come round until dawn, when I'm woken by the sound of my mobile phone ringing.

CHAPTER 17

I don't recognise the number, but I answer it anyway.

'Elvis,' the voice says, 'it's Em.'

'Oh, hi,' I say, my throat full of sleep.

'Elvis, something terrible's happened. Buddy's been attacked. He's in a coma.' She starts to sob.

'God, that's terrible. I'm really sorry.'

She's trying to tell me something but it's a while before she stops crying enough for me to be able to understand it. 'Elvis,' she says when she's finally coherent, 'the police want to speak to you. They're trying to trace Buddy's movements from when he finished work. He was found on a riverbank and no one knows what he was doing there. Did you see him at all yesterday? He must have gone back to the flat because he wasn't in uniform.'

'No, I'm afraid I'd skipped out of your flat by late morning.'

'You silly billy! I bet you haven't been to casualty yet, have you?'

'No, Mum, I haven't.'

'Anyway, I couldn't tell the police how to get hold of you because I didn't have any contact details, and I don't actually know what your name is! All I could tell them was that we always called you Elvis, and that wasn't much help to them. I found this number written down in Buddy's Buddy room just now, and thought I should give you a call.'

'Sure, sure.'

'Now shall I pass this on to the police or—'

'No! No, what I'll do is . . . I'll go to the station myself and make a statement. So tell them I'm coming to see them, there's no need to give them this number.'

'Why not?'

'If you must know, Em, it's a stolen phone.'

'Oh, Elvis.'

'Look, you take care of yourself, OK? I'm sure Buddy will be fine. I'll go and make my statement, then I'll come and see you both in the hospital, how does that sound?'

'OK,' she says weakly.

'Now Buddy's going to be fine. He'll be right as rain in no time. But you've got to be strong for him, OK? Chin up, there's a good girl.'

'Yes, Elvis.'

'So I'll go and make my statement now and I'll see you later, OK?'

'OK.'

'You take care now, bye.'

'Bye-bye.'

Oh my god, how stupid is this woman? It's obviously me who did it! Why can she not see that? Why does she harbour this insane belief that I am in any way a decent person, when all the evidence suggests I'm a drug-crazed loony with no self-control who clearly wants to fuck her senseless. The police know I did it of course, it's just finding me that is proving difficult for them. Just goes to show how being known only by the name of a dead celebrity can work in your favour. Even so, the situation is not good. The pigs will be talking to the bar staff at the pub by the river soon if they haven't done so already, and that will fix me as being with Buddy yesterday afternoon. Also, the description they will give, of a man wearing a pink woman's smock with a bandaged head, will potentially lead to them tracking my movements for the rest of the evening, from the Chinese to the pub, and most importantly, the bus home. I'm beginning to think that maybe I should have thought this all out a bit better, but I guess my rage and desire for Em's wobbly bits got the better of me. Ah, Em, I doubt I will ever gaze on your lovely face again, unless it's in court, or see you naked. Fate has dealt us both a crushing blow, but I fear mine is the more severe. In fact, it's dawning on me that I am in some serious shit. So serious, in fact, that I call Eddie.

There's the usual rigmarole of the male secretary and ten minutes of 'MacArthur Park' on the pan pipes before I finally hear his squeaky, slightly sinister voice. 'Well hello, my boy,' he says, 'how are you on this lovely morning? Not like you to be up before eleven.'

'Eddie, I've got to go away for a while.'

'Do you really? Now what do you mean by that?'

'Eddie, I've done something, which I can't talk about on the phone, which means I'll have to go away. Would you be able to help me?'

'I think so, my boy, I think so. Yeeesss . . . when do you need to go?'

'Right now, Eddie. There are certain people trying to get hold of me, and I don't want them to.'

'Well, listen carefully. I'm going to give you an address. Go there for nine o'clock this evening. Can you keep yourself occupied until then?'

'Sure, Eddie.'

Eddie puts me on hold and 'MacArthur Park' keeps me company while he finds the address, or has it found for him. When he finally gives it, it turns out to be a pub in King's Hedges, one of the less appealing parts of Cambridge. 'Now, don't you worry about a thing,' says Eddie, 'we're going to look after you. We'll keep you snug as a bug in a rug. How do you like the sound of that, my boy?'

'Um, it sounds great, Eddie.'

'Yes, it does, doesn't it? Bon voyage.'

The line goes dead. Now where to? I want to get away from any place I'm likely to be found, but I could also still do with a good lie-down. I'm still not feeling at all well. But I also don't want to go to prison. Thinking about the nick makes me remember my house is full of weed. My mind races forward, exploring all the possible future scenarios, none of them pleasant, that are opening up for me. If the police get a warrant to search the house, there'll be a nice surprise of a whole drawer packed with skunk waiting for them. So if they catch me, even if I somehow get away with GBH, they'll get me on possession with intent to supply for sure. I don't have a huge amount there, but more than enough to make it apparent to any jury it's not just for personal use. So what am I going to do with it? I can't take the stuff with me, and I don't want just to dump it somewhere. Maybe my priorities are a bit skewed, but I spent good money on that skunk, and I'll be damned if I'm not going to get something in return for my investment. Then I have an idea, one that may happily solve another of my problems along the way.

I walk down the country lane into my village. Being in the fresh morning air seems to do me the world of good, and I'm feeling excited about the task I'm setting myself, along with the rewards I might potentially reap from it. I keep my eyes peeled for any of the teenage scum I usually sell to. Being first thing in the morning, they're pretty thin on the ground, but I find one acne-scarred simpleton doing wheelies on his bike up a cul-de-sac. He eyes me with suspicion, contempt and pretty much every other negative emotion going as I walk towards him. 'Hi, Steve,' I say, as I get closer. 'How's things?'

'What's your fucking problem?' he snorts.

'Well,' I say, 'I'm going on a business trip for a while. I'll be gone for some time, and the thing is, I've got to get rid of all my gear before I go. So I was wondering . . . would you be at all interested in . . . Look, Steve, I'll give you a bag of skunk if you can get your girlfriend to suck my cock.'

'You what?' he replies. 'Fuck off, you twat, or I'll fucking batter you.' He rams his front tyre into my leg. It actually hurts a bit.

'OK, just tell your friends, an ounce of skunk for a blow job. From a girl, obviously.'

'You're a fucking nonce. You should be locked up.' He spits on the ground in front of me, then cycles off. 'You're a fucking tranny and all,' he shouts over his shoulder. I don't know what he means at first, and then I remember that I'm still wearing Em's pink top and elasticated trousers, as well as my white Elvisboots. But I don't care, because if I know the moral standards of my clientele, I'm about to have my dick sucked dry. I get stiff just at the thought, and can hardly wait to get back. I expect they'll be queuing round the block for it.

I finally make it back home. I don't have my keys, as they're back in the social club in Elk along with my wallet, so I smash a back window and let myself in. I know I should get some things together, or at least change my clothes, but suddenly I feel very tired again and not that well. I collapse on the sofa, and fight off the urge to black out. Dots are already skimming in front of my eyes and I feel like I'm falling again. I'm not sat down five minutes, though, before the doorbell rings. I feel like ignoring it. It's either the police or a teenage girl wanting to suck my dick, and I find to my surprise I'm not that interested in either. But then, I ask myself, if it's the latter, when will I get an opportunity like that again? Probably never. So, inevitably, my desire for young flesh forces me upwards, and I stagger across the floor of the living room to look out the window. It's Steve's girlfriend, Caroline, along with the bird of one of his friends and another girl I don't recognise. They're wearing the usual alluring combination of tracksuits and gold jewellery. I close the curtains and let them in.

'Hello girls, come in.'

'If we all do it, right, do we get a bag of skunk each?' says Caroline.

'Yes, yes. I can probably spare two each. Gotta shift it.'

'Yeah, well, we better do, or you'll be fucking sorry.'

'You look fucking awful,' says her friend.

'And you smell fucking rank,' says Caroline.

'Look, do you want your skunk or not?'

'Yeah, just saying.'

I take them into the sitting room. 'All right girls, take off your tops.'

'You what?'

'Take your tops off. I want to see your tits.'

'Do we have to?' whinges the one I don't recognise, a podgy girl with bad skin and a stomach hanging out over her belt.

'Just do it, Rach,' says Caroline, a vicious-looking piece of work with a face like broken glass. 'You're about to suck his dick so it doesn't fucking matter does it?'

The other girl is quite pretty, I suppose, although she's stick-thin with a waist so tiny it looks like she'd snap in a high wind. They are all about eighteen, which round here means they look about thirty-five.

It's just my luck, I finally get the opportunity to get sucked off by not one but three teenage girls, and for the first time in forty years, I'm not in the mood. I'm feeling really fucking ill now, and I just want to go to bed for a very long time. I keep on having to fight the urge just to send the girls home and curl up in a ball on the sofa. Still, me being me, by the time they've got their tits out, I've at least managed a semi. Sitting on the sofa, I pull down the elasticated trousers and let it sway in my lap.

'That had better be fucking clean,' says Caroline as it works its way to a full erection.

'OK, you first,' I point to the fat girl.

'I don't want to go first,' she says.

'For fuck's sake, Rach, just fucking do it!' screeches Caroline.

The fat girl steps up nervously and kneels down, touching it, then letting it go, before closing her eyes tight before grabbing it and shoving it in her mouth like she's eating spinach. Her friends stand around with their arms folded, looking round the room and tapping their feet. I have a feeling this may take some time. I'm not feeling it much. In fact it's a struggle to keep it standing. After a few minutes, I push her off and point to the pretty stick girl. 'All right, you take over.' She slouches her way over, before kneeling down and matter-of-factly getting on with it. It's not helping. I don't feel like I'm going to come. Worse, it's going soft.

'Fucking hell, mate, are we ever going to get out of here?' snaps Caroline.

'You,' I point to the fat girl. 'Show me your arse.'

'No, I don't want to.' she murmurs.

'Show me your arse, now!'

'Do as he says, show him your fucking arse, Rach!' screams Caroline. The girl looks like she's holding back tears as she pulls down her tracksuit bottoms and shows me her fat arse.

'OK, you off, you on.' I beckon for Caroline to take over. It slowly gets hard again, and after a few minutes I feel I'm finally going to come. I shoot into her mouth and she chokes, coughing it back up and spitting it on the carpet.

'Fucking hell,' she says between coughs, 'you could have fucking said.'

'My jaw really hurts,' says the thin girl, to no one in particular.

'OK, you lot, you've earned yourself two ounces of skunk each. Now scarper.' I measure the gear out for them and open the door. Waiting for them outside are Steve and his mate. God knows who the fat bird was getting it for. The girls walk out without saying anything. The two boys grunt at them to make sure they got what they came for, and then they are silent.

Stepping back in the house, I notice that there are messages on the answering machine. I don't want to listen to them, but I do. Just various future bookings mysteriously cancelling without explanation. I decide I have to get out of here. I'm just about to get some stuff together when the doorbell goes again. There are four more girls standing there, their boyfriends doing figures of eight in the road behind them. Worse, one of them's brought their mum with them.

'You giving skunk for blow jobs?' she asks. 'I'm not as young as I used to be, but I've got experience.' She lifts up her Bon Jovi T-shirt, flashes her tits at me, and laughs.

Not a fucking chance. I just want to run. 'Just a minute,' I say. I disappear inside, coming back out a minute later with my stash drawer. 'Take it, it's yours,' I tell them as I fling its contents on the forest of nettles that is my front garden. The boys drop their bikes in the road and dive onto it, pushing their girlfriends out of the way and down onto the ground. I edge round them and make my way down the road, not caring that I'm not taking a single thing with me, or that I'm still wearing the fucking pink smock. I just want to get away to somewhere safe, where I can rest my head, and fall into a deep, deep sleep.

CHAPTER 18

'**Oh god, it's you,**' she says. 'What do you want?'

'Jen, please can I come over?'

'Why? Have you run out of paying customers to wave your dick in front of?'

'Ah, so you heard about that.'

'Yeah, I heard. OK, I've got the house to myself for a bit. You can get your arse over here now, but don't outstay your welcome.'

'Thanks Jen, I really appreciate this.'

'Yeah whatever, bye.'

I'm staggering down that country lane again, trying to make it to the bus stop. I can't believe I'm travelling on the bus everywhere again. I only had the new Elvismobile for one day, and now it's abandoned in the car park of that fucking social club in Elk, most likely smashed to bits, or nicked. But like the cancelled bookings, right now I don't care. All I want to do is get my head resting in Jen's furry red bush and fall asleep.

The bus driver nearly doesn't let me on because I look so rough, what with my swollen face, the bloody bandage round my head and the way my eyes keep on rolling upwards. But I tell him I'm going to the doctor's, and he says he's not bloody surprised and sells me a ticket. I can feel myself blacking out on the way over, and falling down that bottomless chasm, but the forward motion of the bus reminds me of the existence of the real world and helps me come to in time for my stop. It's a sunny summer day, and on top of everything I'm struggling with the heat and sweating like a porker. I normally pay less attention to this sort of thing than I probably should, but even I can tell I may be something less than an attractive proposition right now. My wounds are beginning to fester and smell. But nevertheless I stumble on over to Jen's, knowing that until Eddie's people pick me up, rest lies only in her pubic hair. By the time I've reached her neighbourhood, I'm barely standing upright, and nearly crawling on the pavement towards her house. When she opens the door, I fall head first onto her welcome mat.

I must have blacked out, because next thing I know, I'm in the kitchen and Jen is pouring a jug of iced water onto my face.

'What the fuck do you think you're playing at, coming round here in this state?' she says. 'You stink. And what are you dressed like that for? Actually don't tell me, I'm not remotely interested.'

'Jen, I just needed to see you. I'm in a bit of a mess right now.'

'That's the fucking understatement of the year. Well, you're no good to me like this. I mean, you're obviously in no state for fucking, so you may as well just piss off.'

'Jen, I'll screw you later, I promise, I'll screw you silly, just let me lie down with you and get some rest first. Then I'll fuck you, scout's honour.'

Jen considers it, and says: 'OK, this is how we're going to do this. First I'm going to put you in the bath to get rid of that disgusting smell. Then I'm going to do something about your injuries, so I don't throw up at the sight of you. You can sleep for a while when the kids come home from school, but then they'll be going out to scouts. Derek's going round the Fatman's after work to watch more bloody Elvis, so we don't have to worry about him. Once the kids have gone you can fuck me, and you'd better make it decent because you're making me go to a hell of a lot of effort just for one screw.'

'Oh, Jen, you know it'll be great. After all, I do have a very large dick.'

'I wouldn't say that,' she smirks, 'but I'll admit you at least hit my G-spot, which is more than Derek does. Size definitely matters when it's that small. Now fucking get up those stairs before I hose you down.'

Jen runs a bath for me while I get undressed. I'm hoping she'll soap me all over, but once the tub's full, she leaves me to get on with it and goes to do the hoovering. Normally being even in the proximity of Jen would give me the raging horn, but lying in the bath I look down at it and see that it's just a sad, shrivelled stump, like an acorn. It's funny, not only am I not horny, but I don't feel like I want any charlie. I realise I haven't had any for two days, not since I left my packet in the dressing room of Elk social club, along with nearly everything else of importance. Oh well, ain't going to be seeing that again. I expect those trolls are doing lines of it on top of the bar after hours, imagining they're in Asgard, or else they've put it in lost property.

After I've soaked for what must have been an hour, and my fingers and toes have wrinkled in the lukewarm water, Jen comes in with some fresh bandages. 'Haven't you heard of soap?' she moans. 'Oh well, if you get your wounds infected, that's your affair.' She sits me in a wicker chair, where she cleans up my head and my knuckle, and applies fresh bandages. I imagine Jen is a good mother, if a little stern. Or then again, for all I know she might be the worst mother on Earth, with all her kids doomed to end up going on a rampage with a shotgun in Debenhams when they grow up. Seeing as I've never supported any of my children, I'm not sure what good parenting involves. I'm pretty sure not molesting them is a part of it, but other than that, I'm at a loss.

She sends me to the bedroom and tells me not to come out or make a sound, or she'll personally castrate me right then and there. I get between the sheets and immediately find myself drifting into sleep. OK, I'm not using her furry red bush as a pillow, but her normal pillows are pretty fucking all right. The fact that it's Gaylord's hard-earned pay that's allowing me this moment of rare luxury gives me cause for a little chuckle to myself as I go under. Then I sleep so soundly I'm not even bothered by the usual stupid dreams, instead I just sink into a big expanse of gorgeous, velvety black nothingness. It is truly blissful. I'm dimly aware of the sound of children in the house for a bit, then the closing of the front door, followed by quiet. This must mean that it's some hours later already, and that Jen will be coming to fuck me in a minute, but I hope she can spare me a few more minutes' rest. Alas, she doesn't, not even a second, as she immediately storms in naked. 'All right, it's time for you to fuck me now, and do a decent job of it. Don't come before I do, or I'm kicking you out of the house without your clothes. And lick me, before you do anything else.'

She rips the duvet off the bed and lies down on it with her legs open. Groggily I crawl into position as ordered, where she holds my head down as if she's trying to drown me. There, after what seems like days of trying to get to it, I have reached sanctuary. Peace at last in the furry red bush of my dreams. At least that was the plan. But it's more like a medieval torture device, spiky long hairs stabbing into my face. I lick as if my life depends on it, and knowing Jen, it might well do. She feels her breasts as I do it, and I reach up to touch them myself, but she slaps my hand down, snapping, 'I didn't ask you to do that.'

There is only one problem. I'm still not feeling very turned on. Jen lifts my head up by the hair. 'OK, get in,' she says. Then she sees that my cock is only semi-erect. 'What the fuck is this?' she says. 'What fucking good is that to me? Christ, the shit you put me through . . .' She rolls me on my back and sighs as she prepares to suck me. 'I hate doing this,' she mutters.

After a minute or so, she's got me fully erect. She climbs on top and slides it in. Unthinkingly, I touch her breasts again, only for her to slap my face. 'I said I don't want you to do that!' she screams.

Things go OK for a couple of minutes, but it's not long before I feel all the energy drain out of me in a flash. As it goes, I feel my erection slip away with it. Inevitably, it falls out. 'Fuck!' she shouts in my face. 'Oh just forget it. Get out.'

'No, it'll be OK, it'll come back in a minute . . .'

'Yeah, well I can't be bothered waiting. Go on, fuck off.'

'Jen, you can't be serious. I'm sorry the sex didn't work out but . . .'

'Look, the only use I have for you is fucking. If you can't get that right then there's no point you being here.'

'OK, I'm going, I'm going.' I locate my clothes, which Jen had washed and dried in the hours I must have been asleep. This wouldn't have been for my benefit, she just wouldn't have wanted to smell them. These clothes are still humiliating, but at least they're clean, I think to myself as I slip the pink smock over my head. I tie up my white Elvisboots and make my way to the door. It's time to go anyway. 'Right, I'm off now, Jen,' I shout up the stairs to her.

She appears on the landing. 'Elvis,' she says, 'you do know that Derek and the Fatty have been poaching all your bookings by phoning them up and telling them about how you got your cock out on stage the other night, don't you?'

The treacherous little bastards. Of course, they have all the details of any future gigs. That explains the messages on my answering machine. Any other day I'd want to smash their heads into brick walls until their brains formed a pool on the floor, but right now I'm on the run from the police, I feel ill and I really can't bring myself to care. 'I didn't know that, Jen. Thanks for telling me.'

'That's OK. Now for Christ's sake, fuck off.'

That's what I do. It's quite a walk to the pub, especially in my condition, and I don't get far before I pass a newsagent's selling that evening's local paper. 'POLICE SEARCH FOR "ELVIS" ATTACKER' read the boards outside. I pop into the shop and scan the front-page story. They've got hold of some publicity shot of me as Elvis, as well as an identikit photo, complete with bandage and a description of me wearing a pink top, elasticated trousers and white boots. Who put that together for them, I wonder? Presuming that Buddy's still in a coma, it must have been the bartender from the pub, I guess. Or Em. I suppose I'll definitely never get to fuck her now and slap her big arse with my groin, now that they've convinced her I put her husband in a coma. Oh well, you win some, you lose some, and I did get my cock sucked by three different teenagers this morning.

It's a good job the newsagent doesn't read what he sells, or I'd be done for. Instead he's just sitting there behind the counter, flicking through one of his top-shelf magazines. Still, it was pretty stupid of me to go into the shop at all, so I scarper. At least I've found out how much the police know, which is pretty much everything. I ditch the bandage, despite the fact the wound has yet to scab over. If I'd kept it on, though, I'd have been a walking wanted poster. I also take off the pink smock, and walk topless in the warm summer evening. For the first time in many years, my white, flabby belly is exposed to the open air. After a while my man-breast nipples point up as the temperature drops, but I daren't put the smock back on, not now everybody knows I'm wearing it.

I finally get to the pub about half-eight. I take a risk and put on the smock, then I go in and order a pint. I sit in the darkest corner I can find. It's a scummy pub for scummy people, and I feel quite at home here. Even if the barman had been curious about the open wound on my forehead, I don't think he would have cared. He probably knew who I was anyway. I wait there for a while, and drink several pints, before finally, some time after ten, a man with short, shaved hair, obvious muscle under his leather jacket and very good skin comes in and orders a half pint of Coke. I'm certain I've seen him before. He sits at the bar and scans the room until he spots me. He walks over.

'Hi Elvis,' he says, with a cheery grin.

'Don't know what you mean.'

'Eddie says hello. Won't you come with me?'

And of course I follow him out into the street where a stretch limo awaits us, illegally parked outside the doors of about three terraced houses. It's not exactly subtle, and probably not the best vehicle to make a quiet getaway in, but that's Eddie's sense of humour. Elvis has left the building and is being driven away in a big stretch limo. Ha ha fucking ha. I have a feeling Eddie's got more where that one came from.

CHAPTER 19

The limo is ridiculous, a big long white thing with a bar, a television and a mirrored ceiling. I've got enough legroom to breakdance in, and the seat is comfier than any sofa I've ever owned. The bloke from the pub is in the driver's seat. He won't tell me where we're going, saying that Eddie wants it to be a surprise. He will tell me that his name is Dave, and that he's got something I might like.

'What's that, then?' I ask.

'A CD I bought a while back that I've been really enjoying,' he says 'Listen.'

He presses play, and I hear that old familiar voice, singing to me from Heartbreak Hotel.

'I didn't really know much Elvis until that "Little Less

Conversation" song came out,' Dave tells me. 'I mean I only usually listen to dance music and the stuff that's in the charts, but I really liked that song, so when this CD came out with all his number-one records on, I thought I'd try it out. Bought it in Asda actually, only eight quid. Bargain.'

'So you like it then?'

'Yeah, love it, mate. Never heard anything like it. That's why I got to pick you up. Somebody else was going to do it, but I asked Eddie if I could instead.'

'Really?'

'Yeah, well I hope you don't mind, but I just had a few questions about Elvis I thought you might be able to answer for me.'

Christ, this is Fatty and Gayboy's territory, not mine. 'Do my best,' I say.

'Like, you know that Pet Shop Boys song, "Always On My Mind", is it true Elvis did that originally, 'cos someone told me he did, but I thought, that can't be true, it doesn't sound anything like him.'

'Well, umm . . . the very first version was by, I think, Brenda Lee, but it was Elvis who had the hit with it. In 1972, I think.' Sometimes I surprise even myself. Where did I learn that?

'Really? Can't imagine how that would sound.'

'You don't want to, believe me.' That's better. Wouldn't actually want to encourage anyone to listen to the fat buffoon or anything.

'And another thing,' says Dave, 'is it true he died on the toilet? Someone else told me that, and I thought, no way is that right. He died in a car crash, didn't he?'

'No, you're probably thinking of Eddie Cochran, or Princess Diana. Yes, Elvis did die on the bog, from a heart attack, in fact, caused by the strain of doing an enormous dump.'

'That can't be true, can it?'

'That's what his obituary said in the *New York Times*, that he died "straining at stool".' Christ, I shouldn't know this stuff. It's not healthy.

'Wow,' says Dave. 'That must have been a big shit.'

'By the end of his life, Elvis's shits were roughly the size of an elephant's. He would actually break the toilet bowl into pieces with the sheer weight of them. Eventually, he did most of his crapping in a field outside Graceland. It would then be collected and used as fertiliser by local farmers.' OK, I'm taking the piss now, that's more like it. Leave the facts to Fatman and Gayboy.

'You're kidding me.'

'I only wish I were.' Now I'm enjoying this. Maybe it's the relief of finally getting out of Cambridge, or maybe it's because it's the first time in days I'm talking to someone who's glad to see me, but chatting to Dave is getting quite fun. OK, I'm taking the piss with him, but I think I'd enjoy it even if I weren't. Sometimes it's good to be the centre of attention.

'Dave,' I say, 'did you know that at the time of Elvis's death, there were 170 known Elvis impersonators in the world? There are now 85,000. If that rate of growth is sustained, then by 2019, one-third of the population of the planet will be an Elvis impersonator.'

'Is that right?' he says. 'Oh, hang on, I love this song.' He turns up the volume. It would just have to be, wouldn't it, it's fucking 'Hound Dog'. Dave sings along, even though he obviously doesn't know or understand half the words.

'Dave, word of advice. I wouldn't let Eddie catch you singing that.'

'Why not? Eddie loves Elvis.'

'Mmmm. That's just the problem.'

After a while, the conversation peters out and Dave concentrates on his driving. By the time Elvis has entered his movie period on the chronologically ordered CD, we're on the motorway. I try to work out what direction we're going in, but I'm feeling weak again, my eyes hurt, and I have difficulty concentrating on the signs and soon give up. Instead, I find myself thinking about my third marriage, which is strange as that's something I don't usually dwell on, even though technically it lasted the longest. It began when I was in the dumps after Nanette fleeced me for everything I had, doing bits of work here and there and a bit of Elvis through an agency. I'd moved away from London, away from a scene where everybody knew me as a yesterday's man, a right charlie who'd had his wife poked by a top gangster and was too sissy to do anything about it. I don't know why I chose Cambridge. I vaguely knew it from my childhood, I guess, as my mum's parents used to live there and every so often I'd go to stay. I used to like to watch the people punting on the river. But mainly I just needed to go somewhere that wasn't London. I needed a change, make a new start in a place where I had no history, where no illegitimate children would spring out of the woodwork, and where no one would laugh in my face and ask me how the wife was. I was a wounded man. All my pride had gone. I'd been fucked in the arse, first by Eddie for real, then figuratively by Johnny and Nanette. I was practically dead. I realised the only way I could save myself was by doing it to someone else. And that's where Chrissie came in.

I saw her in my local. She was shy but pretty, with glasses, hair that fell in front of her face when she looked down, which was always, and dowdy clothes. She was sexy in the way librarians are sexy. They're all sensible and demure, but you wonder what they'd be like if you turned them on. She must have been in her early twenties then, and I wasn't even thirty. Chatting her up was hard because she was so shy, and even once I'd persuaded her to sit with me for a bit away from her boring friends, it was

like talking to a frightened bunny rabbit, always desperate to get
back to its hutch. But she liked me, or at least she secretly liked
the attention, and I talked her into coming back the next night.
Again, the conversation was a little one-sided, but she opened
up a bit and told me a little about herself, how she lived with
her mum, that her dad had run off, and that she worked in a
film developer's. At the end of the evening, I walked her home,
and kissed her on the lips. She ran to her door, but I asked if I
would see her again down the local the next night, and she
nodded, before disappearing inside without saying goodnight.

I saw Chrissie the next night, and the next, and most nights
after. I took her to the pictures, fancy wine bars, even to a play
she wanted to see. Each night I'd walk her home and snog her
on the way, for longer each time. Of course, I wanted more than
that, and she freaked out when I groped her little tits in an
alleyway, but she let me do it. Finally, I persuaded her to come
round my place. I bought a takeaway and had candles and wine
and everything. Even had a nice dessert. We were snogging on
the sofa and I was feeling her tits, then I took her hand and put
it down my trousers. She backed away and started crying. I
explained that it was something that we'd have to do sometime,
and she finally told me that she'd never done it before, that she
was really scared about it and didn't think she'd be any good. I
told her not to worry, and took her upstairs.

From that point on, it was serious. We were a couple, I was
fucking her regularly, and she was even enjoying it. Her mum
wasn't happy though. She didn't want her daughter living with
her if she was going with older men, or indeed any man, and
pretty much chucked her out. She moved in with me, and it
seemed to make sense for us to get married. And so we did, in
a registry office with just her mum, her three friends and family,
and some bloke I knew from Luton in attendance. I suppose the

marriage was doomed from the start. We went to Brighton on our honeymoon, and I was so fucking bored I ended up shagging some bird staying up the corridor in the same hotel while Chrissie was having a nap. When we got back, I realised the idea of having to screw the same boring bird over and over again for the rest of my life made me sick. I mean, Chrissie was all right for keeping things tidy in the house and that, but in the sack she was, quite frankly, rubbish. So I started going out to the pub without her, and often I'd pick up some bit of stuff and I'd either go back to theirs or just do it down the allotments or something. Chrissie was too timid to make a big deal if I came back late, but if she even mentioned it I'd tell her I could come home any damn time I wanted, and it was none of her fucking business anyway. It went on like that for a bit, until one day Chrissie broke down in tears and told me that her friends were telling her I was going with other women. She wanted to know if it was true. It occurred to me that keeping it a secret was doing me less good than just telling her, so I explained that I had a very high sex drive, and I needed to go with other women so as not to burden her with the responsibility of meeting my needs. I got her to agree that this was reasonable, and with her permission went on shagging my merry way around Cambridge.

But after a while, I got tired of having to trek out to the bird's place if she lived some way off, and I was definitely sick of doing it in the open air up against some shed, so I thought to myself, seeing as I've got Chrissie's permission anyway, I may as well bring them back home. So I walk in one night with some bird, and Chrissie's sitting on the sofa watching telly. I just nod at her and take the bird with me into the bedroom and shag her. Chrissie doesn't say anything to me when the bird leaves a bit later. Soon I'm doing this pretty regular, and Chrissie never says anything. Now round about this time I'd taken to telling Chrissie every day that she's not much to look at, boring in bed and a general fucking pain in the arse who should be grateful for what she gets. Just wearing her down, you know, so it's easier for me to do stuff without any hassle. Anyway, I'm picking up all these birds and taking them back to my place and shagging them, in the bedroom if Chrissie's still up, or on the sofa if she's gone to bed. Then one night, I take a bird home and Chrissie's up watching some programme. Now the bird sees she's watching it, and she wants to see the programme too, so she kicks up a fuss and it ends up that me and her have to sit down on the sofa and watch it with Chrissie. Of course, I've seriously got the horn, and it's a fucking long programme. It goes on and on, and I'm just fed up with waiting, so I start touching the bird up right there, and before you know it, me and the bird are shagging on the sofa, with Chrissie sitting next to us watching the fucking telly!

Pretty soon after that, I'm banged up again, and Chrissie's sodding friends talk her into divorcing me while I'm in the nick. Nice, eh? Kick a man when he's down, why don't you? So there you have it. That's the story of my third marriage. And I suppose after all that you think I'm a cunt of the highest order. Well, maybe you're right, maybe I am. But you know I don't see it like that. I'm certain that I am a psychopath, whatever that test did or didn't prove. I don't believe I have a conscience, and it's like I said before, if I don't have one of those, then there's no way you can really hold me responsible for what I did, is there? It's not like I'm making an informed moral choice. What it comes down to is, you can't tell a snake why it shouldn't bite you, and it's the same with me. I'm an animal acting on instinct, and my instincts tell me to fuck people over, to hurt or destroy them if I gain something from it, or even if I just feel like it and want to get something out of my system, work off a bit of steam. Not that it ever really does the job, because I'll just end up having to do someone else over soon enough. So, no, I don't believe I am a bad man. I see myself more as a prisoner of fate. Come to think of it, I've lived a pretty wretched life.

Christ, I'm feeling ill here in the back of this limo, and it's not just because the CD's up to 'Wooden Heart'. I can feel the ground dissolving and the chasm beneath me beckoning again, and all I can see is a swarm of bees. This isn't right, I think. In fact this is very, very bad. I try to call out to Dave, but he's too far away now, and it's too late, I'm already falling. There's nothing to grab onto, nothing at all. I'm plummeting at what seems like a thousand miles a second. And I fall and fall, further than I've ever gone before. Then, after many millions of miles, and what seems like years, for the first time, I hit the bottom.

CHAPTER 20

It's a funny place, Hell. It's just like you've heard, very dark, fucking hot and everybody's in chains. What they don't tell you about, though, is that you're being incessantly fucked up the arse with something that feels like a road drill. I've been down here so long I've lost all sense of time, and I'm having trouble remembering a moment when I wasn't down here in the dark, being rogered. I know there are people all around me, but there's barely any light, and all I can see are dark shapes. But I can hear them, all of them. It's an incredible sound, almost like a wave, starting out like the moan of someone coming, before slowly building into an awful pained scream, and then starting all over again as a whimper.

There's a smell too, of sex and gore. It's the strangest smell you'll most likely ever come across. Anywhere else it would be abominable, but down here it seems to make perfect sense. All the time I've been here I've wanted to be sick and have sex simultaneously, which is a new one on me. Meanwhile, I'm feeling jism being shot into my arse like bullets every twenty seconds or so, and I'm sure that there's nothing left there but a crater, a gaping wound at the bottom of my spine. I even wonder why it hasn't reached the other side, leaving a hole right through my groin you can see through. I can hardly bear to look, but I've been here for an eternity already, so I suppose it's time for me to investigate. So I turn my head round, and unusually, it travels a full one hundred and eighty degrees. I look down, and my worst suspicions are confirmed. My arse-hole is a bloody pulp, and there is a strange dick-drill thing pounding into it. Then I look up to see who it belongs to. Of course, it's Eddie.

'Well, hello my boy,' he says. 'How absolutely lovely to see you again.'

'Eddie, what are you doing here? You're not dead.'

'Neither are you, old chap. A lot of people down here aren't.'

'Funny, I'd have thought that would be a prerequisite.'

'Oh, a lot of people you know are down here, look.'

Suddenly, faces in the darkness are visible, and I see a whole load of the old gang from London, as well as familiar faces from the nick and a few other places. Somewhere in a flash of light I see Nanette taking it up the arse from Johnny, while she too seems to be pounding away at somebody's gaping wound with her own appendage. I even think I see Jen in the distance, fucking someone over.

'So Eddie,' I say, 'if Hell's not where you go when you die, what is it? And what are we all doing here?'

'Hell, dear boy, is where you and I have been all our lives.

Hell is one great big anal rape, where someone shoots their load into you, and then you do it to someone else.'

'Oh right. So when do I get to stop getting fucked, and get to do the fucking?'

'Can't you see, my dear boy, it's happening right now, look.'

I turn my head round again, and for the first time I see that I have my own drill, and there is a bloody, bleeding arse in front of me, being pounded and mutilated by my own weapon. I come and shoot another bullet of jism into it, and as I do so Eddie does the same into me, and I realise my own voice is part of the mass wave of moans and screaming. Then I see, I am part of one long chain of anal violation that goes on for as far as the eye can see in all directions, and certainly beyond. This is my fate, where I shall always be, and where I have always been. It is where I belong.

And then everything changes.

I hear the beating of giant wings above me. Angels – I shit ye not, a pair of angels swoop down from the sky. They grab me by the shoulders with feet like talons, and pluck me out from the chain. My shackles fall away as we rise. Below me, I see Eddie look up at me forlornly, then move up a place and begin pounding away at the wretched arse that was just in front of me. We climb higher, and the darkness of Hell lifts. Then, in the far distance, I see a brilliant light. It's like the sun, but even though it's the brightest light I've ever seen, it doesn't blind me, even when I look straight at it. The sky around it is yellow, like a sunset. It's beautiful. The angels, meanwhile, are pretty much as you imagine them, only more manly than you'd expect, less gay. More like superheroes than the usual weedy blokes with perms and haloes playing trumpets and harps They even have chest hair. And bird's feet, of course.

We fly closer and closer to the light, and suddenly I see that there is land below us, all green and summery. The angels fly low, and we descend faster than any aeroplane. In an instant, they've set me down on my own, and are already flying away towards the light. I look around, and see that I'm on some sort of riverbank. It's like something from *Swallows and Amazons* or something, a bloody English riverbank. Then I know what riverbank it is. Buddy appears in the distance, looking fit and healthy and all dressed up in his gear, swinging his arms as he walks. Next thing I know, he's right beside me.

'All right, Bud,' I say, 'didn't realise you were dead.'

'I'm not, I'm in a coma, but Heaven isn't about being dead, same as Hell isn't.'

'Oh, right. So this is Heaven is it? Funny they'd let me up here then. I was in Hell a minute ago. I mean, I've always figured I'd be going to Hell 'cos of all the kicking people's heads in and stuff.'

'Yeah, well,' says Buddy, 'we're just kind of letting you look around, see if you like it. Whether you move in or not really all depends on you.'

'Oh OK, I guess, still a bit in the dark though . . .'

'Anyway, I've got to go and see Em. She's over there waiting for me to come out of this coma, so I'll see you later, OK?' And with that he wanders off onto the bridge behind us, where Em waits for him. He pulls a giant bouquet of flowers out from under his Buddy Holly jacket as they run towards each other and meet in a slobbering embrace. I leave them to it and wander up the riverbank. I go up about half a mile, or five hundred, I'm not sure, and there's Bridget, dressed in her dolly-bird gear like it's still 1966, as if she's about to go and see Manfred Mann, sitting on a bench, smoking a cigarette

'Hi, Bridg,' I say, 'how's it going?'

'Not bad, shrimp. You?' She offers me a fag as I sit down next to her.

'I'm feeling pretty good, actually, which is weird.'

'Yeah, you look less like you want to smash my face in with a rock than you usually do.'

'I don't really get what's going on. You're dead, right, so you're in Heaven. But I'm not dead as far as I'm aware, but I'm here, and so are Buddy and Em. Now Buddy might be on his way out, but Em's still alive and kicking. Also, I was in Hell just a minute ago, and there were people who are definitely still alive down there. What is up with all of this?'

'Jesus, you're slow. It doesn't really matter if you're dead or alive. Heaven and Hell are just where you're at in your head. For instance, what was Hell like?'

'Well, it was like one long chain of people fucking each other up the arse, and everyone was ripping each other up in the process. It was pretty fucking grim actually.'

'Exactly. As long as that's your bag, you're in Hell.'

'So you're in Hell if you're a homo? Look, I'm not a fruit, I had my dick shoved in that guy's arse against my will down there!'

'No, silly! It's not about where you put it, but the spirit in which it's put. Hell is the place for people who inflict pain on others in order to serve their own ends. It's not a punishment, it's just inevitable you'll be there if that's your scene. Now look at this.'

She points to the sun, and I see that it's made up of billions of people, again all linked together in a sex chain, but this time it's one of oral pleasure. A bloke would be sucked off by a bird, but he'd be licking out another bird at the same time, who'd be sucking a dick, and so on.

'You see,' says Bridget, 'everyone is giving and receiving pleasure equally. No one's on a power trip, no one's trying to get anybody down, and nobody's getting hurt. It's all done in a spirit of love. And that's what Heaven is. Everything's in balance. The love you take is equal to the love you make. The blow job you send out comes back to you.'

'Well, that's pretty groovy. Hang on, there are some gaylords up there.' I point to where there is a chain of men sucking dick, and in turn, having their own cocks sucked.

'Oh, they're not necessarily gay,' says Bridget, 'just being considerate and balancing out the numbers. Anyway, it's nothing to do with sex really, you dummy, it's all just a metaphor. We figured it was the only way we could get you to understand.'

'Oh right. But listen, this is all very well, but it doesn't really apply to me, does it? I mean, I'm a psychopath. I can't really help being the way I am. I can understand you lot not wanting someone like me hanging around Heaven, but putting me in Hell when it's no fault of my own is a bit harsh.'

'Oh, stop with all this psychopathic crap. You're no more a psychopath than your Auntie Jeanie. This is the whole fucking point. This is why we're showing you all this. You have a choice. Heaven or Hell. It's all up to you. Jesus, how much more do I have to break it down for you?'

'OK, OK, I get your point. Bridget, question for you. Did you really have to top yourself all those years ago?'

'You know full well I did. Dad had been messing about with me since I was a baby and it had sent me mental. What else was I supposed to do?'

'You didn't have to it, Bridg. Didn't you understand I needed you?'

'No, you didn't need me. Nobody needed me. That's why it was OK for me to go. I—'

'I needed you Bridget!' I grab hold of her and shake her hard. 'Don't you understand you tore me apart!' I scream.

She stops protesting. 'I know,' she says softly. 'I could see you crying from up here. I could even see inside you. I guess that's when all your trouble started, when you decided to go bad. Yeah, I shouldn't have done it. But oh, you've been a silly boy, shrimp.' She offers me another cigarette.

'I'm sorry, Bridg.'

'Yeah, I'm sorry too. Now don't worry about it, although I think you've got a shitload of apologising to do to quite a few people back down there.'

'You think?'

'Uh, yeah. Now you're still alive and you're not going to die for a bit, so don't let me down, you mental case. Look, I've got to go, get back to the chain. I'm afraid I can't talk to you again, now that you've finally got the message. So take care of yourself OK? Bye-bye!'

Bridget flies up in the air like Peter Pan and disappears into the mass of fellating bodies, leaving me to make my way back down the riverbank to the bridge on my own, near to where Buddy lies battered and comatose, while Em stands on the bridge, crying and praying.

CHAPTER 21

'**Y**ou ain't nothin' but a hound dog, cryin' all the time . . .'

The words drift towards me in the blackness. I don't want to follow them, but they get their hooks in and pull me forward into a gap in the dark. Light pours in through the slits of my opening eyelids. I clamp them shut again.

'He's waking up.'

'Better go and tell him.'

'You ain't never caught a rabbit, and you ain't no friend of mine . . .'

Against my better judgement, I open my eyes again. They're pretty gunked up, and they won't focus properly, but I can make out I'm in a room somewhere, in a sizable bed, and there's a man sitting on a stool between the bed and the door. 'Hound

Dog' comes to an end, and 'Love Me Tender' begins.

'Thank Christ you're coming round. You gave me a fright when I opened the back door and I couldn't wake you up. Thought you'd died on me.'

'Huh?'

'Elvis, it's Dave. I drove you up here, remember?'

'Oh, yeah.' I can't remember who he is, or why I'd be anywhere I'd not normally be. Worse, I can't even remember where I'd normally be anyway. It hurts to speak and my mouth's very dry. I ask Dave for a glass of water.

He goes to fetch it, and I try to get my brain working as to what's going on. I pick up some fragments here and there – waking up in the country lane, sitting in the bath at Jen's, the barman pointing to my bleeding knuckle, but the loose details lack a skeleton on which to hang them. Then a memory that has the weight of something important hurtles towards me like a boulder. I see Buddy's body lying by the riverbank. It tugs a hidden string, and the sheer enormity of immediate events comes tumbling down on top of me. Fuck, I think to myself, I'm in serious shit here. I feel like being sick for a second as the events of the last week come flooding back. Finally, it comes to me that I was being taken to a place of safety by Dave in the limo, which means I must be there. I relax slightly. But where have I ended up, and what are the chances of me being able to leave?

I scoop the gunk out of my eyes as Dave brings me a glass of water. Instead of handing it to me, he lifts my head up with one hand, and pours it into my mouth with the other. It dribbles a bit down the sides of my mouth, and Dave dabs it away. Once he's finished, I try to raise my arm up to look at my watch, but it's heavy as lead. Anyway, the watch is missing. So are all my clothes. From what I can see and feel, I'm wearing some kind of hospital gown, and to my horror, what seems to be a nappy. I also seem to have something up my nose, a tube I suspect. This is getting very odd. I need information, but I don't feel capable of handling too much, just a little bit to start with. 'What time is it, please?' I ask, just about getting my brain and mouth to work together.

'Half-three,' says Dave. Sunlight is streaming through the window. I can see now that the room is pretty luxurious, like an expensive hotel room, with an elaborate dressing table and a mirror I can see myself in at the far end. As well as that, this might be the nicest and biggest bed I've ever slept in, with silk sheets and a big fat duvet. Maybe I am in a hotel.

'Um, Dave, stupid question, but what day of the week is it?'

'It's Monday, Elvis.'

'I've been asleep for four days? Fucking hell.'

'No, you've been out of it for eleven days. The doctor said you were in a vegetable state or something. He wanted you to be taken to hospital, but what with half the Cambridgeshire Police Force out looking for you, we didn't think that would have been wise. Don't worry, the doc's crooked, he'll keep his mouth shut. Anyway, we took care of you OK. We got nurses in to look after you, but we did a lot of it ourselves too.'

'Uh, who's we exactly? Where am I?'

'Yoouu ain't nothin' but a houuund doggg, cryyyin' aall the tiiime . . .' A voice drawls the song from the doorway across the room. Oh, Jesus Christ, no, it's Eddie.

'My dear boy,' he says, making a grand entrance in summer clothes and sandals, 'it's so great to have you back in the land of the living.'

'Hello, Eddie!' I make an effort to sound pleased, but I doubt I can hide my fear.

'Welcome, welcome, to my humble abode.'

'You mean, I'm at your place?'

'Yes, indeed you are. I am your host and your most humble servant.' He bows, then makes his way to the bed and clasps his hands round my cheeks. 'I was beginning to think we might lose you, and have to dump you in a river somewhere. But no! You're back with us now, and – oh, the fun we're going to have, you and I, now that we're practically cellmates again.'

'Cellmates?'

'Yes, you're going to be living with me! After all, you can't really go back home can you, now that you're a wanted man, a fugitive from the law. Oh, it's so romantic! So this is your hideout, here with me. It's your new home! Isn't that wonderful?'

'Yes, Eddie, that's great, but how long do I have to stay here?'

'Oh, it's not safe out there, my boy. No, better you stay here, where we can look after you.'

I hope to god I'm still dreaming, but I'm pretty certain I'm not. This is beyond my worst nightmare, locked up in Eddie's mansion with him and his goons. Worse, Eddie's choice of entrance music was no joke. It was a signal, telling me what to expect. I'd much rather take my chances with the police. Meanwhile, a nurse enters the room. 'Oh, hello,' she says, 'wasn't expecting you to wake up.' I'm beginning to wish I hadn't.

'Yes, he has woken up, my dear,' says Eddie. 'Now get that nappy off him, for Christ's sake. We'll give our guest some privacy, shall we, boys?' He gestures to Dave and the other goon to leave the room. He follows them as they go, but lingers in the door. 'Youu aint' nothin' but a hoouund dogg . . . cryiiing aall the tiiime . . .' he sings, poking his head round the doorframe. 'I'll speak to you later, my dear boy. Now be good and keep your hands off the nurse, or she'll charge me extra.'

He winks dirtily, and finally disappears. The nurse is a sexy blonde, young and pretty, although her boobs aren't anything to write home about. 'OK, I'm just going to clean you up a bit,' she says in a soft Scottish accent, Edinburgh I should imagine. She unwraps the nappy, and I'm worried that I'll have a boner, but fortunately I don't, it's just caked in my own shit and piss.

'It's all right, I'll clean myself up,' I say.

'Don't be silly,' she replies, 'you're far too weak to be doing stuff for yourself just now. Anyhoo, this is my job. I see lots of dirty botties in my line of work.'

She says that she'll take the tube out of my nose, though, and that I can use a bedpan instead of the nappy. I ask her what her name is. She says it's Tina. She asks me why everybody calls me Elvis. I tell her it's so people don't find out I'm really Alvin Stardust.

Once she's finished wiping my arse, Tina stays with me in the room, sitting in a chair by the bed. We tell each other a bit about ourselves, although obviously I have to skimp on certain details. Well, pretty much all of them, in fact. She tells me about her boyfriend. He's a professional bodybuilder. Eats steak for breakfast. After a while she starts flicking through magazines full of real-life tragic stories that she reads out to me, whether I want to hear them or not. They all have titles like 'Shame of My Vampire Uncle', or 'I Married My Daughter's Killer . . . And I Don't Care'. All hard-luck stories featuring the criminally stupid. Every so often she rings an electric buzzer and a goon, sometimes Dave, takes over for the few minutes it takes for her to have a piss or the little longer she needs to liquidise my food. Apparently my body's too weak to digest solids, so with a spoon she feeds me meals that have been turned into soup. I'm also asleep a lot of the time, which you'd think would be odd seeing as I was out of it for a week and a half. But apparently I've burned up a lot of energy just lying there while my body's been sorting itself out, so I need to rest.

The next day, I wake up to a different nurse. 'Hello Mister

Elvis, my name is Abia,' she says, hovering over each syllable. Abia is a black woman from Nigeria, and her English is very good. She's pretty sexy too, but I don't think she wants to be. Most of the time Abia sits reading the Bible. For some reason, I agree to let her read bits out to me so she can practise her pronunciation. Never really paid much attention to the Bible, not since Sunday school. The bit Abia is reading makes no sense to me anyway. All about the building instructions for a temple already built and knocked down thousands of years ago, and how many cubits each wall in each room had to be. To be honest she could probably skip that bit and I don't think God would mind. I decide I need my own book.

About eleven o'clock, they cart in the crooked doctor to have a look at me. He's a neat little man with hairy hands and a bald head. After giving me the once-over, the best diagnosis he can make without the proper tests and equipment is that I've been suffering from brain damage. Apparently a blow to the head, from the beating I received in the social club most likely, caused my brain to expand and press against my skull, making me shut down until it shrunk a bit and the pressure eased. I should really be having loads of treatment, but I can't get to a hospital, so tough shit.

I don't see Eddie for several days. Dave tells me that he's away in Paris doing business. Just like everything with Eddie, it sounds slightly obscene, even though it wasn't meant to be. I tell Dave I need something to read and he comes up a few minutes later with some car mags. I'm not that into cars, but it gets me out of having to listen to stories about vampire lovers and dead babies in the washing machine, or the measurements for the Israelites' temple, so I suppose I'm grateful. Sometimes Dave sends Abia or Tina away, and sits with me for an hour or so, getting me to tell him stories about Elvis or to recount some of my own experiences as an Elvis impersonator. I tell him quite a bit, but I can't share the really good bits without losing face. Dave tells me a bit about himself too. Turns out he's got a fiancée, which is a surprise, as I'd presumed all of Eddie's goons were homos.

'No, what gave you that idea?' he says when I tell him this.

'Well, just the way you're all so clean, and your skin's so good, and the fact you're all . . . shaved.'

'Just part of the job. Eddie insists we all maintain a very strict skincare regimen, and that we're always smooth. It's just the way he likes things. It doesn't really mean anything.'

'But doesn't he ever try anything? Last time I checked, he was the most predatory old queer on the planet.'

'No, he's smart enough to figure out that it's not in his interest to go in for that. We'd all just batter him if he did.'

And there was me thinking they were all his obedient sex slaves. Just goes to show not everything's as it first seems, I suppose. What I wouldn't count on is any of them stopping Eddie from taking advantage of me in my weakened state, not even Dave. In fact, I'd put money on them helping.

This all carries on for four days or so, with Tina and Abia watching, me sleeping a lot, and the occasional conversation with Dave. I tell him I enjoyed the car mags, but could really do with a good book. Later that afternoon, he comes in grinning with an antique hardback copy of *Oliver Twist*. Says he's heard it's good. On the fourth day, a wheelchair appears, and the nurses lift me into it and push me out onto a balcony outside the window. There I can see the grounds of Eddie's mansion – his landscaped garden, the trees beyond, the pool. I feel quite contented sitting there, I guess.

That night, I wake up. Abia's sitting reading by a lamplight. There's a strange animal noise, like a howling, and at first it sounds like it's outside the house, but the more I listen, the clearer it becomes that it's actually inside the house, and it's coming closer. First, it sounds like it might be in the hall. Then, as if it's coming up the stairs. And finally, it's most definitely in the corridor outside. It's a horrible sound, unearthly. For the first time I'm glad I'm locked in a room with a religious maniac reading the Bible. But Abia doesn't seem to notice it at all. I feel a panic coming over me, and I think I might be about to scream. Then at last, I can hear what it is. It's singing. 'Yoou aain't nothin' but a hoouund dogg, cryyiing aall the tiiime . . .' It gets louder and louder, until he's right outside the door. There, he stands still. 'Yoouu aiin't never caught a rabbit, and yoou aaiin't no friiend of miiine. Good night, my boy.' And he walks away, and he begins to sing it, all over again.

CHAPTER 22

Eddie's gone again in the morning, but the doctor reappears and tells me it's time for me to start getting used to walking about again. The nurses and Dave help me up at first, as I'm unsteady on my legs after not using them for a fortnight, but there's nothing physically wrong with them, so although I still use the wheelchair, soon I'm shuffling about on my own for short spells. Dave locates some casual gear for me to wear round the place, thankfully not from Eddie's old wardrobe, and once I've got enough strength to make it down the stairs on my own, I look to see what Eddie's house has to offer me. After all, may as well make the best of it, seeing as I'm trapped here. Dave tells me that I'm welcome to go into and use anything in any room that's not locked. I daren't try any of the upstairs rooms, just in case I stumble on Eddie's bedroom, which I definitely do not want even to imagine, let alone see. Downstairs, the first thing I discover is the TV room. The set itself is a giant thing built into the wall. When it's turned off, it's like an enormous eye watching me. There are cabinets full of DVDs of films I've never heard of, most of them foreign. Next door to it is the study. I've been in here before with Fatty and Gaylord, but this time I get to look at things a bit more closely. I find the space on the shelf where Dave took the copy of *Oliver Twist* from. I also find that a whole bookcase is fake, the spines of the books forming one large door that swings open to reveal . . . boxes and boxes full of old photographs of naked men and boys, some of them very old indeed, and some of them very dirty. I'd say quite a few date back as far as the nineteenth century, although I can tell from the Tony Curtis haircuts that the most recent ones are from the fifties. Most of the other doors on the ground floor are locked, which leads me to assume that they contain things Eddie does not wish me to see. God knows what that would involve. He obviously wanted me to see the photographs.

Aside from the TV and library, and the gigantic porno bathrooms, of course, there is the garden. It's an enormous thing, and there's no easy way of telling where it ends and the surrounding countryside begins. In it there's a tennis court, a greenhouse full of butterflies, flowerbeds that seem to go on for miles, bushes cut into strange shapes, like pieces in an odd board game, and near the house, with a tiled path leading to it, the swimming pool. I like the garden. I forget about the TV room for the time being and decide to spend my time here.

Eddie has a live-in cook who makes meals for me and the goons, and there's a giant fridge full of booze in the kitchen. Dave says I can help myself, which I do, to a whole range of fancy drinks I've never tried before. Every so often, some of the

goons will take a dip, and shake themselves dry on the side like
Old English sheepdogs, but I never do. I've never been a good
swimmer. I get into a routine of having my breakfast in bed,
lazing there in the morning, having some lunch, then sitting by
the pool with Dickens and a glass of something peculiar, and
working on my tan, for all the good it does me. I do this for
three days. On the second day, the nurses are sent away by the
doctor, who visits for a third and final time, as I am having no
trouble walking or eating, and am obviously capable of taking
care of myself. By the third day, I'm still as white as a sheet.
That's when I get a surprise.

I'm walking from the house to the pool in my shorts and
sandals, book in hand, when I see that someone's taken my spot.
More precisely, two people. Still more precisely, one naked old
bloke lying on a lounger, and a girl, also starkers, jiggling on top
of him, facing the wrong way. It looks odd, his wrinkly old skin
with its liver spots, next to her dark, bronzed smoothness. Her
hair is dark too, with blonde streaks, and it hides her face as it
swings with their motion. He's as bald as a coot, and wearing
big-lensed sunglasses. He's grunting more like he's doing a shit
than he's about to come. Her squeaks are high, like an oriental.
Then he sees me.

'Oi! What the fuck are you looking at? I'll batter you, you
nonce.' He lifts up his sunglasses and pins me with his squinty
eyes. I recognise them instantly. It's Johnny Brooks. She looks
up and shrieks. 'Did I tell you to stop?' he snaps at her. She
starts bouncing and squeaking again obediently.

'Sorry!' I say, waving. I turn and head back to the house.

'Hang on!' he shouts after me, 'it's Elvis isn't it? Get over
here!' Gingerly, I walk over like I'm told. 'Be with you in a
minute,' he says, before letting out a loud moan. 'All right, you,
off.' He slaps the girl's pretty little bottom as she dismounts. As

she does so, I catch her gaze properly for the first time. In that moment, I can say that she is the most beautiful thing I have ever seen. Her eyes are startlingly green. She has the tiniest button nose you can imagine, while her mouth looks warm and wet, and her chin has the loveliest dimple. But, those eyes, they're like precious stones. Also, nice tits. Brown, rather than red nipples. There's something exotic about her, like an old Turkish Delight advert. She can't be older than twenty.

She scurries off to catch Johnny's spunk in a tissue as it plops out, while he vigorously shakes my hand. 'Elvis, my man, how's it going?' he asks. He seems genuinely pleased to see me. 'Heard you're in a spot of bother with the Old Bill. Don't worry, mate, it'll all get sorted out eventually. 'Ere, a little birdie told me that you're the main event at my birthday bash. Brilliant, mate, brilliant. Loved it when you used to do Elvis all those years ago. Be fucking magic to see it again, really looking forward to it.' Christ, the birthday party. I'd forgotten all about it. Of course, I could always cry off sick, but that would probably mean I'd end up kneecapped, or knowing Eddie, buggered senseless, and then kneecapped.

'Yeah, really looking forward to it,' I say. 'So what brings you to this neck of the woods, then?'

'Oh, Eddie lends me this place when I've got some bird on the go. Not that Nanette gives a toss, but she don't want to be around it. And it's a really nice gaff, real classy. A bit fucking queer, but still top banana.'

'It certainly is. I knew Eddie was rich, but not this rich.'

'Yeah, well, let's just say that there are certain prominent businessmen who are walking round with very sore arses. Kind of turns deals in your favour, if you use tactics like that. Look, I can see you want to sit down and read your book, so I'll leave you to it. Got business to attend to myself. Oi, Coreen, move your arse!' He rises off the lounger, his liver-spotted dick swinging as he walks away. The girl joins him and he grips hard on her bottom all the way to the house. She looks over her shoulder at me briefly as they go, her wondrous green eyes gleaming from out of the dark of her skin. Remember, I think to myself as they disappear inside, that man has the power to make you eat your own eyeballs, so be careful what you do with them.

I sit and read until I've got to the end of the chapter where Oliver Twist goes to deliver the books for Mr Brownlow. Then I go to the kitchen to dig out some more fancy booze. I'm standing by the fridge door, working out if it's OK for blokes to drink something called Lambrini, when I sense I'm not alone. I peer round the door, and there she is, wearing a kimono-style robe that doesn't quite cover her crack, but just about keeps her boobs in as long as she holds it together. 'Sorry to interrupt,' she says, 'just looking for a bottle opener.'

I hand her one and try not to stare too hard at her escaping tits. 'Thanks,' she says. 'Um, I was wondering, how come Johnny called you Elvis? That's not your real name is it?'

'Ah, no. I'm an Elvis impersonator. I'll be doing a bit at Johnny's birthday party next week. I expect I'll see you there.'

'No, I'm sorry to say. Nanette will be there and Johnny . . . anyway we'll have our own party.' She smiles a weak smile. I can tell she's not happy with the situation but I'm not sure she can put her finger on what's wrong with it. 'Anyway, it was nice meeting you, Elvis.' She lets go of her gown to shake my hand, and her boobs fall spectacularly out of it. 'Oops, that wasn't meant to happen,' she says with a cheeky glint in her heavenly eyes. And then she turns and goes, her lovely bottom well in view, wiggling away behind her.

For the first time since I came round, I have an urgent

compulsion to play with myself. I decide to leave *Oliver Twist* and the Lambrini for the time being and dart off to one of the needlessly large bathrooms. On the way, I pass the study, where I can hear Johnny on the phone. 'Never mind that, just get hold of him and if he gives you any gip, cut his dick off. No, that's not a figure of speech . . .'

It's the wank to end all wanks, long overdue, and thinking about her – her skin, her eyes, her tits, her crack, her arse, her eyes – makes it all the shorter. I go back to reading my book. The next chapter's got a lot of Nancy in it, and I can't help but picture her as the girl – what did Johnny call her, Coreen? – and sure enough, pretty soon it's all twisted around in my head, and there's an orgy going on in Fagin's den. Christ, I think, it's starting again, all thoughts leading to wanking. Now I'll never finish the damn book. I'm contemplating another hand-shandy when I hear my name. It's Johnny, walking quickly towards me. He's dressed now, although not tidily. It looks like he put his clothes on in a hurry.

'Elvis,' he says, 'something's come up and I've got to go. Can you do me a favour, mate?'

'Sure, Johnny, what?'

'Can you keep Coreen company for an hour or so till someone comes round to take her home? Sorry to ask, but some business is going tits up and I need to sort it out sharpish.'

'Sure, Johnny, it's not a problem.'

'Nice one, mate.' He clasps my shoulder. 'And don't shag her or I'll have to cut your dick right off.' He winks at me and walks away.

I find Coreen in the TV room, flicking channels. She's managed to find some knickers since last time I saw her, but her boobs still threaten to jump out of her robe at any moment. 'Hiya,' she says when I walk in.

'Hi. Do you think it's OK for blokes to drink Lambrini?'

She laughs. 'Why wouldn't it be?'

'Dunno, just seems a bit of a woman's drink from the label.'

'Well, Eddie drinks it, so it must be OK.'

'Eddie does a lot of things most men don't do.'

'Well Eddie isn't normal, and neither are you, you're Elvis.'

'Good point. I'll get us both a glass, shall I?'

She nods. By the time I get back she's made space for me on the sofa. I sink into it next to her and for a minute I think it's going to eat me. When I give her a glass she raises it and clinks mine. 'Cheers, Elvis,' she says and smiles. She soon looks distracted.

'Something the matter?' I ask.

'Oh nothing,' she sighs, 'I just get pissed off sometimes with the way me and Johnny always have to go to such lengths to not get Nanette riled. It's not that she even minds him being with me, as long as she doesn't have to see any of it. I'm so bored with all the sneaking about, that's all. Like half our lives are spent keeping Nanette happy.'

'You wouldn't want to make her unhappy, trust me.'

'Oh, have you met her then?'

'I used to be married to her. Mmm . . . tastes of pears.'

'Jesus . . . Look mate, I'm sorry, I didn't realise . . .'

'No, it's OK, just water under the bridge now.'

'To change the subject, how come you're living at Eddie's place?'

'Do you want the truth?'

'I don't know, mate, do I?'

'Umm, let's just say I had to disappear for a bit.'

'For how long?'

'Don't know. Maybe forever. I'm kind of trapped here, to be honest with you.'

'Yeah, I know the feeling . . .'

So we sit flicking channels, taking the piss out of whatever's on. We drink more Lambrini and we have a pretty good time. And there, I fully grasp the concept of enjoying somebody's company. It means not wanting them to go. I feel natural with her there. Despite the fact she's such a lovely young 'un, I don't freeze up like I usually do. I mean, it's not like I'm staring at her and mumbling 'I like your robe'. But all too soon, a goon comes in to tell us Coreen's ride is here. 'Shit, I'm not ready,' she says. She turns her back to me, takes off her robe and quickly slips into some casual clothes that she takes out of a holdall parked at the foot of the sofa.

'Anyway, lovely meeting you, Elvis,' she says, and gives me a hug and a peck on the cheek. Then she leans close to my ear and whispers, very softly, 'I'll look you up, yeah?'

And she's gone, walking out the front door with her holdall slung over her shoulder. I stand in a daze for a minute, then I go upstairs to sort myself out and try to make sense of the last thing that she said.

CHAPTER 23

I suppose I've got to admit I've changed. Lying by the pool a few hours after Coreen has gone, I can't hide from the fact that something's shifted in my head. Most likely I've got brain damage. But I really don't mind, it's better like this. More than anything, I feel a huge sense of relief. Why? Because the anger has gone, I guess. I don't want to smash things up all the time any more. That means I can get a moment's peace from time to time, without a voice nagging constantly in my head telling me I have to go mental right then and there. Now I can actually concentrate on stuff. I can read a book, I can look at things. I can find something beautiful.

Some things are still the same, however. Not only has my compulsion to play with myself come back, but now I also really want some charlie. It's like my body is remembering what it used to do, and commanding me that I let it do it. Unfortunately, Eddie runs a drug-free house, at least as far as his employees are concerned, and none of the boys have any, or none that they will admit to. So as it gets dark, I have to content myself with opening another bottle of Lambrini, with its sweet pear flavour that I'm really beginning to enjoy, and watching the stars come out, thinking of Coreen and having a fiddle. I guess someone might see, but seeing as sex alfresco seems to be the norm here, I don't see why I shouldn't just fuck myself by the swimming pool and be done with it.

Ah, Coreen, Coreen, how I long for your emerald eyes, your sweet lips, your dusky nipples, and your finely trimmed pubic hair. I want to entwine the very fibres of your being with mine. I also want to screw you on every flat surface in the place, including the garage roof. But not only that, and to my surprise, I want to do normal things with you, like go to Blockbuster or take you to the supermarket. Things like that have never been part of my masturbatory fantasies before, but there they are, slap bang in the middle of one.

I'm just about to spurt into the pool while thinking about food shopping, when a voice shouts, 'No, don't waste it! Leave it for me!'

I'm so startled I come anyway, and it sprays the poolside as I turn to see who it is. Oh fuck, it's Eddie.

'Ah, too late, oh well. Just have to whip some up for me later.' He advances towards me, and I'm already thinking of ways I can kill him should I need to. I grab a towel and cover myself up with it. 'Shame, I was enjoying the view,' he says.

'Sorry Eddie,' I say, 'just had the urge, what with no female company and all.'

'Yes, quite, quite. Sorry I haven't been around for a while,

I've been a terrible host. There's a lot of business I have to take care of. Deals to be made, persuading to do, you know how it is.' I do indeed, although I wish I didn't. 'Anyway, my friend, I see you're looking a lot better. How have you been occupying yourself in my absence, other than the obvious?'

'Oh, just been taking it easy, catching up on my reading.' I indicate the copy of *Oliver Twist* that lies on the poolside, about a foot away from the spunk-spray.

'Ah, Oliver Twist, the little boy who asked for more. Silly twit. Why couldn't he have done the sensible thing and just taken what he wanted, then done damage to anybody who was stupid enough to stand in his way? Ought just to have shoved that gruel spoon right up Mister Bumble's arsehole. Don't you think?'

'I guess. Uh, I really need some charlie, Eddie.' I hadn't planned to ask, in fact it just slipped out. But I can feel the itch, and I know I'll end up going mental unless I scratch it.

'No.'

'Not much, just a little bit to see me through, I . . .'

'Christ, you've been reading that book so much you've turned into the little shit. "Please sir,"' he squeaks in a mocking child's voice, '"can I have some more?" Listen, my son,' he says, raising his voice and turning purple, 'I have no intention of obtaining cocaine or any other drug for you, firstly because I consider it to be a most tiresome habit, and secondly because I am well aware that it affects your performance in quite an extreme manner, and I don't want to see you waggling your willy in front of everybody while making claims of your own omnipotence at Johnny's party on Friday.' Shit, the party.

'So you heard about that too.'

'My dear boy, it made the papers. The whole country knows.'

'Eddie, OK, I'll do without the coke, but I will need some other stuff for the party. Like a costume, a decent PA, and someone to do the sound. It's all things I'd normally organise, but I can't really if I'm stu–, if it's best that I stay here.'

'Oh yes, my boy, anything,' he say, as sweet as pie again. 'All you have to do is ask. And I've been having a little think about your act myself. I was reflecting on that lovely day when you came to see me, and you and your two darling friends sang for me, here by the pool, and I thought, even taking your rather restricted circumstances into account, wouldn't it be just marvellous if they could be there with you?'

'Ah, now that wouldn't really be possible. We no longer have a working relationship.'

Eddie smiles. 'Oh, we'll offer them seven grand each. They'll let bygones be bygones soon enough.' My god, he really knows how to twist the knife in. That's over twice as much as he gave me. Mind you, I'll probably drink that amount in Lambrini by the time I'm out of here, and the medical expenses must have been pretty darn big. Of course, it's now clear Eddie isn't throwing money at me out of any humanitarian spirit, but just keeping me alive long enough to play the party. After that, who knows what he'll do with me. And would there be anything I could do to stop him from doing it?

Meanwhile I decide to concentrate on my more immediate concerns involving Fatty and Gaylord. 'What's to stop them from going to the police and telling them where I am?' I ask.

'Well, that's easy. We just tell them we're going to kill their families if they do.' I'd like to see anybody try and kill Jen, I think to myself. 'Right, my dear boy, how do we go about finding these two fellows?'

I rack my brain. Working on the assumption that they've stolen all my cancelled gigs, I predict that they will be playing a pub in Bury St Edmunds on the Wednesday of this week, if that hasn't already been.

'Eddie, what day of the week is it?'

'Why, it's Tuesday, my boy. Why do you ask?'

'Then I know where they'll be tomorrow night. They've got a gig.'

Eddie flings his arms in the air with delight and shakes me voraciously. 'Marvellous, marvellous. Would you be good enough to go down there and use your powers of persuasion on them? Don't worry, a few of the boys will go with you, and you won't even need to get out of the car if you don't want to, so you'll be quite safe. I should imagine Dave will want to go. He's very interested in Elvis, and in you. I think he may have a crush.'

'I don't think so,' I say, 'he's engaged to be married.'

'That's precisely the sort of fellow you have to watch,' Eddie chuckles, before snapping back to business. 'Tomorrow we shall get hold of everything you require, and in the evening, you shall obtain your boys.'

'Obtain them?'

'Well, we can't give them the chance to run away, can we? They will have to stay here with us, until at least after the party! Goodnight, my boy, I am tired.' He walks away briskly, but pauses before he enters the house. He spins on his heel and points at me, as he sings, 'Yoouu ain't nothin' but a hoouund dogg, cryyiin' all the tiiime . . . Goodnight, sweet prince.' He blows me a kiss and disappears inside.

The next morning, I'm woken from a sleep untroubled by those old strange dreams by a goon who brings a notebook and pen along with my breakfast, and asks me to make a note of everything I might conceivably need for the party. I do this, and he collects it with the breakfast tray half an hour later. I go out to spend another day by the pool with *Oliver Twist*, which perhaps mercifully has been stripped of the bizarre sexual connotations that it had yesterday. Eddie's unexpected interruption last night has put me off my stroke as far as the wanking is concerned, and even the thought of the luscious Coreen is not enough to overcome the faint nausea that accompanies all things Eddie. The man himself makes only a brief appearance, waving at me as he drives past on a little electric buggy he uses to get around his sizable garden, talking on his mobile about the party catering as he passes.

At five o'clock, Dave comes to find me. 'All right, Elvis,' he says, 'you OK to go soon?'

'Yeah, sure,' I say.

'OK, I'll be waiting in the limo out front in quarter of an hour.'

'Christ, we're not going in that are we?'

'I'm afraid we are. Eddie insisted. "If you're going to drive Elvis anywhere," he said, "it's got to be in a limo."'

Sure enough, quarter of an hour later, Dave and two other goons are waiting for me by the limo in the front drive. The two goons agree to sit in the back so me and Dave can sit and talk up front. The divider is up and they can't hear our conversation as we travel down the motorway. Even though I know it's better to keep completely quiet, I can't resist pumping Dave for information about Johnny Brooks and Coreen. Dave just laughs.

'What's so funny?' I ask.

'Just the whole situation. He used to have loads of girls on the go, but when he met Coreen, he cleared them all out. Except for Nanette of course. He's totally smitten with the silly slag. Of course, no reason not to be, she's only nineteen, and she's a total fox.' Nineteen years old, Jesus.

'But who is she?'

'Just some bint. Don't know much about her really. Not much to know as far as I can tell. Obviously, she likes the fine things in life.'

'But how does she feel about it? I mean, does she really like him?'

'How should I know? Look, any slapper who sleeps with someone Johnny's age isn't exactly after love is she? Especially if the old sod in question happens to be as loaded as Johnny is. The really sad thing is that Johnny's fallen head over heels for her. He's even been telling people Nanette's going to be shifted on out. He's in danger of making a right tit of himself if he's not careful.'

'He didn't seem that in love with her when I saw them. He was treating her like she was some prozzer.'

'Yeah, well, that's just his way. Trust me, if you'd seen him with the other girls you'd see the difference. And the boys too, of course.'

My mouth hits the floor of the limo. 'Boys?'

'Don't you know about that? The things I've seen at Eddie's house . . . That swimming pool you love so much has had more than just chlorine pumped into it.'

'That poor girl . . .'

'Hang about. You've fallen for her, haven't you? That's what all these questions are about. No wonder Eddie caught you wanking on the poolside last night.'

'Does anything stay secret round here?'

'Not bloody likely. But seriously, mate, stay away from her. You go anywhere near, you're signing your own death warrant. And I don't want to see that happen. I like you.' Dave saying this makes me worry that Eddie was right about him, and I feel uncomfortable and less talkative for the rest of the journey. So I'm quite glad when we finally arrive in Bury St Edmunds, and park the limo in the grounds of a pub advertising an evening in the company of the Elvis Presley Experience, who bill themselves as the most historically accurate and informative tribute to Elvis Presley in the east of England. Wanted man as I am, this I simply cannot resist.

CHAPTER 24

It's a stupid idea of course. I'm risking being spotted, shopped to the pigs and then a guaranteed spell in the nick, but I just have to see it. If you asked me why, I'd tell you it's so I can laugh at them making a fool of themselves. But that's not the real reason. The real reason is I have to see if they're any good. I need to know just how much they've been carrying me over the past few years. 'Dave,' I say, 'I want to go in.'

'Thought you might,' he says. 'But I think it would be advisable if you went incognito.'

'True. How would I do that?'

'Well, it just so happens . . . I've brought a disguise.'

He lowers the divider and asks one of the goons to hand him a sports bag. Inside are sunglasses, a wide-brimmed hat, a coat that goes all the way down to the ground, and a long, thick scarf. It's July.

'I'm not sure about this, Dave.'

'Look, we can't risk your two friends recognising you before we've had a chance to talk to them can we? To be honest with you, if you don't wear those, I'm not going to let you out of the car.'

I sigh. 'I hate people who wear fucking hats indoors. What's the fucking point of wearing a hat if you're inside? To keep the rain off? If I wear this hat in there, I'll look a right cunt.'

'Elvis, it'll be fun. You'll look like Doctor Who. The good one, I mean, not the crap one who played cricket.'

'What about these glasses? You can't wear sunglasses indoors! If there's one thing I hate more than people still wearing hats when they're inside, it's people wearing fucking sunglasses when they're not even—'

'Elvis, no offence or nothing, but shut up.' I'm blabbering because I'm nervous. What if it turns out they're much, much better than me? I don't think I could bear it if they turned out to be even half decent.

I put on the ridiculous outfit, wrapping the scarf right round my face, while me and Dave get out of the car, leaving the two goons to wait for us. The limo's taking up half the pub car park. A lot of motorbikes are outside for some reason. As I walk in, I see the pair of them standing at the bar, talking to the punters in their civvies. They've only been away from me for a few weeks, and they're already forgetting my rules. Just seeing them do that makes me seethe with anger all of a sudden. I'll give them something to remember all right, I think to myself, imagining the beatings that I could have Dave and the goons give them. But just as suddenly as it arrives, the anger passes. Whereas not so long ago it would have lasted for days, now it slips back into the bog of anxiousness from which it sprung. It's not enough to be angry any more, I realise. I've finally got to start paying attention. Still, even though I'm here to learn, I desperately wish that they'll fail.

Another person I've got to stay clear of is the landlord, last heard on my answering machine, cancelling my services for this evening. I've met him before without my gear on, so he knows what I look like. So immediately I hide myself well away in a corner while Dave goes to the bar. I size up the room through my dark glasses while I wait. This place seems to have changed a bit since last time I was here, three or four years ago. As I remember, it was quite a community place, families, old folk and the like. Now, I can't help but notice, the pub's rather packed full of bikers, real proper ones with hair and tattoos. OK, they're not the Hell's Angels, but they're not exactly a bunch of accountants out on a day trip either. They're big men, some of them definitely going for that marauding Viking look. Their birds look like they'd be pretty tasty in a fight as well. I wonder how Gaylord and the Fatman will go down with them. I didn't do so well with trolls, so maybe they'll have a mess on their hands with Vikings. Perhaps I'll get lucky and they'll roast the pair of them on a spit.

Dave comes back with two pints of Guinness.

'Dave, I have a bit of a problem,' I say, or at least try to, inhaling my scarf as I speak.

'What's that? Couldn't quite hear you.'

'Dave, I can't drink my Guinness. My scarf's in the way.'

'Oh right. Hang on . . .' He skips to the bar again, and comes back proudly waving a straw. 'There. Problem solved!'

'Dave, I'll look a right tit.'

'You look a tit anyway. Come on, slurp it up.'

I resign myself to my ludicrous lot and thread the straw underneath the scarf.

It looks like they're getting ready to start. Gaylord disappears behind the bar with his costume bag, leaving the Fatman to get up on stage and set up a wooden stand, on top of which he places a big folder thick with paper. What could they be planning to do? I ask myself. I can see Soundcheck Stu behind the mixing desk. It looks like they've bought themselves some pretty good gear, which probably cost them a lot more than my last set did, now abandoned of course in that godforsaken social club in Elk. Just goes to show how much the pair of them were shitting me when they said they couldn't spare any cash. I feel the anger rise for a second time, but again it's swallowed up by my growing sense of unease. And also, a thought, inconceivable just a couple of weeks ago, that maybe they were right not to give me the money. But the moment has arrived. The lights go dim, so dim in fact, I can't see a damn thing from behind my sunglasses, except for a single light from Fatty's stand. A sound of a beating heart emerges out of the speakers.

Fat Elvis speaks into the microphone. 'Elvis, man, legend, enigma,' he intones. 'Who was he? Where did he come from? What made him the King of Rock 'n' Roll, the artist of the century, indeed, the greatest musical performer of all time? All these questions and more will be answered as we present to you . . . The Elvis Presley Experience.' Fatty is obviously reading from a script, and his voice has the dead tone of someone unaccustomed to public speaking. And also unaccustomed to reading. The heartbeat gets louder and louder, to the point that I think my eardrums are about to burst, before it cuts suddenly to the sound of a baby crying. A black and white photo of a shack appears on a screen at the back of the stage. Oh my god, they've got slides. 'Elvis Aaron Presley was born on 8 January, 1935,' continues the Fatlad, 'in a two-bedroom shotgun shack in East Tupelo, Mississippi, to parents Vernon and Gladys. Sadly, his twin brother Jesse Garon was stillborn. The Presleys were poor, and often struggled to make ends meet. Elvis loved music from an early age, and at the age of ten made his performing debut when he sang the song "Old Shep" at a talent contest at the Mississippi-Alabama Fair and Dairy Show in downtown Tupelo. Shortly after this he got his first guitar . . .' And so on, and so on. Each fact is illustrated with a relevant slide, usually of a building. Now, biker gangs aren't exactly renowned for their attendance of public lectures, and it's not long before what he's saying is drowned out by, well, them just laughing at him. 'Get on with it!' one of them shouts. 'Sing some bloody songs!' shouts another. Somebody starts a chorus of 'Why are we waiting?' Then the laughter turns into a strange, menacing hooting. Fatty just carries on regardless. Balls of steel, or brains of shit, I can't decide. Me, I can't believe what I'm seeing. Surely they'll never recover from this?

From the slides, I can see that Elvis has arrived at Sun Studios, and is ready to make a record. At last Gaylord appears from behind the bar, dressed as a young Elvis, wearing a suit straight off the cover of the first album, along with a pair of white shoes, and a little wig to cover his bald spot. He's not exactly the embodiment of raw sex that the young Elvis was meant to be, but he's presentable. He begins to wind his way through the punters towards the stage. But the bikers are not letting him through. They've decided it would be much funnier to keep him from getting on. I can see him getting more and more agitated as one after another the bikers block his way. Pretty soon he's squealing at them to 'stop messing about!' because they're 'spoiling it for everybody!' By now, the whole room is laughing, and he's on the opposite side to where he's meant to be, attempting more and more convoluted ways to get to the stage, all the while being pushed from biker to biker in a human version of pinball. Eventually, a Viking elder, who's sitting down and appears to have some authority over the rest of the horde, signals with a gesture that he should be let on stage. As Gayboy clambers up, Soundcheck Stu starts up the backing tape for 'That's All Right'. There's a big cheer. 'About fucking time!' one of them shouts, and they all laugh again.

Gayboy is centre stage like a rabbit in the headlights, visibly shaking and not in a sexy Elvis way. For a moment I think he might wet himself. He doesn't, though. Instead he launches into a performance that is, and there's no way round it, not that bad at all. He can sing, and he can move, and it's certainly histori- cally accurate. When he finishes, he gets a round of applause and quite a few cheers from the mead drinkers that sound sin- cere enough. It's obvious that the pair of them are not beaten yet.

Then, to my delight, the Fatty starts up with the slides again. A groan goes round the room as a photo of Elvis signing his first record contract appears. That is, until one burly gentleman decides to take matters into his own hands, rips the slide carousel off the projector, and throws it at the stage, the slides scattering like bombs from a B-52. Gay and Fat Elvis gawp as their whole plan for the evening falls apart. They huddle together, and I suppose they must decide they have no choice but to carry on without the slides and lecture, because that's what they do, with Gaylord doing a fine set of Sun-era material: 'Mystery Train', 'Baby, Let's Play House', 'Blue Moon of Kentucky'. It's good. Much too good for comfort.

Next he sings the real hits Elvis had in the fifties once he signed to RCA. 'Heartbreak Hotel', fucking 'Hound Dog', 'Blue Suede Shoes', 'All Shook Up', 'Jailhouse Rock' and all the others, and the bikers go crazy for it. I mean, they really do. They're whooping and a-hollering and some are even up dancing with their old ladies. And they're right to, I guess. It's actually very good. Not as brilliant as Buddy, mind, and I wouldn't say it's anywhere near as good as me at my best, back in the old days in the prison rec yard. But the fact is, those bikers are loving it more than anybody's loved anything I've done for many years. I suppose I have to face it, I'm not that good any more. Gayboy and Fatty have been carrying me for a long time. I feel sick as I stare at the truth head-on.

Gaylord keeps up the momentum and works his chronological way through the late fifties and up to the mid sixties with songs like 'Return to Sender' and 'Big Hunk O' Love', as well as some more obscure ones I'd never think of doing. He's on for over an hour, until after he sings 'Crying in the Chapel', when he meekly asks the bikers, 'Can we have the interval now, please?'

The bikers are merciful, and let them have it.

Dave brings me another pint of Guinness and another straw. 'What do you think?' I ask him.

'He's very good,' says Dave. 'I expect he learned it all from you.'

'Pretty much,' I say, but half those songs I've never done. It's never occurred to me to do stuff like 'Little Sister', or '(Marie's the Name) His Latest Flame', and now that I'm brain damaged, I can admit they're pretty good songs. I always did the greatest hits and the greatest shit, and never kept an eye out for the good stuff. If I'm ever going to do anything decent in the future then I'll need to steal some of their ideas. But who am I kidding? I don't have a future. One more gig, then a life of imprisonment as Eddie's sex slave. Meanwhile, in the here and now, I need a piss. I'm getting pretty funny looks from some of the bikers, maybe because I'm wrapped up like it's December, or maybe because I'm drinking Guinness through a straw, so Dave insists on watching my back at the urinal. I'm still not sure about him though, I make sure he doesn't see it. Still, I'm glad he's there.

The second half of the show is about to begin. It's Gayboy who's now sat at the side in his civvies. 'Guitar Man', the main theme from the *'68 Comeback Special* starts up, and Fat Elvis jumps up from underneath the mixing desk where he's obviously been cowering, away from any potential fun and games with the bikers, and bounds on stage dressed in a Vegas jumpsuit. I can see now that they've divided up Elvis's life between them according to waistline, with his later, fatter years recreated through the use of an authentic fatty. The Fatman takes up the story from where Gaylord left off, with the comeback special and on into the Vegas years. He does a good job too, not as well as the Gayster, but then the material isn't as good. Once you get past 'Suspicious Minds', it's pretty much just turgid crap like 'My Way' and 'The Wonder of You', save for the odd OK song. Still, people love that shit, bikers included, and Fats gives it all he can, sweating in his jumpsuit almost as much as I am under this fucking raincoat and scarf.

Finally, Fats sings 'Way Down', Elvis's last hit before he died. The bikers are very happy, whooping in their Viking way and demanding more. No one's taking the piss now. Fatty and Gaylord have won them over all right. Bastards. While the Fatman punches the air in triumph, the Gayster disappears under the mixing desk, then reappears in his Elvis outfit and joins him on stage. Soundcheck Stu starts off the backing track of 'A Little Less Conversation'. Gay and Fat Elvis sing the song together head to head, sharing a microphone and looking into each other's eyes. It all looks very gay.

The bikers let them leave the stage with a big cheer. While they're shaking the hands of men who could crush their skulls, Dave leads me outside.

'You stay here,' he says, as he opens the limo door for me. 'I'll go and round them up.' He takes one of the goons with him. I feel relieved to be taking my coat and scarf off. I'm dripping with sweat.

'Things been OK out here?' I ask the remaining goon as I settle myself down in the front seat.

'Yeah,' he says, 'except for the fucking kids touching the car. Had to wind the window down and point a gun at their knees just to get them to fuck off.'

'That'll learn 'em.'

Already, I can see Dave and the goon escorting Fatlad and Gayboy to the car. They seem to be getting on famously. Dave must have won them over with his enthusiastic curiosity about all things Elvis. Or else he told them he had teenage hookers in Priscilla wigs waiting in the limo. As they get closer, I press the button that winds down the window. Gaylord is talking.

'So Elvis never performed outside the US because of Colonel Parker's status as an illegal immigrant, which he never wanted discovered. This is a shame because Elvis had literally millions of fans the world over, and would have loved to have gone on a world tour . . . Oh Christ.'

'All right, lads,' I say. 'Don't worry, I won't have to put you in a coma if you just do as we say. Get in the back.' The back door opens and they're escorted inside. I know what I'm meant to be doing now. I'm meant to be the bad guy. I'm meant to get angry. The thing is, I'm not angry with them. They've taught me a valuable lesson about passion and integrity. I want to thank them. Unfortunately Eddie's script requires that I make them shit themselves. So that's what I'll have to do, I guess.

CHAPTER 25

Everything's quiet in the limo as we drive back to Eddie's. I let them have it all right. Scared them good. Got them pleading for mercy, begging for forgiveness for all the wrongs they'd done me. I couldn't believe how vicious Dave got with them. Normally he's as sweet as anything, but I could swear he was going to rip their legs off some of the time. Anyway, with Dave's help I managed to convince them that they did me a great wrong by dumping me on the motorway hard shoulder that time, and the only way they could conceivably make it up to me is to return to the fold and play the birthday party of my great friend, Johnny Brooks. I showed them all right. But it doesn't really mean anything. I should feel satisfied that I got my revenge. But, no, I don't feel anything like that at all.

Still, there were some fun and games to be had. I suppose it was quite funny listening to Fatty and Gayboy phoning up their wives and telling them that they'd met a most interesting man at their gig who'd persuaded them to go fishing with him for a few days. But even that couldn't get rid of the feeling that what I was doing was stupid and childish, and worse, just shouldn't be done for reasons I know would hurt too much to understand. I can't open that door. Too much lies behind it. But still it calls to me.

There's a knock on the divider. Dave lowers it, and one of the goons pokes his head round. 'They're asking if they can play a tape,' he says.

'Would it be a tape of Elvis, by any chance?' I ask him.

'Um, yeah it is.'

I sigh. 'Yeah, go on then.'

Thursday afternoon and I've got the pair of them rehearsing on the lawn. We've got backing tracks being pumped out to us from the main house through a pair of enormous speakers that Eddie keeps in reserve for parties. I suppose it's a good job his nearest neighbour lives about three miles away. Anyway, it's been going OK, although it took them a while to slip back into their old supporting role of joke Elvises, or Elvi, or whatever the plural is. It's not all back to my way of doing things, however. In fact we've reached some sort of compromise. We do things mostly the way we used to, but drop some of the novelty numbers and replace them with some of the more decent songs. So out goes 'There's No Room to Rumba in a Sports Car', and in comes 'Mystery Train'. Do away with 'Do the Clambake', and instead sing 'Baby, Let's Play House'. And so on. Call it my first tentative steps towards some sort of integrity. And besides, there's no fucking way I'm standing up in front of a room full of gangsters and asking them if anybody wants to dance in a grass skirt to 'Blue Hawaii'.

I'm just working them through a routine for 'A Mess of Blues' when I shiver involuntarily. It's Eddie. I feel him watching us before I see him, trundling towards us in his little buggy. Not waiting for the song to end, he buzzes straight up and stops in front of us, waving at us like he's royalty in his carriage. 'Well, hello boys!' he squeals. 'How absolutely lovely to see you again.'

'Awwright,' says the Fatman.

Eddie skips off his buggy and gives them both long lingering kisses on their cheeks. He turns to me as they wipe off his spittle behind his back, exchanging worried glances with each other. 'So, dear boy,' says Eddie to me, 'how are rehearsals going? Do you think you're going to be just utterly spectacular for tomorrow evening?'

'Oh, definitely, Eddie. No doubt about it.'

'Good, good, wonderful. Boys,' he says, turning back to Gayboy and Fats, 'I do hope you know how grateful I am to you for giving up your time and energies at such short notice. Is the financial arrangement satisfactory?'

'Financial arrangement?' asks the Fatman.

'Why, yes, of course.' Both of them look at him blankly. 'Don't tell me he hasn't told you! Boys, boys, I'm willing to give you seven thousand pounds each for your trouble. Why did you not tell them? They must have been thinking we'd kidnapped them or something. You've put me in a very bad light!' He glares at me in a way I used to see often, years ago.

'I'm sorry, Eddie,' I say, 'it must have slipped my mind.'

'Yes, well, we can't all just be walking around forgetting things, can we, or the world would just be a big mess, with aeroplanes dropping out of the sky and whatnot. Anyhow, I shall leave you to it. Practice makes perfect, don't they say?' He scootles off on his buggy, leaving me with the two boys, who look at each other, mouthing the words, 'Seven grand. Seven fucking grand . . .'

Next thing I know, they're whooping like bloody Americans, giving each other high-fives and complicated handshakes they're obviously making up on the spot. Soon Gaylord is doing hand-stands and the Fatman is dancing a stupid fatty dance. When they break into a rendition of 'Money, Honey' by Elvis fucking Presley, I feel it's only right to give both of them a slap.

'What's that for?' whines the Fatman.

'You know what for, being an irritating fat cunt, that's what for. Now we're getting back to work.'

'Hang on a minute,' says Gayboy, 'I just want to raise some-thing here. Wouldn't I be right in saying that Eddie only gave you three grand for doing this gig?'

'What I'm being paid is none of your fucking business. Back to work.'

'No, it was definitely three grand. I remember 'cos I was there.'

'Look, stop fucking about. We're getting on with rehearsing, or—'

'Or what?' says the Gaylord. 'You'll have us beaten up? I don't think so. Seeing as Eddie's paying fourteen grand for our services, he's not going to have us done over is he?'

'Yeah,' says the Fatlad, 'we'll do the gig, don't worry, and we'll rehearse to all hours, but you may as well be nice to us, 'cos you've got nothing to back up your big mouth. Now you treat us with respect, which means no calling us names like Gaylord and Fatso, and you'll get a lot of hard work out of us. Deal?' They're right. The moment when I had any genuine power over them passed as soon as they agreed to do the gig. Now we're all in it together.

'OK,' I say, quietly. 'Right, back to work. If that's all right with you fine gentlemen, that is.'

And so we carry on, well into the evening. By the time we've finished, we're as tight as we'll ever be, and may even stand a chance in hell of actually entertaining someone. Eddie himself has disappeared again, but his staff lay on a pretty huge spread for the three of us. It's bloody torture biting my tongue as Gayboy and the Fatman get me worked up at the dining table, I suspect on purpose, with their fucking stupid conversations and constant bloody singing, but after we've eaten I finally get a chance of some peace when they discover Eddie's giant telly.

'Fuck me,' says the Fatman, 'it's massive!'

'We should definitely watch something on this,' says Gayboy. 'Do you reckon Eddie's got *Star Wars*?'

'No he hasn't got fucking *Star Wars*,' I say, the first time I've sworn at the little shit in hours. 'What he's got are some of the finest examples of cinema as an art form.'

'So why hasn't he got *Star Wars* then?' says Fatboy. 'That's the best film ever made.'

'For Christ's sake,' I say. 'Why don't you broaden your horizons for once and watch something with a bit of class? Take this for instance, *Les Enfants du Paradis*. It says here it's the best French film ever. And look, there's a clown on the cover, which means it'll be funny.'

'That's not a clown,' says the Gayster as I show them the box, 'it's a mime.'

'OK, it's a mime, but that's not important. What matters is that we should watch it and actually spend our time on something good for once.'

'OK, OK,' says Fats, 'we'll watch it, if that's what you want to do.'

Twenty minutes in, Gaylord's hitting Fatty in the head with

a cushion. Every time he does so, the Fatman says 'Meep.' They think this is fucking hilarious.

'For fuck's sake,' I scream at the pair of them, 'if you're not going to watch the film, go somewhere else.'

They look at each other for a second. Then the Fatman says to Gayboy, 'Do you fancy a pillow fight?'

'Yaaaay!' screams the Gayster, waving his arms in the air as Fatboy chases him out the room and up the stairs.

I settle down to watch the rest of the film. It's funny, I've never really watched anything like this before, and I'm not honestly expecting it to mean anything to me at all, but it does. As I get drawn into the story, I realise that in many ways, the situation in the film is very similar to my own in regards to Coreen, who's been weighing on my mind quite a lot these past couple of days. You see, it's set in olden times, back in the seventeenth century, or thereabouts, and it's about this bloke who's a mime, like those saddos you see in city centres sometimes who pretend to get out of a box or be pulled along by a rope or get stuck in a lift, when in fact there's nothing there and they're just wasting everybody's time. But the bloke in this, he's really good at it and he can mime all sorts of stuff, not just boxes, ropes and sliding doors. So anyway, he falls for this bird who's a bit of a prozzer and hangs out with criminals. He has a chance to shag her, but he bottles it, and she ends up marrying this rich bloke she doesn't really love. Meanwhile, the mime becomes a big star, and marries this boring bird who he's not really keen on, but he ends up having a family with. But then the first bird comes back, and they still don't end up together, but his wife runs off with the kids anyway, and by the end of the film, nobody's with anybody at all and nobody's happy.

And I suppose it's a bit like that with me and Coreen. I love her, but I'm not with her. She's with Johnny, who's obviously a lot richer than me, but she's not happy. OK, I'm not thick enough to think that she's in love with me, but she could be if we got to spend more time together. Not that that's going to happen, I suppose, with Johnny keeping her chained to his liver-spotted dick. So that means my love for her must be doomed, and that makes me feel pretty fucking miserable. I believe the correct word is 'forlorn'. But then, she said she'd look me up, didn't she? At a stretch, that could be taken to mean she wants to spend some time with me. But then birds say all sorts of crazy shit they don't mean. Probably just said it to wind me up. Bitch. Of course, I don't mean that. It would just be easier for me if I did, that's all.

After all the rehearsing, eating and fancy film-watching, I'm pretty beat and go to bed at one, which is early for me. Sleep comes easily. It doesn't last. I'm woken by the strange sensation that I am not alone in the bed. I can feel another body's heat wrapped around me under the sheets, and a hand holding mine. Someone's warm breath blows on my neck, and it smells of spirits and cigars. Oh, god, oh Jesus Christ, I realise as I wake up fully, it can only be Eddie.

I open my eyes. It's still dark. I try to turn myself over, but I can't. He's pinned me to the bed, pressing down on my arms and legs with all his weight. I can't tell if he's asleep or not, but he's fully clothed. I can even feel his shoes with my foot. 'Eddie?' I ask, feeling a very real sense of dread. 'Is that you?'

'My boy,' he mumbles, 'my dear boy.' He's very drunk, I realise.

'Are you OK, Eddie? Do you want me to help put you to bed?'

'My boy. My lovely, precious boy.' He runs his hand through my hair, and then he kisses my neck and cheek.

'Eddie, don't do that. Please.'

'My boy, you're so beautiful. Let me kiss you, you beautiful angel.'

He kisses me on the lips, running his tongue over them.

'Why won't you let me kiss you?' he pouts. 'Am I not good enough for you? Don't you know who I am? I made you, you bastard!' For a second I'm sure he's going to turn violent, and even though he's pretty old, he's in good shape, but his tensed muscles soon relax as he sinks further into me and the bed.

'It's not that, Eddie,' I say to him, 'I'm just not . . . like you, that's all.'

He's silent for a few seconds, then says, 'No, no, you're not. Of course you're not. You won't let me down will you? You'll be a star tomorrow for me won't you? You'll be an angel for your Eddie, won't you, my boy?'

'Of course. I won't let you down.'

'You're a good boy. I love you, you know.' He begins to sob.

'Eddie, what's wrong?'

'I'm old. I'm old, and I'm ugly, and I'm fat. I'm going to die by myself. You know, I must have fucked a million boys, but I never let any of them stay. None of them would have wanted to stay anyway. And now I'm going to die. I'm going to die without ever having been loved.'

'You're not going to die, Eddie,' I say, cradling his head for reasons I can't quite explain. 'You've got years to go yet.'

'My dear boy. I've got cancer. I am going to be dying very soon. And I can look back on my life and say, without any doubt, none of it's been worthwhile. Not the money, not the sex, none of it. It's all been a total fucking waste of time.' He cries softly to himself while I run my hand over his head and soothe him to sleep. Despite his weight pressing down on me, I somehow fall back to sleep myself, until I'm woken in the early morning for just a minute by the opening and closing of the door. I see that I'm alone again in the room and go back to sleep.

CHAPTER 26

Eddie's not around when I get up Friday morning, and there's still no sign of him the rest of the day. We do a bit more rehearsing, but mostly lounge around until about six o'clock when we're bundled into the limo to be taken up to London. Unfortunately, it's not Dave driving us, so I have to sit in the back with the pair of them. They start singing Elvis songs as per fucking usual, but I hit on an unusual tactic in order to shut them up. I actually engage them in conversation. Not to make things too painful, the subject I settle on is myself.

'So was there a lot in the papers about me then?' I ask.

'Quite a lot, yeah,' replies the Fatty. 'They dragged it out a bit, I guess because people found it so funny that an Elvis

204 • *Richard Blandford*

impersonator would kick the crap out of someone who's pretending to be Buddy Holly. You putting him in a coma, people didn't find that so funny, but still . . . when they investigated your last known movements and it turned out that you'd got your todger out in a social club while dressed as Elvis and pretending to be Jesus, they couldn't get enough of that.'

'Hasn't gone down well in the Elvis fan community though,' chips in Gaylord. 'The general consensus is that you've brought Elvis into disrepute through association, and made a laughing stock of the profession of Elvis tribute artist.'

'Yeah, 'cos they really needed my help on that one.'

'There is a minority opinion, however, on the militant fringes of Elvis fandom, that you only gave that bloke what was coming to him for liking Buddy over Elvis. However, this is, I stress, a stance taken by a tiny number of Elvis extremists, who advocate a policy of total Elvis separatism away from the mainstream of general rock 'n' roll appreciation.'

'Where the fuck do you get this shit from?'

'The Internet mostly,' says the Fatman. 'In fact, thanks to Elvis message boards and chat rooms, you're being discussed all over the world, from South Africa to New Zealand, even Memphis itself.'

'Fame at last,' I say. 'Maybe I should go on tour.'

'If you did, you'd be arrested,' says Gayboy. 'You should just be hoping there are no undercover policemen there tonight. Otherwise, you're fucked.'

'Yes, thank you for bringing that to my attention, as if I didn't have enough to worry about already.'

'Well, you're going to be caught eventually aren't you,' the Gayster says. 'Unless you spend the rest of your life in Eddie's garden, you're not going to get away with it.'

'Look, you gaylord, if I ever have a vacancy for a nagging

voice inside my head that points out my every mistake, I'll let you know. Until then, shut the fuck up!'

'Don't call me Gaylord. If you fucking call me that again, I won't go on stage tonight.'

'If you don't go on stage tonight, you'll be using disabled parking spaces for the rest of your life and you know it. Don't make idle threats, you fucking gay cock.'

'Lads, lads,' says Fatso, 'let's keep it civil, shall we, for all our sakes.'

'Ah shut it, Fatboy,' I say under my breath, but I know I can't take it any further. There's an awkward silence for a few minutes, which the Fatty breaks by bursting into 'You Don't Have to Say You Love Me'. I can see there's no point in even trying to stop him, and by the time he's on the second line, the Gayster's joined in too. It's not that long a journey though, and I only have to endure their rendition of the entire second side of Elvis's *That's the Way It Is* album before we arrive in Soho, at the back door of Eddie's Trunk Club. A goon we've never seen before waits for us outside, and unsmilingly grunts at our arrival before bundling us in. It's not that nice in the back, it's cold, no carpeting and the paint's peeling. And there's a funny smell, sickly sweet. I can't explain it, but it just makes me think that something's wrong. It's particularly strong as we pass the dressing room.

The unsmiling goon unlocks a door. 'Wait in here,' he says, 'toilet's that way. Don't go anywhere else.'

We walk into the lounge. It's OK. At least it's got heating and a carpet, and an old brown three-piece suite. Makes me think of a dentist's waiting room. They've even laid out a finger buffet for us in there, along with a crate of beer. Nervously, the three of us sit down. I pull the crate of beer towards me and throw them a can each. No one says anything. Fatty takes a swig of the cheap supermarket beer and belches. I'm about to swat him round the head, when unexpectedly, he says, 'I'm quite looking forward to this actually.'

'Yeah, me too,' says Gaylord. 'It'll be good to do the old act one last time, and really do it properly. You know, you are loads better than us, at least when you put your mind to it.'

'Yeah, boss, you're the best,' says the Fatman.

I'm so taken back by their unexpected appreciation, I don't know what to say. A couple of weeks ago I'd have just told them they were pointing out the fucking obvious, but I know that's not good enough now. 'Thanks, lads,' is what I do say, after a moment's thought.

There's a knock on the door. It swings open, and a friendly face appears. It's Dave.

'Hi, guys,' he says, beaming. 'Just thought I'd wish you good luck for tonight.'

'Thanks, Dave,' I say.

'That's OK, I can't wait. Listen, if you want to pop out and have a bit of a soundcheck, now would be a good time to do it.'

'Yeah, that's an idea.'

'OK, just follow me. I'll see if I can round up the sound-guy we've found for you.'

Dave leads us down the cold corridor, past the dressing room and into the club. I can see a platform for dancing in the centre of the room, as well as a few smaller podiums throughout. At the side are alcoves, I should imagine for more intimate shows. The place is empty save for a few cleaners, wiping down the tables and the poles, and a couple of goons, stalking the place with their mobile phones. The club itself looks oddly clinical with the lights up. It's all chrome and leather padding. Funny to think in just a few hours' time, women will be showing their crotches to strange men here. Then I have a horrible thought. 'Uh, Dave,' I say, 'where is it we'll be performing exactly?'

'Well, up there of course.' He points to the main pole-dancing stage. It would have to be, wouldn't it, yet another of Eddie's little jokes. Oh well, there's no way we're getting out of it, I think to myself, so with resignation I pull myself up, the pair of them following behind. I see myself in the mirrored floor, caged in by the maze of poles around me. 'Fuck me,' says the Fatman, 'we don't have to strip do we?'

'Only if someone stuffs money in your trousers.'

Dave brings in the soundman, a big ball of denim and hair who sets up a couple of microphones on the stage. We give him our CDs full of backing music and do a run through of 'Burning Love'.

'Was that all right?' I ask Dave.

'Magic, mate, magic,' he says.

We go back to the lounge and eat the canapés and get pissed. We must be in there for hours before it's even time to get changed. By that point I'm rationing the beers as the Gayster is losing his coordination. I also fit in several visits to the lav to sort myself out. For my nerves, you understand. After a while we can hear the party starting. Banging techno is playing loudly, and making the base of my skull throb.

'What are they playing that crap for?' asks Gayboy.

'Yeah, bloody beeping robot music,' says the Fatman. 'Not like the old days when people played real songs on real instruments.' Ah, Coreen, Coreen, even though you're not here, I feel your influence.

Meanwhile, we change into our outfits and wait for our call. The other two are wearing their costumes from their last gig, Gayboy as fifties rockabilly Elvis, the Fatman in the Vegas jump-suit. I've gone for something a bit different this time round. I'm dressed as *'68 Comeback Special* Elvis, all in black leather. I'm too fat for it, but then, really, so was Elvis. What it means is we'll be presenting the three ages of Elvis, side by side like Charlie's Angels. It's not what people will be expecting, and when your public's a bunch of psychotic gangsters, not satisfying them's a dangerous thing. But it all feels a bit more honest, and that's been striking me as important these past couple of days.

'Elvis in five minutes, please,' someone shouts. And even though I've been downing it for hours, right now I feel very sober. I feel that something is at stake here. Maybe it's no coincidence that this is the first time in absolutely years I've been Elvis without doing any charlie. I've been dying for some all day, but now it's clear I'm not going to get any, I feel like I've passed through it, and I don't even want it that much. I just want to go out there and be Elvis, do it right, and show people, even if they are a bunch of sociopathic mental cases, what it is I'm doing here, why it is I'm on this fucking planet in the first place. Right now I feel that I could drop down dead out there and it wouldn't matter, I'd be doing what I was made to do. Even Gaylord and Fatty seem to sense that all of this is in some way important. After getting on my wick all bloody day with their singing and nattering, they've finally got round to shutting up these past couple of hours, and both look pretty serious. Not that they're ever not serious about Elvis, but it's rare that they'd be quiet about it.

And then it's time to go. Dave calls us and leads us down the corridor. We wait by the door, peering round it to have a peek at the party. It looks pretty wild. Even though the main stage has been cleared for us, there are still girls dancing on the podiums, wild-eyed gangsters hypnotised by their shaved slits while their girlfriends hang docilely off their arm. I recognise a few faces from the old days. Most of them I don't, though. Younger, newer faces, more vicious, harder than the old gang. These ones can't be bothered to hide their thuggery behind a smile.

The thumping of the music cuts out, and there's a squeal of feedback. Someone's up on the stage by the microphone. 'Ladies and gentlemen, your attention please . . .' It's Eddie. 'It is my very great pleasure to introduce to you a young talent that I myself discovered many years ago. And do you know, ladies and gentlemen, if I were to die tomorrow, then I could honestly say, that the one thing that I am most proud of, the one thing that when all is said and done I can say is really any achievement at all, is finding this boy. He's hot, he's sexy, he's the king of rock 'n' roll, he's a no good lowdown hound dog, put your hands together for . . . Elvis.'

The applause all but drowns out *Also Sprach Zarathustra*, and it takes the whole of the intro of 'See See Rider' for us to run from the door to the platform. Fortunately nobody tries any funny business and we get through pretty easily, although Fatty has difficulty clambering up on stage, which gets laughs, and a few cries of 'You fat bastard!' as I pull him up behind me. No sooner are we up there, however, I realise we will not be performing alone.

Girls. Girls to the right of me. Girls to the left of me. Girls behind me. Girls! Completely naked girls! They run onto the stage, and each of them quickly wraps herself round a pole as I try and remember what the hell it was I was meant to be doing. This I really wasn't expecting. True, I'd imagined it, and even wanked over the thought of it a few times, but here it is happening, it's actually happening. The Gayster and Fatlad are so surprised they're bumping into each other, and it's still taking me a few moments to recover. But I snap out of it when I realise

I'm about to miss my cue, and bound over to the microphone just in time for . . .

> I said see, see see Rider
> Oh see, what you have done . . .

They're blanketing the stage in light, so I can't make out any of the faces of the very bad men I'm singing to, but the room's whistling and clapping and hollering. Obviously the Elvis and naked women combo is really working for this crowd.

And for the rest of the night, we are truly kings. This is the best I've ever been, and the boys aren't bad either. We lead the audience everywhere, from fifties rock 'n' roll to seventies schmaltz, from the big hits to more obscure numbers. And what's more, I believe in every minute of it. And besides, it's fun. Every so often one of the girls frees herself from her pole and drapes herself briefly round one of us, and after a while, once I'm confident enough that I won't get taken outside, I do the same to them. Soon, even the boys are doing it, which is funny seeing how scared of women they are. The girls are good movers too, proper dancers. There's something not right, though. When I get close up to the girls, nearly without exception, there are marks. Big black bruises on their backs and torsos. Welts. Christ almighty, Eddie's excelled himself this time. He's made a choreographed dancing troupe out of what are probably migrant sex slaves. The girls come and go in half-hour shifts. God knows how many Eddie has back there, but I see each of them only twice.

Finally, two-and-a-half hours and three encores later, we're done. We did it. We wowed a discerning audience of criminals, downright nutters and their mistresses, and surely there can be no harder task in showbiz. Well, I'd like to see Cilla Black do it. And at one moment, somewhere in the middle of 'In the Ghetto', just for a second, I saw Johnny, and I saw Nanette, who's looking terrible by the way, tanned to a crisp with vari- cose veins, and for the very first time, the very sight of them together didn't make me feel like shit on a shoe. For that moment, in fact, I felt way above them, simply because I was Elvis and they were not. Sure, Johnny had the money, the former girl of my dreams, also the current girl of my dreams, and a nice big birthday party. But he wasn't Elvis. And right then, that was the most important thing. Because, I now see, for me to be Elvis is to be part of a chain, a good chain, not the sick chain of exploitation that I've been part of nearly my entire life. As Elvis, things flow through me. Something is given to me from some- where, and I pass it on. It reminds me of something someone said to me once, but I can't put my finger on it. Maybe I dreamt it. Or saw it on telly.

'Well done, boys,' I say, putting my arms round the shoulders of my two comrades as we make our way off the stage. 'You've done yourselves proud. It was really good to work with you again.' I don't know where it came from either, but they look at each other as if I'd just turned into a unicorn or something.

'Well, it's nice of you to say so,' says the Fatman. 'It was fun.'

'Yeah, it was,' says Gaylord, stunned.

Dave's waiting for us in the corridor.

'Oh my fucking god, you were brilliant!' he says.

'Yeah, we did OK,' I reply.

'Well, gentlemen, if you'll just follow me, Eddie has a little present for you.'

He leads us back to the lounge, opens the door for us, then leaves. There, standing in a row, are three of the dancers, two blondes and a brunette, naked except for G-strings. They look terrified. One of them is holding an envelope, which she gingerly presses into my hand. 'This is for you,' she says. Her accent is Russian or thereabouts. I open it, and inside is a note on some very nice paper, which says:

To Elvis (x 3)

Enjoy.

Your friend
Eddie

The two boys are standing in shock. I show them the note.

'No, I can't do this, I'm married. I can't do it,' says the Gayster.

All three of the girls rush to wrap themselves round him. 'Please,' says the brunette, 'you must or, umm, how you say, it will not be good for us.'

'Look,' I say, 'I think you're going to have to, or one of these girls will get beaten up.'

'I can't do it, I'm sorry,' says Gaylord. 'I'm married, and that's that.'

'Ah, you do know that Jen hasn't exactly been faithful to you, don't you.'

'Yeah. I know that, and I know that the lad . . . isn't mine, before you point that out.'

'So, what are you waiting for, my son? Get in there!'

'OK.' He looks up. 'I want the one in the middle.'

'Oh, I want that one,' says the Fatster.

'Lads, lads,' I say. 'You can swap over at half-time. You can do what you like with them. You don't even need to chat them up or anything. They probably wouldn't understand you anyway.'

They each pick a girl and clumsily lead her over to the sofa.

After twenty minutes of needless conversation, they finally get round to fucking them, and quite frankly, that's something I never want to have to see or hear again, especially as they're singing 'The Wonder of You' while they do it. Me, I take the one who's left over, the dark-haired girl. She's just skin and bone. She has marks all over her back that I have to close my eyes from seeing as I take her from behind, which, for the first time, I'm doing not because I get a kick out of it, but because I do not want to have to see her face.

CHAPTER 27

We're driven back to Eddie's in the early hours of the morning. We crash out as soon as we get there, and I'm thinking that I won't get up for another day or two. It doesn't work out that way.

'Elvis, Elvis, you've got to get up.' It's Dave, shaking me into consciousness. 'Ah, Eddie wants to see you. He's down in the garden. You don't need to get dressed or anything, just put this dressing gown on. It's just he wants you down there fast.'

I can barely get my body to move, but Dave lifts me up and puts the dressing gown and a pair of slippers on me before I even know that he's doing it. He leads me out of the room and down the stairs. As I get to the bottom, I see that Gayboy and Fatty are being shepherded by another goon behind me. They're also wearing only dressing gowns and slippers. The Fatman

yawns like a walrus. 'Gor blimey, guv, it's a bit early innit?' he
says to the goon. The goon says nothing.

'Dave,' I say, 'do you have any idea what's going on?'

'No, not really,' he mumbles.

Eddie's waiting for us by the swimming pool. He's still dressed
up to the nines in a tux, from last night.

'Boys, boys,' he says as we approach. 'You've made an old man
so happy. You were spectacular last night, and amazing, and beautiful. I love you all so much. Thank you!' He throws his arms
around me and hugs me tight, patting me hard on the back.

'Thanks, Eddie,' I say.

'No, thank you, my boy. And you too, of course!' He hugs
Fats now. He can't quite get his arms round him, so instead he
clasps his face in his hands. He reaches up and kisses him lightly
on the lips. 'Thank you, my son,' he whispers.

I can see the look of fear in Gaylord's eyes as Eddie approaches
him. 'And you, why you are such a little darling!' He grabs
Gayboy's head towards him. Then, Eddie plunges his tongue deep
into the Gayster's mouth, with a force he couldn't possibly resist.
He holds it there for what seems a hideously long while. Gay
Elvis makes a terrible whimpering sound as Eddie takes his tongue
from his mouth and licks his face, all the while pressing down
hard on his skull with his hands. Eddie doesn't seem even to be
here at all. Finally he lets go. As Gaylord tries to regain control
over his breathing, Eddie turns away to face the rising sun. Then
he returns to face us again, as if nothing had happened.

'Of course, I am so grateful to you all,' he says. 'You helped
me do something special for Johnny, who I think of as being
like a son to me in many ways. As are you, my dear boy.' He
stands next to me and ruffles my hair. He's teary-eyed. 'Oh how
I wish I could have all my boys around me in these last days.
But that is not to be. I will die alone no doubt . . .' His voice

trails off as he goes back to stare at the sunrise. 'How many more I wonder? How many more days?'

Then he comes back to us, a smile on his face. 'Lads,' he says to Fats and the Gayster, 'I owe you some money.'

'Yeah, it was seven grand each, fourteen in total,' says the Fatty, as if he were talking to the plumber.

'Of course, of course.' Eddie reaches into his jacket. 'And who should I make the cheques payable to?'

I know what's going to happen. I see that the swimming pool is lined with Eddie's goons. There is no chequebook. Instead, Eddie whips out a pistol and shoots the Fatman in the face. The back of his head sprays behind him on the tiles, as his life seeps out of him and he crumples on the ground in a big blubbery heap. Derek lets out an ear-splitting wail and looks to see where he can run, only to find that there is nowhere. In the end, he hides behind me, pleading with me to save him, but Eddie just walks round, and I have to step away, if only to make sure the inevitable bullets don't pass through him and into me. He takes several slugs to the chest and gut.

Me, I know I'm not going to die. It just doesn't feel like it's my time. Sure enough, Eddie puts his gun away, and his goons pack the bodies away in bags they had hidden away in the shrubbery, while others clean the poolside with mops and buckets. 'Don't let it drip into the pool!' Eddie shouts at them.

'I'm sorry, my boy,' he says to me finally, 'they had to go. They'd seen too much. Plus, their fees were quite exorbitant. But don't you worry, you're safe. Johnny likes you, and I do too, of course. In fact, Johnny sent you a message. He said, "Don't you shave". You hear that, my boy? Those are specific instructions, and if I see you without facial hair from this moment on, I'm authorised to shoot you too. Of course, you know I couldn't do that to you, my dear, dear boy. I'd have to get one of the boys to do it.' He smiles at me weakly, and goes inside. I sit by the pool and watch the goons carry the bodies away, and the rest of the sunrise.

And so the days go by. Most of the time Eddie's not around, but every so often he turns up, sings 'Hound Dog' at me from across the lawn, makes sure I haven't been shaving, and goes away again. I think he must be going out of his way to work until he drops dead. And me, I just sit, eat, wank, sleep, get hairy, get fat, educate myself on world cinema and read. I get to the end of *Oliver Twist*, but its happy conclusion does not satisfy me. In real life, doesn't everything good end badly? I bet if it were a true story Oliver would be hanged and Fagin would walk away scot-free. I suppose I'm jealous of him and his bright future and new life with Mr Brownlow. Nothing like that awaits me, I'm sure. I look about for another literary classic to keep me occupied. Eddie's got a set of books by some birds called the Brontë sisters, and I recognise some of the titles, but I flick through them and they look to me like they're women's books. There's a copy of that book *Crime and Punishment* by Dostoevsky on the shelf, but I can't imagine it will tell me anything I don't already know. I finally settle on more Dickens, *Great Expectations*. You know where you are with Dickens.

Like I said, I'm left on my own most of the time, and I find it harder to talk to Dave since they shot Gay and Fat Elvis, knowing that he knew about it before and lied to me about it, and even stood there at the side of the pool waiting for it to happen. He still wants to be my mate though, so I try and make an effort, if only for the company. I tell him about rock 'n' roll records, and he even goes out and buys some of them on CD. Says he can't listen to dance music now, says it winds him up. Dave's pretty much the only person I speak to round here.

Nothing really happens, except this one time. You see, I'm sitting in the TV room quite late, and Eddie comes in, roaring drunk, dressed up but all dishevelled. He just stands there shouting abuse at me, and he says that he'd get the boys to pin me down right there and then and he'd rape me, but Johnny had made him promise not to touch me. 'You're a prickteasing little shit,' he tells me, 'but I love you, you beautiful bastard. One day I'm going to fuck you, then I'm going to kill you, then I'm going to fuck you back to life again, then kill you for a second time, you lovely, adorable, evil little swine.' Then he collapses, and I fetch some of the boys to put him to bed.

I must have been there for weeks, and summer feels like it's on the cusp of autumn, when Johnny turns up one day with Coreen. A goon summons me to the hall from the garden. 'Aeeyy! It's the King!' he says to me as he greets me. His lovable geezer act sometimes makes it hard to remember that he's actually a vicious killer who fucked my wife. Eddie's absent as usual, so it's just me and them, plus the usual assorted henchmen. He shakes my hand with both of his and pats me on the back. 'Nice one, my son, nice one. Best birthday I ever had. Look, mate, sorry about your friends and everything, but Eddie just blew his cool on that one. There was no need for it, bang out of order. Gave him a right bollocking over it, I can tell you.' He's lying of course. If he didn't directly order it himself, he would have certainly authorised it. 'But I'm going to make it up to you. Well, I can see you've been growing a beard like I told you, that's good. It could actually do with a bit of a trim now, and your hair, you look well scruffy. But that's OK, Coreen here's going to tidy you up, aren't you love?' She nods. 'And once she's done we're going to take your picture. And once we've done that . . . well, you're just a hare's whisker away from getting out of this poof's place.'

He leaves me alone with Coreen in a bathroom. She's looking as beautiful to me as she did before as I see the reflection of her precious green eyes in the bathroom mirror. Seeing her makes me giddy, and a bit scared, but for the first time since Gaylord and Fatty were shot, I can truly say I'm in a good mood. 'Johnny says you were bloody amazing at his birthday party,' she says as she wraps a plastic sheet round my neck. 'Wish that I could've seen it.'

'Oh well,' I say, 'I could do it again for your birthday.'

'That would be fantastic. My dad loved Elvis you know. You remind me of him.'

'He could watch too, I guess.'

'Nah, he's dead.'

'I'm sorry.'

'It's OK. He got what was coming to him.'

Coreen shaves my hair very short, so it's difficult to tell where my bald spot begins and ends. Then she trims the beard so that I look like Ming the Merciless or something.

'What do you think?' she asks.

'Um, it's not what I would have chosen, but it's . . . nice.'

'Well, that's kind of the idea. We need to make you look as different as possible. And the hair's just the first part.' I realise all her sentences go up at the end when she says them, as if each one's a question.

'Ta-da!' She hands me a pair of thick-rimmed spectacles, the type poncy Londoners wear.

'I don't wear glasses,' I say.

'You do now. It's normal glass, see? They don't make you see better or nothing. And that's not all. Johnny sent me shopping for you, look.' She leads me to the TV room. In there is a mountain of bags from the sort of shops it's not occurred to me to shop in for about thirty years, not since I discovered British

Home Stores. Some very nice stuff here, very stylish. I recognise some of the names. Fcuk. Benetton. It's smart, but casual. 'This is your new wardrobe,' she says, 'I hope you like it.'

'I do,' I say, 'I like it very much.'

'Good. Now get your arse into some of it so we can take this photo.' Johnny is standing by the door. 'We'll be in the study when you're ready.'

'Johnny's being very hands on about all this,' I say to Coreen once he's gone.

'Oh, well it's my special project really,' she says. 'It's something he's given me to do to keep me quiet 'cos he never did get round to leaving his wife like he said he would. So he's working on it with me today, and I do my bit like a good girl and keep my trap shut.'

'Well you've done a good job,' I say, as she turns her back while I put on some new trousers. 'How did you know what would fit me anyway?'

'I worked it out from looking at you,' she says. 'Just a talent I have.'

'That's very impressive.'

I'm genuinely not expecting it when she turns round and puts her hand down my boxer shorts, grabbing hold of it hard. 'No, that's impressive,' she whispers, and kisses me on the lips. 'And besides, I have many other talents. Bet you want to know what they are.'

'Needlepoint?'

'Close.' She giggles, and draws back. 'Go on, put your trousers on and go and have your photo taken.'

I try to finish getting dressed, but I have to send her out of the room because my erection just won't go down while she's there. Then I go to the study, where one of Johnny's men takes my photo. I am born again in the flash of his camera.

CHAPTER 28

It's autumn in Manchester, and the leaves are falling. I've been walking around for hours, round the nice areas and some of the bad, and my legs hurt, but I can't stop. This is where I've ended up, wearing the clothes that Coreen chose for me and living off the few grand Johnny doled out to get me started in my new life. There isn't much to it yet, other than a rented flat in Victoria Park, the clothes, a new mobile and number, and my new name, backed up with fake ID: driving licence, passport, courtesy of Johnny. I need to look for work, but I haven't got round to it yet. When I do, I'm allowed to give Eddie and Johnny as references. Johnny offered me some bent work, but I said I didn't want it. I'm too old, and if I got caught I'd go down not only for that, but everything else most likely. Besides, I'm really sick of all that crap.

I'm all wrapped up in a big thick coat Coreen thought to get for me. It's been pissing it down, and all the brown leaves are soggy and sticking to my feet like cornflakes. I've walked all the way through Moss Side and Whalley Range, and now I'm going back again. I need a few weeks to get my head together around here. Things have really changed for me. You could say that door flew open. I think it was seeing Fatty and Gayboy shot down that did it. All those years, I had nothing but contempt for the pair of them, but seeing them dying, it struck me as being so unfair, such a waste. But more than that, afterwards it felt like I lost something that was important to me, that a part of my life had ended along with them. And there's no getting round it, I have to admit, I miss them a little bit, and the thought of them not being around makes me sad. I suppose what I'm saying is that it's occurred to me that really, I quite liked them.

A truck drives through a puddle and drenches me outside the school for the deaf. If you want a place to be depressed, you can't do better than Manchester. I've been thinking about what happened to my sister lately, what my dad did to her, and how she ended up hanging herself in her bedroom. I remember it happening, with my mum screaming and crying, and my dad cutting her down. Me, I just stood there. It tore me apart inside for weeks afterwards, at times I felt like doing the same thing too. But mostly I was angry. Angry at my dad for sending her mad enough to do it, but mostly angry at her for leaving. I went a bit crazy for a while, smashed up a whole load of stuff, beat up a few kids. But pretty soon after, I got my bird knocked up, and then I had my own problems, so I never really dwelt upon it again that much. But now, like Fat and Gay Elvis, it just seems a total shame. There's somebody dead and there's no good reason for it, other than my dad couldn't keep his pervy hands to himself. I've been thinking that maybe my life would have been better if my big sister Bridg was in it, but who knows?

I haven't been in Manchester for years. It's a lot different now, a load of the tower blocks have gone, and you can't move for students in a lot of places. It's worse than Cambridge. I've had to think about lots of different stuff since I got here. A whole load of stuff fell out of that door, stuff I never wanted to look at again, let alone think about. Some of it's easier to deal with than the rest of it. I'm not too sad about my first wife and kid, and that lady and her daughter. I mean it's all pretty stupid, and it's bad that the boy grew up without a father and all, but really, I was just a lad. Even if I'd stayed, he wouldn't have had much of a dad with me being the way I was, so it was probably all for the best. He turned out all right anyway, so I heard. Karen had a hard time of it for a bit, people said, but she got married again eventually, and I think to someone who had a bit of cash. So I don't feel that bad about all that. It's like when I was doing the thieving afterwards, and I got caught and sent down. I mean, I was still very young, and no one was really hurt, so that doesn't bother me that much. But I suppose what does bother me quite a lot is what I did to my third wife Chrissie. I was just plain bad to her. After all, when it comes down to it, what I did was find a girl who didn't know how to stand up for herself, and pushed her further than anybody's meant to go. There's no excuse for that sort of thing. Everybody deserves some respect, even when they don't know that themselves. I only worked that out the other day. Chrissie's just the beginning of course. After that, there was the fire.

I cut through Moss Side. No students here, just normal people. Why on earth I got involved with the fire I'll never figure out. OK, it was the money. And it all goes back to Eddie. Back then, he wasn't quite the millionaire businessman he is these days, and he needed a favour. He was trying to open up another strip club up in London, but a local shopkeeper was kicking up a hell of a fuss, saying it would lower the tone of the area and all that. Eddie reasoned that if the man's little grocer shop wasn't there any more, he'd most likely lose interest in complaining. He offered me the job of taking care of it. I was a good choice, because if I got caught, I wouldn't squeal, and if I went down, no one would miss me. Plus, I was fucking broke. Now, the grocer and his family lived above the shop, but Eddie was impatient, and he couldn't be bothered to wait for the property to be empty before it got torched. Instead, Eddie just told me to go over there and do it. So, at two o'clock one morning, I poured a can of petrol through the letterbox, dropped in a match, and ran. Then I got in my car and drove away while the fire took hold. Now, the shopkeeper was woken up by the smoke alarm from the shop below, called the fire brigade, who put the fire out no problem, and got everybody out OK. Quite a few cabbages were lost, but the damage wasn't irreparable. Turns out I hadn't even done that great a job. But that didn't stop the police from paying me a visit soon after. Turns out the shop was opposite a garage with a CCTV camera on their forecourt. Not only did they catch me on tape pouring the petrol through the letterbox and then speeding away half a minute later, but they also managed to get the car number plate. I'd driven up and filled the can with petrol there not five minutes earlier.

As you can expect, Eddie did and said nothing. The police were working their arses off trying to connect him to me. There were loads of links of course, dating back to us sharing a prison cell together, but nothing that would have stood up in court. So it was me that ended up in the nick again for a good few years, while outside Eddie built his empire. But I don't mind that now. What really bothers me, so much so that it makes me want to do myself damage, is that I could have killed an entire family, including the little 'uns. And I didn't have a twinge of conscience about it. I keep on telling myself things were different then, that it just wasn't in my nature to think about things like that, but what sort of excuse is that? It's nowhere near good enough is it?

And as of today I've now got an even bigger weight to carry round. I don't normally read the paper, but this morning I was waiting for a haircut, and I was flicking through one and there it was, tucked away on page seven. The final part of a near-forgotten summer silly season story. 'ELVIS ATTACK VICTIM DEAD'. It said that Buddy never woke from the coma. He had a brain haemorrhage and they ended up switching the life support off. There was no mention of Em. And so I walked right out of the hairdresser's then and there. And I haven't stopped walking yet.

I felt bad before but now I feel the worst I can imagine anyone can feel. I can't stop thinking about Em. If she feels half as bad as I did when I lost Bridg, then I might as well have killed her too. I want to find her and put my arms around her and comfort her, but I know I can never do that. What I should do, I know, is walk into the nearest police station and turn myself in. Not for me, I've been punished for the fire already, and it's still torturing me. But maybe seeing me banged up for the rest of my life would give Em some comfort. I won't do it, though. I'm too old and I'm too scared and I'm too lonely. Em will most likely never have peace because I'm too much of a coward to give it to her. End of story.

I walk up Oxford Road, past the university, with all the cool students in their cool clothes milling about and not looking where they're going just like they do in Cambridge. Looking at them makes me realise that my need for sex has nearly completely fizzled out since coming here. Normally, all these girls in their autumn-wear would be making me hard and filling my head with duffel-coat fantasies, but the old thing's just hanging there, limp and shrivelled, like a deflated balloon. I never want charlie any more either. My desires may have been inconvenient and made me act rather strangely, but at least they were mine. Now they've been taken away from me too. I miss them like lost friends. I miss them like I miss Gay and Fat Elvis. I miss them like Buddy. I miss them like Em. I miss them like Bridget.

I don't know where or why I'm walking now. But I can't think of a reason to stop or go back, so I just keep going. Keep going all the way down this long road, past the Cornerhouse cinema, where I sometimes go to watch boring old art films now that I don't deserve anything entertaining, until I reach the point where a flight of steps leads you down to the old Manchester canals. I walk down and stand on the side, leaning over the railing, looking into the water. I spot a polystyrene cup far in the distance where the sun is setting, and watch it as it makes its long journey to underneath where I stand.

'Look at that fella, he's going to jump!'

'Don't do it, mate!'

A bunch of scallies laugh at me as they whiz past on their bicycles. It's getting dark now, and where light isn't reflected in it, the water is black like tar. And I think, why don't I? Why not just jump? Why should I keep on going? I can't think of a single reason that doesn't come down to cowardice in the face of death. But still I don't jump.

CHAPTER 29

Five days later, Coreen is on my doorstep.

'Fuck me, what are you doing here?' I ask.

'Well, I just thought I'd drop by.'

She's wearing tights and trainers, a denim miniskirt and a tracksuit top, and carrying her holdall, stuffed full. She's drenched from the rain and looks just lovely.

'Can I come in?' she says. 'I'm soaked. It wasn't raining when I left London, but I got past Birmingham on the train and it started pissing it down.'

'Yeah, that happens. But how the hell did you find me?'

'I asked people didn't I? Your flat upstairs?'

'Yeah, follow me.'

We go upstairs and I open the door. The flat's pretty tidy.

What with me not having much to do all day, I've finally taken
to learning how to take care of myself properly. The furniture
came with the flat, and I haven't really added much, other than
a TV. The walls are completely bare, so it's pretty depressing,
but it's only when I walk in there with Coreen that I notice.
Maybe I've been too depressed myself for it to register.

'Well, this is . . . nice,' she says.

'You don't mean that do you?'

'No, not really.' She giggles. 'Can I put this bag down somewhere?'

'Yeah, anywhere will do. Sit down, please. So, um, what are
you doing in Manchester, Coreen?'

'Oh, this and that, do a bit of clubbing, do some shopping.
Gonna be 'avin' it large in Manchestah!'

'Right, right. So are you staying with some mates or something?'

'Ah, I was hoping I could stay with you actually.'

'With me?'

'Yeah, well, I don't really know anybody else in the area, and,
well, you know, you're my mate, ain't yer. Christ, I'm soaked
through.' She unzips her tracksuit top and takes it off.
Underneath it, she only has on a V-neck that clings to her breasts.

'Um, would you like a cup of tea?'

'Do you have anything stronger?'

'Actually, no.' This is true. The desire for alcohol has gone
the same way as that for charlie and wanking.

'Oh, well, tea it is then.'

I go to the kitchen. As I make the tea I can feel two months'
worth of depression drain out of me. When I come back she's
texting on her mobile. I put the tea down on a coffee table and
she smiles. 'Cheers, my dears,' she says.

'So how long were you thinking of staying?'

'Oh, not too long. Wouldn't want to outstay my welcome or anything, but you know, I thought we could spend some time together, have a laugh, hang out.' She leans forward to pick up her cup of tea. I can't help looking down her top.

'We could go to the cinema,' I say.

'Yeah, we could do that.' She stays hunched forward and drinks her tea. My gaze is torn between her cleavage and the floor.

'So, um, what does Johnny think about all this, you going away and that?'

'Ah, Johnny.' She stares into her mug of tea and while her mind is elsewhere, allows it to slip. The tea spills onto her hand. 'Ahhh, shiiit!' she cries, 'Ow! Ow!'

'Come with me,' I say, 'we'll run it under the tap.' I put my arm round her waist and quickly lead her into the kitchen. There I hold her wrist as the cold water flows over her reddening hand. I don't have any bandages so I have to make do with wrapping it in a towel.

'I'm such a mong,' she says.

'No, no you're not,' I say. 'You're not a mong. You're a joey.'

'You what?'

'Joey. A Joey Deacon. Oh never mind.'

'I don't get it.'

'No, I guess you'd be too young.'

'So why am I a Joey?'

'Do you remember the programme *Blue Peter*?'

'Yeah, it's still on.'

'Well, years ago they did a campaign to raise money for spastics. And so kids could learn about them, they had this guy on called Joey Deacon, who was one and had to use a wheelchair. But all the kids just thought he was really funny and laughed at how he talked and dribbled, and how one week he lost his shoe in the Thames. Anyway they all called each other Joeys or Deacons as an insult. And once the kids did it, their parents took it up as well. Now people say it and they don't know where it comes from.'

'That's not funny. It's really cruel.'

'So's mong.'

'Why? It just means stupid.'

'No it doesn't. It's short for mongoloid. You know, Down's syndrome.'

'Oh. My. God. I'm so sorry, I didn't realise.' She hides her head in the palm of her hand.

'It's OK.'

She puts her arms around me and rests her head on my chest. 'You've got to help me,' she says softly. 'Johnny doesn't know where I am. I had to get away from him, he's mental. I know he'd have ended up killing me. He was getting really obsessive and weird.'

'Why did you come here?' I ask.

'He wouldn't think to look here. You see, I couldn't be by myself. I wouldn't be able to stand it. Anywhere else he'd figure it out and find me. And you seem . . . kind. I think you're a good person.'

'I wouldn't be too sure of that.'

'You are. I can tell. You have a good aura.' She looks up at me. 'Don't you worry, I'll look after you. I'll cook, clean, do anything you want.' She reaches her face close up to mine and kisses me. 'Anything you want.' She slides down my body and tries to open my flies with her good hand.

'You don't have to do that,' I say.

'I do, I do.'

When she eventually manages to undo them and pull it out, it's not even erect. 'Oh, what's wrong?' she says. 'Don't you like me?'

'Of course I do. I just haven't been feeling that way for a while.'

'Well, we'll have to see about that, won't we?' She takes her top off and slides down to the floor on her knees. There she kisses it, and licks it, and sucks it, until slowly, very slowly, it fills with blood and grows. 'There, see? Magic,' she says.

She leads me into the bedroom, lies me down, undresses me and then herself, ignoring the growing redness on her hand, and climbs on. When I come, it feels for a moment like I'm floating, travelling through space. When I finally reach my body again, I'm exhausted and can't move, and breathing very fast.

'There, there,' she says. 'I'm here. I'll look after you.' Then she lays her head on my chest. 'You'll look after me, won't you?'

'Yes, I'll look after you,' I say.

And so begins my life with Coreen.

Three weeks later and things have turned round pretty fast. First thing she did when she moved in was decorate the flat with lots of cushions and posters of waterfalls and the like. So now the place looks great. Second big change is that I don't need to look for a job for the time being. Seems that Coreen's picked up quite a few quid from her time with Johnny, so right now, we're both taking it easy. Also, I'm actually eating decently for once, might even be losing some weight, because Coreen is a really good cook. Her mum was from the Caribbean and taught her all sorts of recipes, and she cooks me loads of stuff I've never eaten before, like coconut prawns. Who'd have thought that would work? Mind you, she's a weird mix of stuff herself. Her mum was a half-caste, and her dad was Tunisian. All that stuff together makes her seem like she comes from some other place that you can't find on the map, like Shangri-La or something.

The place is actually messier now that she's here. It's all the boxes of shoes she buys, she just chucks the paper they wrap them in on the floor. She's really not that good at cleaning up, which is strange for me seeing as all the other women I've lived with have always been walking after me with a dustpan. Now it's me that's doing it. But every so often she'll have a cleaning frenzy and the kitchen will be scrubbed from top to bottom in about five minutes, and it'll be spotless. We have sex nearly every day. In fact, for the first week or so we were having it several times a day, until she admitted she was getting sore. My drive for it has recovered pretty fucking miraculously, I can tell you. Coreen knows a whole load of positions I've never bothered with before – putting her legs over my shoulders, facing the other way, and all that. I don't mind so much, it doesn't make it feel that different to me, I just don't understand why it has to take so long. But I'm not really bothered, as long as she's enjoying it. Sometimes the new stuff doesn't work anyway, and we go back to doing it the old-fashioned ways.

A lot of the time we sit around watching telly, but she likes to go shopping a lot. There's a place called Affleck's Palace she's mad on, and she dragged me in there once, and it was pretty freaky, loads of tattoo and piercing parlours, and weird magic shops for druids. Found some good record stalls there, though. I'm thinking of buying a turntable and rebuilding my collection of rock 'n' roll 45s. I used to have loads of stuff, but I sold it all to get money for the charlie. Fucking stupid, looking back on it. Sometimes we go out for a drink, but I get tired of people staring at us. I suppose the age difference is hard to take for some people. It's OK for an ageing millionaire gangster to have a nineteen-year-old girlfriend, but just some old bloke in a pub, forget about it. I also take her to the Cornerhouse to watch the art films. She doesn't like them much, but at least people don't tend to stare in places like that.

Coreen reckons I have a problem with gays. She says that I'm always making really prejudiced remarks, and I don't know what I'm talking about. I tell her about being violated on a nightly basis by Eddie, and point out that sort of thing can affect a person. It's funny, I can tell her stuff like that. Anyway, she says I have to re-educate myself, because most gay men aren't like Eddie. So she takes me to Canal Street, or Anal Street as it says on the road sign, and makes me sit in a bar full of gays to show me how lovely they are. I guess she's right. They're no more or less likely to be arseholes than anyone else, and I don't feel like taking my anger out on anybody much these days anyway.

So there you have it, my new life. You know, the really weird thing is, I'm happy. For the first time in my life I'm happy. I'm not that angry about stuff any more, and I've forgiven myself for a lot of the stuff I've done, so I'm quite relaxed about things. In fact I don't think about all that old stuff at all, and I don't feel that I have to. So is everything perfect? Well, no, I guess not. I suppose I have my suspicions that Coreen is actually quite fucked up, that she has a thing about being with older men who she looks after and has sex with, in return for some sort of security. So, I don't know how much she's here because she wants to be, or whether she's just acting on a strange compulsion that means she has to be. I don't call her on it though. I don't want to jinx it. In fact, I don't want to know the truth. I want to keep things the way they are. I want to stay with her because I love her. Simple as that.

I mean take today for instance. I was lying on the couch, just beginning to read the book of a film we saw the other day, *The Tin Drum* by Günter Grass. And Coreen comes in, wearing nothing but her underwear, with a plate of something for me that looks really tasty.

'What are these?' I ask her.

'Coquitos,' she says. 'Coconut balls.'

'You didn't have to do this for me,' I say.

'I know, I just wanted to,' she says.

Now why would I want to walk away from that? I don't think anybody's said they've done something for me just because they wanted to before.

OK, I admit it, I think about Buddy sometimes. You know, I can't help dwelling on the fact that I am a murderer. I killed him, and left Em on her own. I have to admit I did a terrible thing. But, I tell myself, I was a different person then. Yes, it was 'me' who did it, but it wasn't me. Not the me who I am now. Anyway I've got away with it by the looks of things. In fact my life is loads better because of it. So I can't give myself up now, can I? Not now things are finally turning round for the better. That just wouldn't be fair.

The coquitos are very sweet, and I know I shouldn't eat them all at once, but I do anyway. By the time I've put the plate down, I'm feeling quite sick. Coreen undoes her bra and presses my face between her breasts. I don't have the heart to tell her I'd rather she didn't do that right now.

CHAPTER 30

'It's OK, but it all sounds the same,' says Coreen.

'I guess, but it all sounds good. Not like what you call R & B, which isn't real R & B anyway.'

I've given up on my idea of rebuilding my rock 'n' roll 45s collection, now that I've found out you can get CD sets with sixty tracks on them for a tenner. They sound loads better too, no crackle or anything. I've just got back from the shops with a Sun Records compilation. It's got nearly everything, Jerry Lee Lewis, Roy Orbison, Carl Perkins, plus a whole load of rare stuff I've never heard. My favourite's 'Flying Saucer Rock and Roll' by Billy Lee Riley, a song about how rock 'n' roll was brought to Earth by Martians. Well, it might have happened.

There's no Elvis, but that's OK, I can do without him for the time being.

'What do you mean it's not R & B?'

'R & B stands for rhythm and blues. There's no blues in what you listen to.'

'Am I bothered? I don't think so.'

The whole rock 'n' roll thing has been troubling me. I've been remembering the amount of pleasure that I used to get out of my old rock 'n' roll records, and it's like I've been going out of my way to forget it all these years. I recall that I started buying them in the late sixties when there was that rock 'n' roll revival, and Teddy boys marched on Radio 1 protesting about how they didn't play Elvis and Gene Vincent records any more. I was still buying them in the mid seventies when I got out of the nick the first time. Then you had pub rock, which was a heavy type of rock 'n' roll that cleared the way for punk, and I listened to that quite a lot, followed some of the bands. Didn't like punk so much, but there was a band called the Cramps who were good. Did a sort of rockabilly thing with a horror-movie look. Then soon after that I just stopped caring about music, I guess, and convinced myself I never liked it that much in the first place. But now I'm wondering why, and to be honest with you I don't like the answers I'm coming up with. I remember now how the records used to make me feel less angry, a little less hateful towards everybody. I could put one on and find some peace. And that makes me think, if I could be like that then, which is pretty much the way that I feel now, then why did I walk away from it? All that crap about being a psychopath. I mean, how pathetic is that? Just a stupid, childish excuse. And in those moments that I'm now remembering, I think to my shame that I must have known what it was to have conflicting emotions, to have a conscience, to have guilt, affection, even love, basically

what it is to be a human being. I must have chosen to hide from
all those things, just to make my life easier. When? I guess some
point after Nanette dumped me, but in truth, I think it began
much earlier. With Bridget, probably. But as long as I had the
music, then I was still holding onto something of me that was
human. That's why it had to go.

'Anyway, I thought you said you liked Elvis. He's rock 'n'
roll.'

'Did I? Oh, I was probably just trying to get into your pants.
I liked that "Little Less Conversation" song. Don't like the old
stuff so much.'

'What's wrong with it?'

'It's old.'

'So am I.'

'Your point being?'

Things aren't going so well with me and Coreen now. I don't
think she's that keen on me any more, and now I doubt she ever
was. But now, not three months into the relationship, I can see
her contempt for me. I'm more in love with her than ever, but
even so I'm not going to delude myself. Oh, she's using me,
that's for sure, but you know what, I'm happy to be used. I'm
a charlie, I know, but I can't bring myself to care. Right now,
I'm happy to be one.

Her phone plays the theme tune to *The A-Team*. She takes
it into the other room to answer it. She's very good at not making
herself heard when she doesn't want to be, but I pick up the
occasional 'oh, shit' and 'fuck' that indicate things are not well.
When she comes back in, she has a nearly convincing grin on
her face.

'You OK?' I ask.

'Fine,' she says.

'Who was that on the phone?'

'Just a mate. Why?'

'Just wondering.'

'You jealous or something?'

'No. Just wondering who it was, that's all.'

She walks towards me gingerly. 'Look, um,' she says, 'I think it's time I moved on. It's not you, I just want to go, OK?'

I grasp for words. I find many. 'Wow, that's unexpected. Ah, I don't understand. Is there something that I need to do that I'm not doing? I could get a job if that's what's wrong . . .'

'I said it wasn't you. Look, we had a good time, but I'm too young to be tied down anywhere. I had enough of that with Johnny. Please understand.'

'Sure, I understand.'

I've understood from the moment she got the phone call. She's running, and if I had any sense, so would I. She starts packing stuff up in her holdall. She's bought far more than she can take with her since moving here, and she leaves most of her old stuff in the closet. I hear her on the phone checking train times, but I go out of my way not to catch where she's going. I sit silently on the sofa watching the telly as she gets her last few bits and pieces, and then, when she's done, she joins me.

'So where are you going to go?' I ask her.

'Haven't decided yet.'

'What time's your train?'

'Soon.'

'Is it a special train for people who don't know where they're going?'

'Oh, shut up, you Joey,' she grins.

'I'll miss you.'

'I'll miss you too.'

'No, I really will miss you.'

'I know you will.'

We don't say anything else, and then it's time for her to go. Her taxi arrives, and we hug awkwardly on the doorstep, and then we wave goodbye.

I go back to watching the telly. Of course, I'm torn in two by it, but it all feels right somehow. I can see that it was inevitable and there was no point trying to change it. That's not to say I don't want to run after her and beg her to change her mind. It's just that I know that would be a virtual death sentence for her. Johnny's coming, I know it, and he may well kill me, but that's OK, I don't mind. Whatever he does, I'll consider it my punishment for what I did to Buddy. And if by some chance I survive it, then maybe I can enjoy my freedom without the nagging feeling that I don't really deserve it. It's a screwed up way of looking at it, I know, but I feel like it's fair. Or in other words, I'll do anything rather than go back to prison.

So what am I going to do when Johnny gets here? Deny that she was ever here? If I'm planning on doing that I should get rid of that wardrobe full of her clothes in the bedroom. But no, I won't deny it. I want him to know. I want him to know that I had his woman, like he had mine. OK, it's juvenile, but it still hurts, damn it. And also, I love her. I want to testify to that, not to hide it, not even from Johnny. It was the purest thing I ever felt, and I want him to know that, if only for him to see how different we are, or at least how different we are now.

No, I'm going to tell him that she was here, and that we were lovers, and that I'm in love with her. And then he'll probably kill me.

My new mobile rings. It's never rung before. Needless to say I don't recognise the number. I take the call.

'Hello?'

'Elvis, it's Dave.'

'Oh, hi Dave.'

'Are you totally fucking mental? What did you think you were doing, shagging Johnny's bird like that?'

'Yeah, like you didn't.'

'What do you mean?'

'How else would she have found out where I was?'

'OK, she sucked my cock, but that was it. Anyway, you've got to disappear. Johnny's on his way up now to fetch her back. He'll give you a right kicking, probably pull your bollocks off or worse.'

'Well if he does, he does.'

'He won't if he can't find you. Make a fucking move, now!'

'I'm staying where I am, Dave.'

'Oh my god, you've really gone flipping mad, haven't you. Elvis, I'm phoning from a motorway service station. I'm coming too. I'm driving Johnny up, but not only that, I'm also driving Eddie. If they find you, it's going to be very, very bad, and I won't be able to stop them. In fact, I'll have no choice but to help them do whatever they're going to do to you. So please, don't put me in that position. Go, now.'

'I can't, Dave. I have to stay. I'll take whatever's coming to me.'

'Damn right you will, mate. OK, I'll see you when we get there, and if you don't come through it in one piece, I'll say it now. It's been good to know you. You're a good bloke.'

'Thanks, Dave.'

He hangs up. Well, this is it. I'm most likely going to die within the next twenty-four hours. Maybe it'll be quick, and they'll just shoot me, or more likely, it will be long and painful, with much buggery and singing of 'Hound Dog' involved. Still, it's a fitting end to the life I've lived, so there's a kind of poetic justice there. Except sitting here, it occurs to me I can do without justice right now, poetic or otherwise, and I still have a chance to make a run for it. And that's what I decide to do. I pack a bag with a few basic things, and in two minutes I'm out of the flat, making in the direction of Oxford Road where I can get a bus to the train station, or at least somewhere I can hide until it's likely they've been and gone.

I don't get far. As I turn a corner, an American-style SUV comes to a screeching halt down the road in front of me. Dave must have braked the instant he saw me. I turn and run back the way I just came, but over my shoulder I see two goons I don't recognise, but who must be Johnny's rather than Eddie's because of their acne, jump out and run towards me as the SUV drives alongside. It's winter now, and the pavements are slippery with ice, as the bleakest, greyest sky hangs above me. I make a good go of it, but I'm so out of shape, there's not much hope of my getting anywhere. In less than a minute, they've got me by the arms and are bundling me inside. There, Eddie waits for me, sprawled out on the back seat. He looks ill and much thinner than the last time I saw him.

'My dear boy,' he says, 'how wonderful to see you again. We've driven all the way up here just to visit. Tell you what, why don't we go round to your place for a nice cup of tea. Don't you think that would be lovely, Johnny?'

Johnny turns round from the front passenger seat and winks at me. 'All right, Elvis my son? Just want to ask you a few questions.' Dave looks round briefly from the driver's seat and gives a little half smile.

'Not a problem. What can I help you with?'

'Cup of tea first, then questions,' says Eddie. And so they drive me back to the flat. A goon presses a gun at my back as I walk to the door, but it's hidden away inside a sportsbag. From a distance, there's no way you could guess what was going on.

I unlock the front door and lead them up the stairs. We enter the flat, and I watch as one goon shuts the door, and the other pushes an armchair in front of it. I realise that I've been completely encircled. No one seems to be smiling. Johnny's sniffing the air.

'So who wants tea?' I ask.

CHAPTER 31

Johnny smacks me in the mouth, very, very hard. I fall backwards on the floor, as my mouth fills with blood.

'Nobody wants any fucking tea!' he shouts. 'Where is she, you little shit? I know she's been here, I can smell her!'

It takes me a while to get my jaw to work, but after making a strange bleating noise that I've never made before, eventually I manage a few words, although my diction is far from clear. 'I nnon' know wha you mean whonny . . .' is how it comes out.

'Don't fucking mess me about. Tell me where she is before I kill you, you fucking. Ungrateful. Little. Fucking. Scab.' Each word is punctuated with a kick to my chest. Now my breathing resembles the neighing of a donkey. Strangely, the urge to share with Johnny the purity of my love for Coreen has entirely left me.

A goon has been scouting round the flat. He comes in from the bedroom. 'Johnny, there's a wardrobe full of her clothes in there.'

Johnny slams his foot into my groin. 'Tell me where she is, now!'

I really want to answer his question by now. But of course, I don't know where she is. So I have to make something up. 'Nnivernnoo. Nee's nonng ne Nivernnoo.'

'What the fuck's he saying?'

'Nnivernoo. Ing Nivernoo noonay.'

'Johnny,' says Dave, 'I think he's saying Liverpool.'

I nod my head. 'Nivernoo! Nivernoo!'

'You fucking liar! Now where is she?' He kicks me in the stomach and I scream. It takes a good few minutes for me to be stop the involuntary noises long enough to be able to speak. 'Liv-er-nool,' I say softly, 'She's in Liv-er-nool all nay.'

'When does she get back?' says Johnny, much calmer now.

'Non't know, sorwy.'

'Don't fucking mess me about! What time will she be back? How's she getting back, bus? Train?'

'Nrain! Nrain nis evening!'

'What time train?'

'Awoun alf-seven.' It must have already gone six.

He turns to his goons. 'OK, we're going down the station, see if he's telling the truth. Eddie, you and your man stay here. You can do what you like to him except kill him. I'll do that myself later, once I've found the slut.' He stands over me, his foot resting on my face. 'You hear that, my son? Your number's come up. Now don't you look at me like that, it's your own stupid fault. I liked you, Elvis, but you had to go and take the piss, didn't yer? Now I'll have to make you eat your own eyes or whatever it is I'm meant to fucking do to people. Yum yum.' He raises his foot. It looks like he's about to stamp on my head, and I prepare for my brains to fly out of my ears, but instead he just taps me on the chin with the toe of his boot. 'Later,' he says, with a wink and a point. Then he and his men are out the door. I hear them drive away. I'm alone with Dave and Eddie.

'Dave, take his clothes off, please,' says Eddie. It was inevitable, obviously. I'm going to be buggered one last time by Eddie, then I'm going to die. Dave does as he's told, and peels the bloody shirt from me, and yanks away my trousers, pants and socks.

'Dave, fetch my bag please. Now open it up, take it out, put it on him, that's right.' It's hard to turn my head enough to be able to see what he's doing but I manage to look up as he towers over me, holding, and I recognise it instantly, an Elvis outfit, the most ridiculous white jumpsuit type from the last of the Vegas years. Of course, I realise, it's the one Fatboy wore on the night of Johnny's party. Eddie must have kept it as some kind of trophy. Dave rolls me on my back and packs my legs into the trousers, then holds me up to pull them round my waist. They're way too big of course, and I have to hold them to keep them from falling down, which they do briefly, when he puts the jacket on me. I can't stand up without Dave holding me, and I fall down a few times when he has to let go. I crouch on the floor as he puts the cape on my shoulders and the scarf round my neck.

'OK,' says Eddie when most of the outfit has been put on me, except for the wig and shoes, 'leave him on the ground. Now why don't you pop out for a bit, go get yourself some supper?'

'No, it's OK. I'll stay, just in case you need help.'

'Go, young David. That's an order, my good man.'

'Right. I'll come back in an hour or so, shall I?'

'That will be more than sufficient for what I have to do, thank you.'

'OK, um, see you in a bit then.' He waves at me on the way out.

Eddie crouches beside me, and strokes my hair. 'You used to be so beautiful,' he says gently. He kisses my forehead with what appears to be affection. 'Not now, now you're old and fat like me. But if I squint, I can just about make out the beautiful boy you used to be. And that's enough.' He picks up the wig and rests it on my head. 'I crown thee Elvis, the King of Rock 'n' Roll.' He stands and begins to pace the room. I stay crouched on the floor, partly because I know I'm meant to, and partly to avoid the pain that moving creates.

'I'm sorry, Eddie,' I say, 'I know I messed up.'

'Yes, yes, you did, you did,' he replies, 'but to be honest I'm not really interested in what you did to Johnny's bit of fluff. But the fact that you did it gives me the opportunity to do something I've wanted to do for all of these past few months that we've been reacquainted. You see, I'm dying, and as you know, I'm going to die lonely and unloved. So, here at the end of my life, the only thing I can say about it is that for the vast majority of it, I was always powerful. It was a very rare occasion for anybody to get one over on me, and if they did, I made sure that they paid. Even in prison, as you no doubt remember, it was me that ran the place. And now, when I look back on a life characterised by the physical and psychological domination of my fellow man, of all those who I have bullied, beaten and buggered, the one person who I think of most fondly is you. Elvis, you have a very special place in my heart. You are truly my favourite victim of my destructive desire. I think it's even fair to say that in my own way, I love you.'

'I'm flattered.'

'No, you're not, you're repulsed. But that's understandable. I'm faintly repulsed by you, what with the state you've let yourself get into. But that's not what this is about, no, not at all.' He crouches next to me, places his hands underneath my jacket, and runs them up and down my bare skin. 'No, this is all about ... In the twelfth century, Gerald of Wales observed a pagan ceremony in Ireland, in which the leader of the tribe engaged in sexual intercourse with a horse, then killed it and fed it to his tribe. The Christian Gerald saw this as evidence of the utter sexual depravity of the Irish pagans. But what he failed to understand was that the point of the ritual was not sex, but power. By conquering the animal with his penis, the leader was also symbolically conquering the forces of nature that the horse represented. And so, here we have a similar situation.' He moves round behind me, and runs his hands down over my arse. 'I don't find you particularly sexually desirable any more. Nevertheless, I am about to give you the buggering of your life, because I need to feel it again, I need to feel my power over you utterly, just once more, before I die.' He places me in position, pulls down my oversized Elvistrousers, and I hear him unbuckle himself behind me. 'Now, be a good boy and sing "Hound Dog" for me.'

He jabs it in with one thrust, and it hurts like it never hurt before. I'm too busy crying out to sing anything, but he doesn't seem bothered. He pummels fast and hard, and I recall a dream I must have had not too long ago, where I was in a very similar situation, but the cock was a drill, ripping my flesh apart. It feels like that's precisely what he's doing now. And then, without coming, he stops. He stops and keeps still, breathing heavily.

'Oh, this isn't what I want at all,' he says, like a disappointed schoolboy.

I hear him buckle up, and I turn round to see him resting his back on the foot of the sofa.

'Um, pull your trousers up, and come over here, would you?' he says.

I hitch up the trousers, and feel the white polyester stick to my backside, with blood no doubt. I manage to get my body to move over to where he is, and place myself next to him. There he wraps his arm around me and cradles me like a baby.

'Would you . . . hold me for a minute?' he says, and I put my arms round him too, and we sit there in quiet for some time. I even rock him a bit, which in that moment it occurs to me is something I've never done for any of my kids. 'Thank you,' he says finally.

'That's OK.'

'It's just . . . that . . . I don't want to be on my own when it happens.'

He pulls up his trouser leg and reveals a pistol, perhaps the same one he used to kill Gay and Fat Elvis with. 'I'd stand back if I were you,' he says.

I pull away as he stares into the barrel. He fires.

My first instinct is to get away, but I can barely stand, and I don't get halfway across the room before I trip over my Elvistrousers and fall flat on my face. I can't get up again. And lying there, for I don't know how many minutes, sprayed in Eddie's brains and wearing a white Elvis outfit coated in my own blood, of all people, I think of Em. I think of her losing the one she loved, and having no comprehension of why it even happened. It's a great big wrong that resounds through the universe. Going through this ordeal with Johnny and Eddie was meant to act as punishment for what I did to Buddy, but I feel no less guilty than I did before. It was just more of the same old thing, a few more links in that stupid chain. It doesn't help

Em any, and I'm still carrying the weight. I know I have to set both of us free. And so I call the police.

I tell them I wish to report a suicide, and confess to a murder. No, I didn't kill the person whose suicide I'm reporting, they killed themselves. That's why it's a suicide. I'm the Cambridgeshire Elvis killer. I killed Buddy Holly. No, I'm not having a laugh. They nearly hang up on me, but I finally convince them to send officers round to the flat. Then there is nothing for it but to wait.

Almost immediately, there's a banging on the door. I can't imagine the police would have got here this quickly. Which means it could be Johnny, and if it is, then I'm a dead man. 'Wh-who is it?' I ask.

'It's Dave.' Thank fuck for that.

'Dave, I can't open the door. I'm on the floor.'

'Where's Eddie, Elvis?'

'Eddie's dead. He shot himself.'

'Fucking hell.' Immediately, Dave hammers at the door with his shoulder. After a few blows, it flies off its hinges. He runs in, jumps over me, and stands over Eddie's body. 'You didn't do this?'

'Ah, no. Look, Dave, you've got to get away. The police are on their way here.'

'The police, shit. OK, I'll break into a car and get us out of here. Hang tight, OK?'

'No, I'm staying here. I'm turning myself in.'

Dave looks at me incredulously. 'Don't be daft, man. I can get us both out of here, away from the police as well as Johnny.'

'Dave,' I say, 'I can't run any more. I don't even want to. Now get your arse in gear or you'll be dragged down the cells and all.'

'Don't make me do this, Elvis. Like I said before, I like you.'

'Thanks Dave, but I'm staying here.'

He reaches down and shakes my hand. 'You're a good bloke, you know that?'

'No, I'm not, but I think one day I might be.'

He hugs me tight, straightens himself up, smiles one last smile, and hurries out through the space where the door used to be.

I wait for the police. Maybe Johnny will get here first, who knows? That would make the situation interesting. But whichever way it turns out, at least I know I tried to be noble, and with Eddie's bullet hole staring at me like an all-seeing and judging eye from the centre of his face, it's a big deal.

So as the minutes tick by, far too slow, and much too fast, for old time's sake, I sing for him:

> You ain't nothin' but a hound dog
> Cryin' all the time
> You ain't nothin' but a hound dog
> Cryin' all the time
> You ain't never caught a rabbit . . .